The Second Life

BY THE SAME AUTHOR

Jonathan the Visionary

The Second Life

by
X. B. Saintine

Translated, annotated and introduced by
Brian Stableford

A Black Coat Press Book

ISBN 978-1-61227-750-9. First Printing. May 2018. Published by Black Coat Press, an imprint of Hollywood Comics.com, LLC, P.O. Box 17270, Encino, CA 91416. All rights reserved. Except for review purposes, no part of this book may be reproduced or transmitted in any form or by any means, electronic or mechanical, including photocopying, recording, or by any information storage and retrieval system, without permission in writing from the publisher. The stories and characters depicted in this novel are entirely fictional. Printed in the United States of America.

TABLE OF CONTENTS

Introduction 7
THE SECOND LIFE 21
Error and Truth 21
The Golden Gnat..24
The Venetian Mirror 30
A Nocturnal Ascension of the Jungfrau............................35
The Large Armchair...45
The Marionette Theater 48
The Taking of Ptolemais...53
The Two Hunts 56
The Doctor's Hallucinations 69
Insects and Flowers...82
Lise's Dwelling..85
The Song of the Nightingale 90
A Little Hand 91
A Night in the Woods 101
The Cup of Tears 108
Psylla, The Gold-Eater..111
China in Paris...118
The Ibises of Ysamboul 131
The Dream of an Inquisitor..135
Prometheus 138
The Flight from Saint Helena 149
The Great Discovery of Animules 153
On the Pedestal 162
The Three Lights...168
Timothée Jerry's Five Rungs...174
I Become a Barbel...187
The Victims' Ball 189
Another Solomon..195
Saint Babylas' Day 197
The Paradise of Flowers 212
My Funeral...234
A Shadow's Dream...248

Lalagé 251
The Journal of my Dreams..253
    I. Advice to Travelers...253
    II. A New Wandering Jew 255
    III. Astronomical Journeys 258
    IV. Another Visit! Another Planet!................................265
    V. What Is A Dream? 273
    VI. Wellbeing at a Bargain Price...................................277
APPENDICES 280
The Ballad of Jane Stilich..280
The Valley of Souls 285

Introduction

La Seconde Vie by X. B. Saintine, here translated as
The Second Life, was first published by Hachette in
1864. It was the author's last book, and was probably
intended as such; documentation of his life is sparse, but
one of the observations on record is that he was in poor
health in his final years, that his death was not unexpected, and that he approached it with resignation. The
text of the book adds some weight to that assertion, in
certain aspects of its subject matter, and in its wry tone;
it contains a summary of sorts of a lifelong preoccupation, and also a doubly ironic judgment of that life's
achievements. There is also some evidence in the text,
however, that the bulk of it had been prepared for publication some years earlier, and that the final section was a
late addition.

The present translation is one of a pair, following
Jonathan the Visionary, a translation of the author's first
volume of prose fiction, *Jonathan le visionnaire* (serial-
ized 1823-25; book 1825), which also includes the supplementary items that the author added to that portmanteau text in subsequent editions. The two portmanteaux
provided book-ends of a sort to the author's long and
prolific career, exhibiting marked affinities. *La Seconde
Vie* takes up many of the themes broached in *Jonathan le
visionnaire*, reaffirming some of the points made in the
earlier volume, with a similar deft obliquity. In fact, the
final version of *Jonathan le visionnaire* appeared after
La Seconde Vie, in 1866, following the author's death in

1865, but it had certainly been prepared beforehand, probably in 1861, the year in which he published his penultimate story collection, *Contes de toutes les couleurs*, which includes all the stories published in earlier versions of the Jonathan portmanteau but omitted from the final one. Translations of two of the new stories from that collection are included in the present volume as appendices, the latter of which—the final story in *Contes de toutes les couleurs*, "La Vallée des Âmes" (tr. as "The Valley of Souls")—could easily have been included in *La Seconde Vie*, and has a similar elegiac feel to it.

The author of the article on X. B. Saintine featured in Pierre Larousse's *Grand Dictionnaire* (1866-76) seems to have been unable to find any information about his life except that he was born in 1798 and died in 1865—a dearth of information that was inherited by several subsequent reference books, extending all the way to Wikipedia—and did not even record the elementary information that the author's baptismal name was Joseph-Xavier Boniface, and that he was born in Normandy, in the region surrounding the city of Cambrai. Other sources record, however, that Xavier Boniface was conscripted into the National Guard in 1814 (at the age of sixteen) and was embroiled peripherally in the conflicts of the Hundred Days in 1815. While in garrison, he met his fellow conscript Eugène Scribe, who was already a successful playwright, and in order to pass the time profitably, the two of them collaborated in writing a vaudeville, under the pseudonym of "Xavier."

After being released from military service, Boniface returned to the studies in medicine for which he had previously been destined, but his life had already taken a different course, and his commitment to a career writing frivolous amusements for the stage had been determined.

He continued to use the signature Xavier occasionally, and also a mere "X," but soon selected "Saintine" as his preferred pseudonym, the prefatory X. B. being the initials of his real name (Joseph was merely the name of the saint to whose feast day he was born, attached for reasons of convention).

As well as writing for the stage, Saintine wrote poetry—for which he won a prize awarded by the Académie Française in 1817—and soon began writing short stories, but it was his vaudevilles, mingled with the occasional longer comedy and a few ventures into earnest drama, that provided his principal income and reputation. The Larousse article credited him with approximately two hundred, but in a brief obituary note added to a review of *La Seconde Vie* in *Bibliographie Catholique* in 1865, Alphonse Berthet quotes an exact figure of 157—approximately one every three months throughout his long career. Eventually, prose fiction provided a significant second string to his bow, when his second novel, *Picciola* (1836; tr. as *Picciola; or, The Prison Flower*), became a best-seller and was rapidly established as one of the core prose works of French Romanticism. None of the novels he produced thereafter matched its success, but they all sold well enough to warrant reprinting, and he became sufficiently prosperous to buy a house in Marly, to which he retired with his wife and children, while still retaining many friendships in Parisian society.

Prior to the attainment of that celebrity, however, Saintine appears to have struggled to reach print, and the original publication of his early short stories was in a periodical that he helped to found and finance, the short-lived *Mercure du dix-neuvième siècle* , which was advertised as being published by "the members of a Society of Men of Letters." The prime mover of the society in question, the periodical's most frequent contributor and the signatory of the editorial in the first issue, appears to have been Pierre-François Tissot (1768-1864), a radical Republican journalist and a significant pioneer of the Romantic Movement.

Tissot had previously worked on the newspapers *Le Constitutionnel* and *La Minerve*, both of which had been suppressed by Louis XVIII's censors because of their political activism, and the *Mercure* had to maintain a careful diplomacy in order not to suffer the same fate. Other members of the Society included the then-radical Adolphe Thiers and his friend and associate Félix Bodin. Among the poets whose work the periodical published during that phase of its existence were Victor Hugo, Alphonse de Lamartine and Madame [Marceline] Desbordes-Valmore, then at the beginning of what were to become glittering careers, and its reviews routinely contained fervent propaganda for "*romanticisme*," not only in French literature but German and English literature as well.

The seventeen stories that Saintine published in the *Mercure*—one of which contained three subsidiary stories—were the only items of prose fiction the periodical published, and were genuinely pioneering, in an era when prose was still regarded as inherently less prestigious than poetry; their example helped to pave the way for an explosion of Romantic prose in the 1830s. They were preceded by an introductory item introducing the mysteriously immortal Jonathan as their collective narrator and occasional protagonist, and that defensive packaging material was subsequently to be expanded very considerably in the two later versions of the portmanteau, *Les Soirées de Jonathan* (1837) and the posthumous version that recovered the original title. The 1837 version added four new stories to the original seventeen, but dropped five, while the 1866 version dropped eight of the twenty-one but added as a supplement a longer item originally published in the *Revue de Paris* in 1932, "Histoire d'une civilisation antédiluvienne," which was the most ambitious item the author produced in the course of his career, the controversial nature of which might well have been responsible for the postponement of the publication of the final version of the portmanteau until after the author's death.

The author's career spanned several different reigns, his first vaudevilles being produced while Louis XVIII was on the throne and his first volume of fiction during the even more repressive reign of Charles X. He reached the height of his fame after the July Revolution of 1830, during the reign of Louis-Philippe, but continued his career with no loss of prestige through the turbulence of the Second Republic, following the Revolution of 1848, and long into the Second Empire established after the *coup d'état* of 1851. Although he rode out all of those transitions, that survival required a certain diplomacy even in the beginning, and considerably more toward the end. Although Saintine seems to have recanted, in large measure, the radical Republicanism of his youth, as well as the dogmatic materialism that he espoused briefly during his days as a medical student, that recantation would not necessarily have kept him out of trouble during the early days of the Second Empire, when Napoléon III's censors clamped down hard on anything that could be construed as political satire. Several of the pillars of the Romantic Movement were exiled by virtue of their Republican allegiance, including Victor Hugo, Alexandre Dumas and Edgar Quinet, precisely in order to set a sharp example to their former fellows.

Saintine escaped that penalty, but had to live nevertheless with the rigorous censorship, and must have been keenly aware of the fact that his personal history might well lead the censors to inspect everything he produced with particular attention. His vaudevilles were careful to cause no offense, and the fiction that he produced during the 1850s was almost all historical fiction, safely distanced from any suggestion of relevance to the present day—a defensive move made by all the surviving members of the Romanic Movement, which had a profound effect on the pattern French fiction in the relevant period.

Although none of the stories contained in the original version of *Jonathan le visionnaire* were likely to attract the ire of the Second Empire's censors, having helped to establish a fashion for temporally and geographically remote settings, "Histoire d'une civilisation antédiluvienne" was a different matter, in spite of being set in Ethiopia before the origin of history, and its scathing satire might well have raised hackles in 1861 that it had not raised on its initial publication in 1832, when the political climate was milder. There is, in consequence, some significance in the fact that *La Seconde Vie* contains "Prométhée" (tr. as "Prometheus"), which reiterates one of the core arguments of the earlier item, albeit more elliptically, seeking further safety in the protective clothing of a dream, and in a more querulous fashion, reflecting the change of mind that had brought him back from his youthful flirtation with materialism to the very particular anti-materialism manifest in his resolutely flippant and multiply hypothetical reflections on the "Second Life" of the soul.

The possibility of political suppression was, of course, not the only factor that probably inhibited

Saintine's adventures in satire and speculation at various points in his career. The introduction to *Les Soirées de Jonathan* looks suspiciously like an aborted novel—an impression augmented by the further text inserted into supplementary material of the posthumous version of the portmanteau—and if that is the case, it might well be a symptom of the difficulty that authors have always had in marketing fantastic fiction, in the teeth of editorial and critical disapproval. Although a few of Saintine's shorter stories are flamboyantly fantastic, all of his published novels and the greater number of his longer stories are naturalistic, as are the vast majority of the dramatic productions that represented the main strand of his production, and it was not until the 1860s that he began to indulge his evident love of fantasy one a lavish scale. He did so primarily in collections of tales for children, including two collections of traditional tales and an exercise in the popularization of science similar to those undertaken in the same era by S. Henry Berthoud, *La Mère Gigogne et ses trois filles* [Mother Gigogne—a character featured in popular puppet shows—and Her Three Daughters] (1864; reprinted several times as *Science enfantine* [Children's Science]).

The pattern of his career, in fact, suggests strongly that Saintine might well have been one of several members of the Romantic Movement who would have liked to give their imagination freer rein in their serious endeavors, but who were obliged to operate under the burden of an editorial yoke in that regard for much of their careers. In *La Seconde Vie*, however, he cast caution to the winds in no uncertain terms, and indulged his eccentricities wholeheartedly, in a fashion that he might never have permitted himself but for the conviction that it would be his swan song. It is a truly remarkable book, as much in its self-indulgence as in its strangeness, and it is notable that it is not only one of the very few works of prose fiction that he produced that was never reprinted, but one of the few not to be reproduced, at least at the time of writing, on the Bibliothèque Nationale's *gallica* website.

The use of dreams as a literary device is, of course, as old as literature itself, and as a stratagem to excuse fantastic material it had become a cliché long before *Le Seconde Vie* was produced—as is obvious in the manner in which several of Saintine's stories deliberately play with the clichéd appropriations, varying them and commenting on them. The adaptation of the fundamental device to the purposes of Voltairean *contes philosophiques* had been widely practiced in the eighteenth century, most prolifically by Louis-Sébastien Mercier in the two collections *Songes philosophiques* (1768) and *Songes d'un ermite* (1770) and the notorious *L'An deux mille quatre cent quarante, rêve s'il en fut jamais* (1770; much augmented in subsequent editions; tr. as *Memoirs of the Year 2500*). The stories in *La Seconde Vie* recapitulate some of the purposes for which Mercier employed the method, not only in its adaptation to innovative apologues but also its adaptation to futuristic speculation, in "La Chine à Paris" ("China in Paris"), and cosmological whimsy, in "Courses astronomiques" ("Astronomical Journeys") and its sequel.

In general, Saintine's dream stories are less earnest than Mercier's, careful in their refusal to take themselves too seriously, and they clearly bear the imprint of his long career as a writer of vaudevilles. There is, however, one aspect of them that is more serious than Mercier, writing in a much earlier period of history, was able to be, and that is their continual interest in examining the nature of dreaming from a viewpoint infused and infected by contemporary psychological science. In that regard, the book was written and published in an intermediate era, when the phenomena of dreams, hallucinations and psychotropic had begun to attract serious attention and venturesome hypotheses, but had not yet begun to produce dogmatic assertions and analyses of the kind that flourished in the Freudian era.

Early quasi-scientific theorizing about dreams and hallucinations in France was closely connected with the popularization of Anton Mesmer's theory of "animal magnetism" and its connection with the phenomenon of "somnambulism," which preoccupied such proto-psychologists as Alexandre Bertrand. The writers of the Romantic Movement took a keen interest in such work, most especially Charles Nodier, with whom Saintine was acquainted, and who was one of the few writers in the Movement who preceded him in writing abundant prose fiction in that context. Not only did Nodier write such intense hallucinatory fantasies as "Smarra, ou les démons de la nuit" (1821; tr. as "Smarra")[1] but he attempted a philosophical analysis of "De quelques phenomènes du sommeil" [On Some Phenomena of Sleep] in an article published in the *Revue de Paris* in 1831 a year before Saintine's "Histoire d'une civilisation antédiluvienne" appeared in its pages and two years before Nodier published two futuristic fantasies there seemingly influenced by Saintine's story. Honoré de Balzac also seems to have taken some influence from Nodier, as well as the mystic visionary Emmanuel Swedenborg, in writing his own quasi-autobiographical ac-

---

[1] In *Trilby * The Crumb Fairy*, Black Coat Press, 978-1-61227-455-3.

count of the augmentation of a "second life" in "Louis Lambert" (1832).

The word "hallucination" appears to have been coined in France in 1817, by the pioneering psychiatrist Jean-Étienne Esquirol, although it did not reach the Académie's official *Dictionnaire* until 1835. That notion complicated previous hypotheses about the possible relationship between dream states and madness, broached by Voltaire, among others, and also by the physiologist under whose influence Saintine briefly became a materialist while studying medicine, Pierre-Jean Cabanis. One of Esquirol's most enthusiastic disciples, Jacques-Joseph Moreau, who preferred to style himself Moreau de Tours, became famous for employing the literary Club des Haschichins in order to assist him in his research into the effects of hallucinogenic drugs, recruiting one of the pillars of the Romantic Movement, Théophile Gautier as his most prestigious volunteer. The Club briefly involved Hugo, Dumas, Balzac, Charles Baudelaire and Gérard de Nerval, the last-named of whom figures significantly in the longest story in *La Seconde Vie*. "La Saint Babylas" ("Saint Babylas' Day"), and who built his celebrity on hallucinatory stories that were both symptomatic of his own mental turbulence and an attempt to relieve it by decanting it into literary endeavor. Another leading light of the Movement, Alfred de Musset, had earlier translated Thomas de Quincey's *Confessions of an English Opium-Eater* (1821; Fr. tr. 1828) into French, making it into a key reference-point for the Movement's writers.

Saintine does not seem to have involved himself in the Club des Haschichins, but his interest in the kind of research that Moreau was doing is very obvious in the connected narratives "Les Deux chasses" (The Two

Hunts") and "Les Hallucinations du docteur" ("The Doctor's Hallucinations"). If, as seems likely, the stories are quasi-autobiographical, it is not impossible that the doctor featured in them is, in fact, Moreau de Tours; the description offered by the doctor in the story of the hallucinogenic effects of henbane is strongly reminiscent in several respects of the account of the effects of hashish offered by Gautier in "Le Club des hachichins [*sic*]" published in 1846 in the *Revue des deux mondes* as an item of fiction rather than an honest documentary. Seen as an ensemble, in fact, *La Seconde Vie* is an exercise of the same kind as Gautier's literary hybrid, deliberately conflating fiction and autobiography in such a way as to make it impossible to detect where one begins and the other ends—or, more importantly, whether there is, in fact, any discernible boundary.

By the time Saintine published *La Seconde Vie*—although at least some of the materials on which it is based might have been written many years before—Baudelaire, following in Gautier's footsteps, had popularized the notion of assisted hallucination as a quest for *Les Paradis artificiels* [Artificial Paradises] (1860). Baudelaire's ultimate conclusion was skeptical, and Saintine's attitude appears to have been more so, even though he does endorse the magnetic force of the lure. The fantasies in the collection that advertize their paradisal element—most flamboyantly, "Le Paradis des fleurs" ("The Paradise of Flowers")—do so with conspicuous irony and a deliberate surrealism. Deliberate surrealism also features in some of the other metaphysical fantasies in the collection, as in the striking "Grande découverte des animules" ("The Great Discovery of Animules") and the cosmological fantasies of "Courses astronomiques." There is, however, an earnest pole to

Saintine's speculative fiction as well as a whimsically surreal one, and "Les Cinq échelons de Timothée Jerry" ("Timothée Jerry's Five Rungs"), which deliberately revisits the speculative theme of one of the most outstanding stories in *Jonathan le visionnaire*, "L'Enfant du sorcier" ("The Sorcerer's Child"), is an effective and sternly logical thought-experiment, the humor of which is purely apologetic.

The collection was, of course, published well in advance of Sigmund Freud's attempts to decode the symbolism of dreams in sexual terms, and in terms of the eroticism of the dream-imagery featured therein Saintine's work cannot begin to compete with the imagery of Gautier, Nerval, Baudelaire or even Nodier. That element is not, however, absent, and is, indeed, ever-present, albeit slyly, in the intriguingly mysterious person of Lalagé. Freudians would be bound to find much to amuse them in the laconic "Psylla, la mangeuse d'or," and something to fascinate them in the grotesquely disturbing "Une petite main" ("A Little Hand"). By contrast, "La Glace de Venise" ("The Venetian Glass") and "Le Logis de Lise" (Lise's Dwelling") are deliberately conventional stories, perhaps weakened by the conspicuous dilution of their eroticism, when compared to similar exercises by Gautier; the same cannot be said, however, of the deliberately elusive but strangely ubiquitous presence within the ensemble of Lalagé.

In fact, the marginal and barely-explained presence of Lalagé within the collection mainly serves to call attention to her liminal nature, and she is not the only recurrent element in the collection that gives rise to the suspicion that, in spite of his relentless good humor and liking for happy endings, the narrative voice of the stories is nursing a secret but deep regret about with he does not like to think, let alone speak—a regret that cuts deeper than the disenchantment and self-dissatisfaction deliberately and self-indulgently paraded in "La Coupe des larmes" ("The Cup of Tears"), "Sur le pavois" ("On the Pedestal"), "Prométhée" and "Mes Funerailles" ("My Funeral"). Partly because of that deliberate evasion, *La Seconde Vie* is an even more ambiguous and more ambivalent text than it pretends to be, and perhaps more than it set out to be. It deliberately breaks its own frivolous surface continually, alternating prose with doggerel, the farcical with the philosophical and the sentimental with the horrific, but beyond that contrived fracture there is an ominous element within its relentless playfulness that is both complex and thought-provoking.

La Seconde Vie was not the first collection of works of fiction to consists entirely of fictitious dreams and hallucinations, although it is consciously and deliberately very different from its most august predecessor, Gérard de Nerval's *Les Filles du feu* (1854), but it is nevertheless a pioneering work, which attempted to do something quite new, as well as providing a supplement and a complement to the author's first literary portmanteau, written forty years before but never conclusively set aside, and which still had to take its definitive form, as least as a printed book if not in manuscript. *La Seconde Vie* is a very entertaining book, which can be read purely for its entertainment value, and it is certainly satisfying in its vaudevillesque aspect, but it is also more than that, by no means entirely detached from the sentimental intensity of the classic *Picciola*, and from the heart of the esthetic endeavor of the Romantic Movement that X. B. Saintine had played a significant part in formulating and impelling.

The translation of *La Seconde Vie* was made from the London Library's copy of the Hachette edition. The translations of the two appended short stories were made from the copy of the 1861 Hachette edition of *Contes de toutes les couleurs* reproduced on *gallica*.

Brian Stableford

THE SECOND LIFE

Dreams and Reveries. Visions and Nightmares

Dreaming is still living.

Error and Truth

Error and truth, how to recognize you?
You contrast in everything today, but tomorrow,
     Perhaps I shall encounter you
With the same features, on the same road,
Passing by like two sisters, holding hands.

The things of life and the things of dream
     Act by turns, leading us astray
Amid the eddies of their dual current;
What is the sun that rises during our nights?

To whom, for certainty, can I have recourse,
Verity, which everyone pursues and fears?
Our sages, whose study has filled long days,
What have they left us to light the route?
Theories, words, what do I know? Doubt!
So many objects have stuck our gaze and mind
     Which the memory wipes out!
So many other memories take their place,
And which, perhaps, hatched out in mists,

Are residues of dreams! One finds their trace,
One mingles them with life, and, close to amity,
     In intimate company, one recalls
Some event of which they were the fraction;
One talks about it, with astonishment and irritation
At finding it forgetful and incredulous, and sudden-
ly
Doubt seizes you: Was it only a vain dream?

Error and truth, how to recognize you?
You contrast in everything today, but tomorrow,
     Perhaps I shall encounter you
With the same features, on the same road,
Walking like two sisters, holding hands.

Man thinks he knows everything and does not know
himself,
    Science deceives him, and amour even more!
    Circling our horizon with deceptive beacons,
    Each of which, through shadows and vapors,
    At the whim of winds and waves, pushes and pulls
us
    Over a double ocean into a double arena;
    The woman one loved, the day we had her,
    Did we dream them, or have they fled us?

Dream! Oh, how dominant that word is in life!
     How much room it takes up! Awake, we
dream;
    In the midst of our woes, while dreaming, we can
    Create a happiness that no one envies us;
    And who among us would want to erase from his
days,
     Those sweet moments, so full and so brief,

When thought launches far away to vagabond,
Lifting before our steps the barriers of a world,
And there, surrounding us with pleasant visions,
Houris with pure faces, glories and trophies,
Replace in our hand the magician's wand
          In the land of illusions!

          Well, if, intermittently
          Eyes closed, or eyes open,
We possess within us that double existence,
          O my soul, rightly or wrongly.
          Go forth into that other universe,
The unlimited world of the Second Life!
To the possible, to the real, you are not enslaved;
          Realms by you discovered,
Hands full of facts, come back and tell me
Your crazy visions, your various dreams
          And whether in prose or in verse
I will take faithful account of them
For the distraction of minds in confusion.

The Golden Gnat

I had just read the work in which the powerful dia-
lectician Proudhon, supporting himself on the philosopher Hegel, the learned Ancillon,[2] a minister of the Holy
Gospel, and the wise Portalis,[3] the eminent jurist, and
many others no less respectable, glorifies war in all its
aspects, and declares it an inspiration of God indispensable to the dignity, the glory and even the happiness of
humankind. In spite of the vigorous logic of the apostle,
I separated from him not completely convinced.[4]

In order to rest from Proudhon, I had taken, somewhat at random, from a friendly bookshelf, *Les Soirées
de Saint-Petersbourg*. The title seemed to promise me
something fairly relaxing, as did the name of the author,
Maistre. I thought it was the work of Xavier le Maistre,
the charming author of *Voyage autour de ma chambre*,
but it was his terrible brother Joseph whom I was about
to encounter.[5]

---

[2] The German pastor, historian and philosopher Friedrich
Ancillon (1767-1837), the descendant of a notable French
Huguenot family, he was the professor of history at the Mili-
tary Academy of Berlin for many years.

[3] The jurist Jean-Étienne-Marie Portalis (1746-1907) was one
of the lawyers commissioned by Napoléon to draw up the new
Civil Code.

[4] This is a surprisingly selective judgment of the philosophical
position of the anti-militarist anarchist Pierre-Joseph Proudhon
(1809-1865), and is surely a trifle tongue-in-cheek.

[5] The Savoyard philosopher Joseph le Maistre (1753-1821),
was a central figure of the "Counter-Enlightenment," a

On opening the volume, almost at random, as I had taken it, I perceived my mistake easily, I read this:

"In the vast domain of living nature, a manifest violence reigns, a kind of prescribed rage, which arms all beings *in mutua funera*... Already, in the vegetable realm, one begins to sense the law; from the immense catalpa to the most humble grass, how many plants die, how many are killed? But as soon as you enter the animal kingdom, the law suddenly takes on a frightful evidence... There are insects of prey, reptiles of prey, birds of prey, fish of prey and quadrupeds of prey. There is not an instant of duration in which a living being is not being devoured by another. Above those numerous races of animals is placed man, whose destructive hand spares nothing that lives; he kills in order to nourish himself, he kills in order to dress himself, he kills in order to adorn himself, he kills in order to attack, in order to defend himself, in order to educate himself and in order to amuse himself, and he kills for the sake of killing."

So well indoctrinated by one blow after another, I interrupted myself to say: "I don't have the habit of struggling against something stronger than me."

Until that day, I had had the stupid mania of playing Don Quixote to birds, and even insects—all animals in general. Many a time I had had occasion to intervene in quarrels between dogs and cats and get myself bitten or

---

staunch monarchist who blamed rationalist opposition to religion for causing the horrors of the 1789 Revolution. He was an ambassador in Russia for many years, and published the title cited in 1821. His brother Xavier (1763-1852) was a soldier, but took time out while temporarily under arrest to dramatize his experience in the parody of travel literature *Voyage autour ma chambre* [Voyage Around my Room] (1794).

scratched; in fights between two cocks, two rams, and even two humans, and receiving thrusts of a spur, a horn or a fist. I would not get involved again; since beasts and humans are destined to devour ne anther, since magpies eat warblers, warblers eat beetles and beetles eat the good God's creatures too, what does it have to do with me?

Half-lying on a bench in my garden, still holding Joseph le Maistre's volume in my hand, I was arguing with myself in that fashion when I sensed my eyes closing—but not completely, for I saw then, on a branch of a maple that was hanging over me, a spider completing the spinning of its web. Having terminated its network of fine mesh, it had scarcely begun to lie in wait in its little tunnel when a pretty fly with brilliant reflections came recklessly to run into it. First I saw it take a few tottering steps on the edge of the artfully-woven trap, and flutter its wings in order to resume its flight, but its feet were already retained by the sticky threads, and the spider, sensing its web vibrate, attentive to what was happening outside its hiding-place, put its head out of the window.

That pretty fly, I would have been able to save. But according to what I had just read, would that not have been trying to oppose the decrees of fatality itself? In any case, movement, the necessity of getting up from my bench and taking a few steps, would infallibly have troubled and annihilated the gentle slumber that was overtaking me. I therefore let things follow their course.

Soon, there was a muted hum around me, and something like a golden spangle vibrated before my gaze. After a gesture to chase it away, I resumed my pose as a sleeper, but every time slumber closed my eyelids, the gnat—for it could only be a gnat—sounded its fanfare again, with enough force to become entirely importunate to a man who, emerging from lunch, only wanted to take his siesta peacefully.

I half-opened an eye. The golden gnat had taken on larger proportions and appeared to me to be entirely similar to the pretty fly with the metallic reflections that had fallen into the spider's trap.

"Good," I said to myself. "It's got out of it on its own; it's surely the same one."

But I heard a murmur in my ear: "No, villain, it's not her. I wish to Heaven that I had died in her place, for she was about to be a mother; the cradle of her children was already prepared, coated with gum and furnished with appropriate aliments; we had disposed it under the bark of a willow, sheltered from all attack; the most precious moments of our existence had been devoted to that holy labor imposed on each of us by the great providential law, to which we submit without understanding it and without contenting it. Now my companion is no more, and neither of us will have accomplished our task down here. Curse you! Curse you!"

He interrupted himself for a few seconds; I thought he had gone. Suddenly, the buzzing recommenced, and, as if it were responding to the thought that was traversing my brain at that moment, it resumed forcefully: "No, it isn't that hideous spider that I'm accusing, it's you, you alone! The spider has obeyed the law of her nature, her instincts and its needs. Perhaps she too has children to nourish, who are crying out with hunger, and a victim was needed to be shared among them. But you were only obeying a sentiment of cowardly egotism; in order not to change position, in order not to give yourself the trouble of taking three steps forward, you allowed an innocent and inoffensive creature to perish, who, like you members of a superior race, perhaps better than you, appreciated the joys of life, amour and duty. You let her perish, and her posterity with her. Curse you! Curse you!

"Curse you! As well as the destructive law of nature with which your authors have indoctrinated you, there is the law of God that wards off the excessively disastrous effects of the other: the law of pity and protection that confides the weak to the guard of the strong. Don't you know that one? If you don't know it, you're not a man; if you do know it, curse you! Curse you!"

The intense, strident buzz resounded like a trumpet then, and the golden gnat went on, in a tone of challenge: "Yes, is it not true that struggle is divine in essence? To hinder its effects is to quarrel with the sage plans of nature; the right of might makes all other rights fall silent! But where does it reside, that right? Don't you also know that the creature most infimal in appearance is sometimes sufficiently well-armed to cast down man himself and throw him as pasture to the worms? There are certain terrible substances, of which we are the depositaries; aliments for us, they can turn against you into devastations, into poisons. You wanted it—well, then, it's war! War! Defend yourself, I'm a coal-black fly!"[6]

And I felt a profoundly piercing beneath the eye. I uttered a cry and, greatly alarmed, ran into the house calling for help. But no trace could be found of the bite.

No matter: I have remembered the lesson. Since that day, above the pitiless law of nature I put that of

---

[6] *Charbonneuse* [coal-black] can also mean "like anthrax" in French, so the statement is more sinister than it seems. It is probably not irrelevant, either, that Saintine had lived through the era when the Italian *Carbonari* had inspired Revolutionary groups all over Europe.

God, and above the magnificent but desolate argument of Joseph de Maistre that of my golden gnat.

The Venetian Mirror

Having arrived in the evening at the country house of one of my friends, Monsieur N***, after a long walk taken under the direction of the owner, during which I had to visit his woods, his fishing-lake, his dairy farms and even his fields of beets, I returned to my room and threw myself on my bed, intending to rest for an hour or two.

My sleep was agitated. Not that my fatigue went as far as curvature, and, in consequence, as far as fever...no, I didn't have a fever; my pulse remained calm and regular—but I don't have the habit of sleeping in broad daylight: that was the entire mystery of my agitation.

During one of my bouts of slumber, a domestic had come in to close the shutter of my window, on which the sun was shining directly. On waking up, I thought I saw a figure designed in front of me; then other figures came in its wake: the figures of women, pretty women, so far as I could judge from a rapid inspection, for they only appeared and disappeared.

There was a round opening in the upper part of the shutter. I thought at first that it was through that gap that my curious visitors were coming, in turn, to watch me sleep.

But who could those charming individuals be? Nothing in their physiognomy recalled the ladies in whose company I had found myself that morning in N***'s house at breakfast.

Then I perceived that I had turned my back to the window and the shutter, and from the depths of the gap behind the bed I saw new apparitions rising, still feminine apparitions. This time, it was not only faces or profiles; each of my visitors showed herself in her gracious ensemble, her neck disengaged, her shoulders bare, and so close to me that I could surely have seized them in passing

Lying under my coverlet, I played dead for a while, but with my eyes alert; I waited for one of my charmers to return to the scene; when that happened—without any evil intention, I swear—I extended my hand abruptly in her direction…with the sole result that I bruised my fingers against a mirror.

A Venetian glass with beveled edges, framed with finely-carved modern scrollwork, the existence of which I had not suspected until that moment, was placed at the back of the alcove I occupied. It was in that mirror that the pleasant mirage was reproduced, brought by a ray of sunlight coming through the circular opening in the shutter—at least, that was what I thought.

Certain henceforth of only dealing with reflections, I examined my beautiful ladies at my leisure and with the appropriate calmness.

Some of them were completely unknown to me, but as for the majority of then, I had surely encountered them elsewhere—where? I could not recall, and I strove in vain to understand by what fortuitous circumstance they were assembled in my friend N***'s house, and holding their decameron in the part of the garden located outside my window. What was equally singular was that almost all of them, apparently, were wearing theatrical costumes, the robes and coiffures of another era; there were even a few whose hair disappeared under powder.

Was our hostess preparing a dramatic surprise for the evening? That seemed probable.

And my beautiful actresses filed before me. One was displaying an Henri III ruff, another the weighty high collar of the Medicis, some of them silky elastic corkscrew curls, crepes and arrangements of hair in stages, or wigs surmounted with pouffes from the reigns of Louis XIII, XIV and XV.

In truth, I could hardly comprehend how such various adornments could figure in the same play, when all of a sudden, without hesitation, I recognized the models of two famous portraits by Larillière and Latour: Madame de Montespan and Madame de Pompadour had just appeared in my mirror.

Once on the track, the names of my other characters came to memory easily. They were nothing less than the favorites of our old kings, Valois and Bourbons: Diane de Poitiers, Gabrielle d'Estrées, Mademoiselles de La Fayette, d'Hautefort, de Fontanges and de la Vallière. Madame de Maintenon, clad in black with a Book of Hours in hand, was leading the mourning for one reign; Madame Dubarry, costumed as a bacchante, was closing the march of another.

But how had so many beautiful ladies come to find me in my alcove, through the hole in my shutter? I searched for the cause of the phenomenon, and thought I had found it when my friend N*** came into my room. He opened my window, toward which I launched myself, casting a fearful glance outside. Everything had disappeared.

"You have a fine collection of portraits," I told him. "Is it to give them a breath of air that you're exposing them in your garden?"

And I told him the story of my visitors, and how I had every reason to suppose that those portraits, placed outside the house, thanks to the reflection of solar rays, doubtless by a procedure identical to that of the *camera obscura*, had come to be reflected in the mirror in my alcove.

He smiled.

"I know what it is," he told me, "and I regret having neglected to warn you. It's not a matter of any *camera obscura* effect; it's the mirror itself, the mirror alone that has the gift of reproducing images that were once reflected in it."

And as I opened my eyes wide with incredulity, he went on: "That Venetian glass, bought by my grandfather, came from the pillage of Versailles in 1792. Brought to France by Catherine de' Médici, it initially decorated the Hôtel Saint-Pol and the Louvre; it passed from there to Fontainebleau, the Tuileries and Versailles, always ornamenting the private cabinet of the reigning king. As all the beauties in question habitually frequented that cabinet, their image, by virtue of being reflected there thousands of times, has, so to speak, become encrusted therein. From time to time, especially in dim light, by virtue of an effect of optics or catoptrics, for which I'm not sufficiently learned to give you a valid reason, by emission or luminous vibration, the image appears spontaneously on its surface. You see," he added, "that there's no question of a *camera obscura* here, nor of a collection of portraits, and the phenomenon that seems, at first sight, to be somewhat marvelous, is, in sum, quite simple."

I was convinced by that, only raising a single objection: "Why aren't the images of the men conserved as well as those of the women?"

"That's self-explanatory, of course!" he replied, laughing. "Women look at themselves in a mirror more often than men."

I know that since then, for a reason I don't seek to understand, my friend N*** has denied ever having had that conversation with me, but I affirm that that is exactly the explanation he gave me regarding the singular properties of his Venetian looking-glass.

A Nocturnal Ascension of the Jungfrau

A deputation of the English Mountaineering Club expected in the Bernese Oberland, was due to attempt to climb the Jungfrau.

I am not madly fond of the English. Perhaps they are very amiable people at home, I have never had the whim of going to seek them there; but I have encountered them everywhere else in Europe, and everywhere, even in my dreams, I declare that I have found them stiff, angular, formal, surly and unsociable, defending themselves against any approach in the fashion of thistles or porcupines. Thus, the idea that their Mountaineering Club was soon going to give us more proof of the sole kind of superiority that I grant them over us irritated me extremely.

The English have their flag planted in the five continents of the world; the seething sea has hardly given birth to a tiny fortuitous island, and before it is even consolidated, while it is still nothing but liquid mud, they have plunged a long spike into it surmounted by their leopard banner.[7] With that same spike and that same banner, it is necessary for them to decorate the peaks of all the highest mountains of the globe, commencing with Switzerland. It is for the latter operation that the Mountaineering Club has been instituted; it is the final word in that system of invasion pushed to the point of madness.

---

[7] A heraldic "leopard" is a lion in a particular posture, the one in which the three lions displayed in England's royal coat-of-arms are represented.

With a few tourist friends, I was then in Lauterbrunn, in the same wild valley from which the Jungfrau launches herself to a height of four thousand three hundred meters. From our inn we could see her dominating the entire northern chain of the Alps. I had her incessantly before my eyes, and the sight of her gave birth within me to thoughts as elevated as her.[8]

Among my companions some were painters, the others botanists or mineralogists; all of them dispersed into the surroundings in the early morning. I gladly guarded the luggage, with a book in hand. Now, as the book in question was a guide-book, an Ebel, a Richard or a Joanne, I was able, before them, while remaining where I was, to bring myself up to date with all the beauties of the Bernese Oberland—but I was too often distracted from my reading by the sight of the mountain.

When we met for dinner, when my friends joked, as always, about my immobility during the voyage and my insouciance regarding Alpine explorations. I made them a proposition that astonished them. That was to steal from the Mountaineering Club the honor of the first ascent of the Jungfrau. The Englishmen were due to arrive the next day; I proposed enrolling all the local guides that same day and thus preventing any competition.

---

[8] The summit of the Jungfrau has first been reached in 1811, by an exceedingly difficult route, and it was not until 1865—after this story was written—that a route more easily accessible to climbers was discovered. The world's first Mountaineering Club was the English Alpine Club, founded in 1857, although Charles Barrington had previously led three English ascents of the Jungfrau in 1856.

The idea seemed audacious to them, especially coming from me. Nevertheless, it was adopted unanimously, and I was charged with recruiting our escort.

The master guide, the man who rightly presided over all the great expeditions of that sort, lived in Lauterbrunn. I went to his cottage, were I only found his wife and three grown-up sons, already of an age to hunt chamois. I informed all four of the motive that brought me, and it was agreed that, as soon as the father returned, they would send him to my inn to settle the conditions of our agreement.

When night fell, weary of waiting, I went to bed, instructing the maidservant to wake me up as soon as he arrived. Scarcely was I in bed than someone knocked on my door; it was him, and to my great surprise I recognized him as Christian Roth, the most worthy guide in the world, who had been warmly recommended to me by Cyprien Fournier, one of my good friends.[9]

Christian Roth grasped the situation immediately. The English climbers were due to arrive in Lauterbrunn early the following morning, doubtless with an escort hired either in Unterseen or Interlaken. In consequence, if we wanted to anticipate them and not follow on their heels, there was not a minute to lose. The night was magnificent, the moon full; in such circumstances, he thought the night more favorable to an ascent than the

---

[9] The naturalist Cyprien Fournier is a character in a story by Saintine called "La Femme baromètre," in his collection *Les Metamorphoses de la Femme* (1845), which was separately translated into English as a pamphlet entitled *Woman's Whims; or, The Female Barometer*, with the by-line M. Xavier. There actually was an Alpine guide named Christian Roth, however, active in the 1860s.

day, in view of the more resistant solidity of the snow. Furthermore, we could furnish ourselves with lanterns and resin torches in case of fog or obscurity.

His opinion, therefore, was that we should set out immediately, and that opinion became mine spontaneously, so keen was my desire to put one over on the Mountaineering Club.

In all haste, I went to knock on the door of each of my companions, but sleep kept both their eyes and ears firmly closed. I knocked, rang, called out and turned the house upside down in vain, nothing came of it.

A thought, formidable in pride and temerity, went through my head then, which was to steal a march not only on the English but my Parisians as well, and to concentrate on myself alone the glory and the perils of the great expedition.

Christian Roth had two experienced guides to hand; with his three sons, that was as many people as we needed. We equipped ourselves with iron-tipped staffs, ropes, rope-ladders, shoes fitted with crampons, hooks, axes and even firearms, in case of trouble; not that we needed to fear thieves at those altitudes—one does not encounter any once past five or six hundred meters above sea level—but there was a risk of being violently robbed by bears. It was as well to take precautions in that regard, as in all the others.

We set forth. Horses took us rapidly to the first slopes of the mountain and helped us to cross them. Forced to abandon them until our return, we tethered them to the protruding roots of an old fir-tree, exposed by an avalanche. For an hour we traversed a gravelly and crumbling terrain where the only vegetation consisted of black mosses and lichens, a few gentians and a few microscopic buttercups. Stimulated by the pure, keen air of the high regions, I followed my route at a firm and assured pace, even giving myself the pleasure on the way of collecting a few plants by moonlight. We drew nearer to the abode of the perpetual snows.

Who would believe it? On those heights that only know one season, winter, where all vegetation seems to cease, animals can live. I saw chamois standing like sentinels on inaccessible peaks; I saw foxes in pursuit of snow-hens. Christian told me that during the day, one even encounters birds—not eagles but snow-finches pursuing flies, and even butterflies that the winds from below send up, half-stunned and scarcely fluttering their wings.

On the inferior plateau I had already had the good fortune of nocturnal plant-collecting; here I had that of fox-hunting, which nearly cost me dear. I don't know whether I hit the target, but the detonation of my rifle although scarcely perceptible to the ear, imprinted the mass of air surrounding us with a shock that was sufficient to cause the fall of an avalanche. That avalanche engulfed one of our guides. I made a movement to run to his aid,

"No imprudence!" said Christian Roth, perfectly calm and extending his arm. "The flow has no thickness; it's probable that he'll get up again."

He made me understand, however, that if he did not get up, that might modify the total of my bill considerably.

Fortunately, the man rejoined us, shaking himself from head to foot.

We did not take long to arrive at the most arduous part of our enterprise. Sometimes we had to avoid moraines, erratic stones that, impelled by the flow of invisible waters, descended the same slopes that we were scaling with so much effort; sometimes, a torrent of muddy water, half-congealed, blocked our passage; once the torrent was crossed, it was the crevasses of a glacier that opened before us, several feet wide.

As a conscientious guide, my friend Christian Roth, who wanted the excursion to be instructive for me, placed a torch between the gaping lips of the glacier, and enabled me to admire in its depths a series of prisms reflecting all imaginable shades of blue, while brilliant layers of the purest celadon green extended along the edges.

Ten years before, a member of the Mountaineering Club had disappeared into that same crevasse; he was still there, perfectly preserved; I could see him. Ten paces away, Christian lowered his torch again; Mechanically, I leaned over the gulf, but I closed my eyes; a current of air, charged with ice-particles, was escaping from the entrails of the glacier, and I had no doubt that it was the dead man who was blowing snow in my face in that fashion.

Of what happened afterwards I have only retained a confused memory. I only know that ropes were hoisted up, rope-ladders established, and that we continued climbing, climbing perpetually.

Almost asleep, exhausted by fatigue, I wanted to sit down on a granite boulder; Christian declared that I was a dead man if I stopped there for ten minutes; as proof of it he told me the lamentable story of all the travelers who, having reached the extreme point at which we had arrived, gripped by the cold, had gone to sleep, never to wake up again.

While talking to me, he made me drink from his own flask a liquor composed of half eau-de-vie and half vinegar, and forced me to eat a mouthful of black bread accompanied by a morsel of grilled cheese, a sustenance indispensable to all Alpine mountain-climbers.

After that, supported on one side by his arm and on the other by my iron-tipped staff, my feet biting the ice thanks to the crampons on my shoes, tightly surrounded by my escort of guides, my living rampart, I walked for a few minutes more, still ascending, or rather being taken and hoisted upwards...but the need for sleep took hold of me more ardently, my brain was disturbed; I mistook the cries of marmots, the last cry of life, which rises up even in the highest Alpine summits, for the cries of my predecessors, all those dead men lying in their shrouds of snow in their tombs of ice. Those tombs I thought I recognized in seeing a certain number of erratic stones lined up in rows in one of the valleys down below.

It was too much; my strength and courage were exhausted, and, renouncing the glory of being the first to tread the virgin summit of the Jungfrau, I was about to give the signal to go back...

Suddenly, I saw a shadow gliding along a ledge; a human form loomed up through the blue-tinted nocturnal vapors. Like me, it was climbing those previously-immaculate carpets of snow...

I thought about the Mountaineering Club.

My ardor was renewed; I hastened my stride with such determination that my guides were outdistanced. Carried forward by a supernatural force, leaving my iron-tipped staff behind, I descended slopes slowly and scaled them at a run; the snowy peaks drew closer ahead of me, in order that I could pass from one to another with a single bound. I did not take long to attain, finally, the culminating peak of the mountain. Then I remained dumbstruck with shock.

The same human form that had appeared to me on the ledge, which I believed that I had left behind me, was standing on the plateau in an attitude of triumph and defiance.

I approached. It was a woman…Lalagé! Lalagé! Don't ask me yet who Lalagé is.

"Oh!" she said to me, in a tone of bitter mockery, "not content with wanting to dispute with the Mountaineering Club the honor of being the first one on this summit, which already departs from a bad sentiment, you've excluded your own friends, to the benefit of your vanity—a treason, this time! Well, it's me who got here first; you've wasted your efforts and the glory of the enterprise. It's only just that you fail, when you've only employed shameful means to succeed."

Nonplussed, I was still listening when she had disappeared.

A moment later, Christian Roth arrived, carrying a flag with the French colors. He planted it—or, rather, wedged it in an upright position by means of two boulders, filling the interstices with snow. I saw him do it with a sort of apathy; numbness took hold of me again; I no longer aspired to anything but departure.

How did we contrive our descent? The only thing that I remember clearly is that when we reached the place where we had left our horses tethered to the roots of the old fir tree, we found nothing there but bones; the bears had eaten the rest.

Finally, at dawn, exhausted and bent over, half-brutalized and half-frozen, I reinstalled myself in my bed, where I hoped for a reparative sleep…but that sleep, which, after such fatigue, was so necessary to me, was almost immediately interrupted by my Parisians.

"Wake up! Wake up! It's time to set forth; the Virgin is holding out her arms to us; let's go! Get up, idler!"

"Idler!" I said, trying to open my eyes; "I haven't closed an eye; I've been on the march since yesterday. I've taken advantage of the full moon and the splendid night to make the ascension of the Jungfrau with Christian Roth and his three sons. I've only just got back."

They burst out laughing. "A pretext as adroit as it is implausible, for not quitting the inn," murmured one of my tourists. "That fellow is the god Terminus!"

"What!" said another. "It was your idea; you're the one who engaged us is the enterprise, and you're deserting it!"

"Far from deserting it, I've accomplished it alone, at my own risk and peril," I replied, this time with my eyes wide open. "Put your nose out of the window, look at the summit of the mountain, and you'll see our glorious tricolor flag floating there, under the folds of which the Mountaineering Club will read from afar the words: *Too late!*"

No one budged. They looked at one another in bewilderment.

At that moment the maidservant came to tell me that the chief guide, to whose home I had gone the previous day without encountering him, was there and asking to see me.

He came in. It was not Christian Roth.

After exchanging a few words, I told him about my nocturnal adventures, and although he had begun by saying that a moonlit excursion on the Jungfrau seemed impracticable, he had to recognize the exactitude of the observations I had made and the reality of the objects I had encountered there: the bare fir-tree, the gravelly plateau only strewn with gentians and dwarf buttercups, and a thousand other details of the route. When I reached the incident of the dead man still visible in the mouth of the glacier he interrupted me.

"Very good! That's the Englishman's Crevasse. As for those white tombs, lined up next to one another, that's the Valley of Moraines." It's true that he added: "But all that could have been learned from books; and as for the master guide charged with the route, it was certainly neither Christian Roth nor me, for I slept in Rosenlaui last night opposite Mettenburg, and Father Christian has been sleeping for five years in Meyringen cemetery. In any case, Messieurs, let's postpone the expedition until tomorrow; the Jungfrau will remain unapproachable to everyone today—with no exception," he concluded, in the self-important tone of a man who seems to be saying: *I have the key in my pocket.*

My comrades asked me then whether I still had the design of accomplishing the climb other than in a dream.

"Good God, no!" I replied. "What I've seen is sufficient for me."

I have had occasion since to talk about the Jungfrau to simple folk who have made the ascent without the aid of slumber, an ascent fairly common nowadays; I could talk about it as easily as them, without taking the trouble, like them, to scale the five hundred stages of the mountain. I was even able to recall certain details effaced from their memory.

One sometimes sees more with closed eyes than open ones.

The Large Armchair

Opposite me was the large armchair, already empty for a long month.

For a month, stationed by the extinct hearth, its back turned to the daylight, it had been there, as solitary and lamentable as a house deserted by its owner.

O large armchair, how the sight of you wrings my heart!

But is it permissible for me to change the location of that venerated item of furniture, become forever holy for me?

By touching it, I would seem to be suddenly effacing those precious imprints, scarcely graspable by anyone else, but which surge forth before my eyes, numerous and palpitating with memories.

That large armchair, with its high back slightly hollowed out in the upper part, its sagging seat and the scratches in its fabric, and even its stains, speaks to me; it appears to comprehend my grief and to share it. Has it not witnessed, in my company, the supreme adieu? I can still see the marks made by its castors on the parquet when, the dear invalid having said to me "I'm cold, move me closer to the fire," I carried out his order, the last one that I was to receive from him.

Aiding himself then with the chair's two arms, he raised himself up slightly, articulating my name in the midst of a groan, and fell back with all his weight. And the arms of the chair testified to his last effort, as the parquet did to his last movement.

Could I think that I would never see the man I was mourning again, never hear him again, when his traces, almost alive, permitted me to follow him so closely?

How long did I stay there, my eyes moist, my head inclined and full of those dolorous preoccupations? I don't know. When I came round, two red morocco slippers that I scarcely recognized struck my gaze.

Incredibly, they were not empty! To my profound surprise, I saw the two feet that filled them move slightly, and support themselves, crossed over, on one of the fire-irons.

I trembled; I scarcely dared think and pursue my examination. Although my gaze remained fixed on the same point, however, I glimpsed a floating object, brown in hue. It was a long dressing-gown, under the folds of which the feet and the slippers immediately disappeared.

Was someone sitting in the chair, then?

My heart palpitating with anguish, gently and gradually, I raised my eyes, unable to believe in a profanation. Half way up the dressing-gown, on the double angle emphasized by the knees, two hands were resting...

Those hands! Oh, how many times they had passed over my forehead and into my hair! How many times I had raised them respectfully to my lips!

I dared...I looked higher. His head inclined over his chest, my father retained a mild attitude of meditation, or slumber...nothing else...

At that moment, I heard someone call me. It really was his voice. That appeal had, however, come from the next room, and he had not budged; he was still asleep, or meditating.

Again, with more force, my name was pronounced behind me; I turned around; and when I returned my eyes to the large armchair it was empty again…and empty it has remained, until this day.

The Marionette Theater

Neatly clad in black, in the Venetian style, with their plumed toques tipping over their eyes, their jade pins and clasps, quivering on their little cardboard legs, how light they were, and how gracious, the two puppets!

The dance they executed on a semblance of a tight-rope extended across the proscenium, an arm's length at the most, had kept me attentive immediately, the spinet tune that marked the measure and regulated their movements completed my satisfaction.

How did I come to be thus installed in the auditorium of a marionette theater, where hardly anyone goes but children accompanied by their nursemaids? I have no idea. At any rate, I had to be making a singular figure in the midst of those brats. In order to take stock of my situation, turning my eyes away from my charming puppets, I paraded my gaze around momentarily.

The hall, sparkling with candlelight, was richly decorated from top to bottom, and I did not see any brats or nursemaids there, but elegant women, men wearing épées, and ecclesiastics clad as bishops.

I had arrived late, it appeared, and only in the latter part of the spectacle, for I heard grave men placed on the same bench as me affirming that in his drunkenness and his quarrel with the policeman Polichinelle had been perfect; that Pierrot, having visibly eaten all of his stolen pâté, including the crust, had been incomparable. For myself, I thought that my two pretty Venetian puppets must at least equal them in merit. Without the strings that activated them being visible, they went back and forth along their rope, leaping, performing entrechats and cartwheels, and falling upside-down, suspended by a hand or an ankle. Could one see anything more curious on the part of mechanical characters?

No one, however, in the stalls or the boxes, was showing the slightest mark of satisfaction, either at the skill of the mechanician or that or the spinet-player, who composed the entire orchestra and seemed to be holding the souls of the two puppets in his hands.

Hoping to enthuse that starchy public, I uttered a "bravo," accompanying it with a few signs of approval. My applause and my bravo did not find any echo in the hall. A few of the grave men, my neighbors on the bench, turned toward me with surprised, almost shocked expressions; but the man at the spinet also turned round, and thanked me with a smile. Under a little round wig, lightly powdered, I perceived a young face with large, expressive blue eyes, which were sympathetic to me to the highest degree.

The two puppets were still dancing; the one-man orchestra was playing his tune, still the same, scarcely ornamented by slight variations. No matter! I even liked the monotony of the tune; it lulled me in a mild rapture, and I was listening even more intently than I was watching, when a noise of moving chairs, doors and banquettes came to distract me from my blissful state.

In a box opposite, an important individual—I was able to judge that by the numerous decorations suspended from his buttonhole, around his neck and over his breast, cut diagonally by a broad yellow and black ribbon—had stood up, and everyone else had stood up too. He had inclined his head slightly, and everyone, men, women and ecclesiastics, had curbed their heads as low

49

as they could. Finally, he went out, and everyone jostled one another in the doorways in order to leave in their turn, with the exception of half a dozen enthusiasts, of which I was one.

After having let the torrent flow away, setting an example to the others, I was the first to resume my seat, which attracted a further salutation and smile from the young musician.

The puppets had not interrupted their evolutions on the tightrope; he continued, even while bowing and smiling, to run his fingers over the keyboard.

It was getting late; the illumination was only throwing out a few dubious gleams; among the aficionados, five out of the six withdrew.

In spite of that general desertion, the orchestra and the actors kept going; I held firm too, alone in the empty and darkened hall; I composed the audience—which earned me a third bow and a third smile from the man at the spinet.

Soon, my pretty Venetian puppets disappeared in their turn; I don't know how. Nevertheless, my musician remained at his post and continued playing his tune.

The same tune, the same bow and the same smile led me to think now that the man, as well as the dancing puppets, Polichinelle and Pierrot, was part of the marionette troupe, and that his spinet and he were only a single machine set up for a certain number of hours.

I waited for it to stop; it didn't.

Then something extraordinary happened. I looked at the orchestra; my musician was no longer there. He had gone to join the important person, the beautiful ladies, the churchmen, the five aficionados and the two puppet acrobats, and yet the unique tune executed by him could still be heard; and I found myself at home, in my bed. It was broad daylight, and it was not on a spinet that the tune was now resonating but in my head.

I tried to bring it to my lips; it came of its own accord. Although I was wide awake at that moment, it seemed to me to be more charming than ever. What a triumph for me! Was not my conviction regarding the routine work of the imagination during a dream receiving there its definitive sanction? While dreaming, I had become a composer of music; I had composed a melody, a charming melody, with variations—me, who could not play a note!

Fearful of losing my precious discovery, I dressed in haste and immediately went to see one of my friends, a young poet and musician, in order that he could write down my tune, to fix its on paper. And I hummed it as I got dressed, I hummed it on the way and going up the stairs, and while pulling the bell-cord I was still humming it.

But while I was explaining to my friend Honoré M*** what it was about, my tune seemed to want to escape, as a bird does at the sight of the cage that will retain it forever. I could no longer find the beginning, the end, or the middle. After much effort, a few measures of the refrain came back to mind.

"Good! I've got it!" interjected my young composer, whose head is a complete music library. And he went to take from his shelf an old bulky volume of music, opened it, sat down at the piano and played, note for note, with the variations, the famous piece of which I had truly thought myself the inventor.

"It's one of the first tunes composed by Haydn," he said, "for the marionette theater of Prince Esterhazy, of whom the young maestro was then a supplier as well as the humble orchestra leader, as you know."

I did not know that, and I had never known it, I told him. I had scarcely heard mention of Haydn, and his works were completely unknown to me. With vehement protestations, I would have claimed even so the property of my tune if the phrase "marionette theater" had not diverted me into another, much more important, train of thought.

I remembered the two puppets, the handsome gentlemen and the beautiful ladies of my dream. Was the important individual with the yellow and black ribbon Prince Esterhazy, then?

At that moment I uttered a cry of surprise and amazement. My young poet-composer had just reopened the stout volume at the frontispiece, where the name of Haydn was radiant, and below his name was his portrait. The portrait was that of my man at the spinet, striking in his resemblance, with the same little round wig, the same gaze and the same smile.

Well, then, no. No, I admitted that I was not the author of the tune that had charmed me so much. But that tune, I had heard played by Haydn in person, toward the second half of the eighteenth century, at a court spectacle, in the noble marionette theater of the powerful Prince Esterhazy.

What can one think of that musical revelation, that retrograde vision, in which the event and I had been able to look one another in the face at a distance of a hundred years?

The Taking of Ptolemais[10]

I was browsing along the quay,
When I left for the crusade;
The king, who had noticed me,
Designated me for the escalade.

We camped outside Ptolemais,
Starving, living on little more
Than millet and on maize;
Little enough for men of war.

The day arrived anyway
Tightening my belt,
I made ready for the fray,
The cards of fate were dealt.

I listened to the mass

---

[10] Ptolemais was one of five cities on the coast of what is now Libya, which formed the Pentapolis of Cyrenaica. The Pentapolis was devastated by an earthquake in 365, but Ptolemais remained the capital of Cyrenaica until 428, when it was destroyed by the Vandals. Although rebuilt, it was destroyed again by Arabs in the eighth century, long before the crusades, and was buried in the sand; its ruins had not yet been excavated when Saintine wrote the poem. This is the only poem in the volume of which I have been able to conserve the rhyme-scheme; although it is arguable that as most of them are doggerel, it might have given a fairer impression of their quality to save the rhymes by compromising the meaning, I took the view that preserving the meaning was more important.

And intoned a prayer or two,
I'll say nothing of the fast,
That everybody knew.

The ladder shook in my hand,
But not because of fear,
The hunger fires being fanned
As the great attack drew near.

Penetrating like a dart
I crossed the ditch and wall
And first on to the rampart
I sounded the holy call.

Blood flowed beneath my sword
When at the battle's height,
I was seized and drawn toward
A man of size and might.

Was it one of Saladin's Turks?
No, it's a notary, a friend,
Who laughed at all my quirks
And made me comprehend.

In my hand was Montmerqué,
Poujoulat, Michaud and Poujade;[11]

---

[11] Louis-Jean-Nicolas de Montmerqué was an obscure publisher whose book collection was sold by auction in 1861; Saintine, a collector himself, might have attended the sale. Jean-Joseph Poujoulat was a historian who published a book of *Correspondence d'Orient* in collaboration with the more famous historian Joseph-François Michaud, whose books in-

While browsing along the quay
I had set forth for the crusade.

cluded *Histoire des croisades* (1841). Eugène Poujade published a book on *Le Liban et la Syrie* in 1860.

The Two Hunts
(A Consultation)

"There are dreams, then which take us by surprise, as it were, when we are fully awake and rational? At the moment when we least expect it, after lying in wait for a moment of weakness on our part—an involuntary, momentary lowering of the eyelid—the deceptive bird falls upon us; our senses have not completely ceased their ordinary exercise when, extending its wings, it carries us away through the turbulence of the second life, and a great magical spectacle is played out before our eyelashes, scarcely intersected.

"If that magical play, which can surprise us in the middle of a conversation, without interrupting it entirely, without our interlocutors suspecting our state of somnolence, and without our having lost any sentiment of reality ourselves, is not a dream, what is it? It is up to you, Doctor, who have made a special study of the matter, to see clearly in my darkness, and up to me to enable you to appreciate the fact. This is the most gripping example that I find in my own memories.

"I was young—it was twenty years and more ago. During the vacation, I had just installed myself in the house of my great aunt, in a semblance of an old château near Blois. An invitation arrived for me to take part in a hunt in the woods of Chambord, where wild beasts have multiplied excessively, to the great detriment of the farmers.

"The day before the opening, my friends and I went to install ourselves at a turning, in the house of a man named Chotiau...there! The name of our host, which I thought erased from my memory permanently, just returned suddenly! Sometimes Doctor, in spite of the time that has gone by, my memories transport me once again to the uneven banks of the Cosson; I see once again a certain crossroads in the forest, the wild and picturesque scene that witnessed the most curious incident of our hunt.

"Why should I not tell you about that incident, my dear Doctor? We're chatting here amicably, with our feet in the fire-irons, and without taking anything away from the main event—which is to say, the dream, which, in my stories, always has to occupy the foreground—I can risk that preamble, perhaps necessary for the consultation that you are kindly granting me.

"So, we were hunting, and wild boar, if you please—which is to say, with bullets, with the precautions usual in any serious war.

"On the first day, we did marvelously; eight pigs were slain and, like Masséna, I was declared on the battlefield 'the dear child of Victory.' On the second day, which was to be that of our return to Blois, early in the morning, three yearlings and a few piglets had been killed without favor having given me a glimpse of one. They had emerged from cover in my line of sight.

"Having risen at the same time as the sun, my body motionless, my eyes fixed and my thumb on the action of my rifle, I held my position nevertheless for four hours, attentive to the point of anguish, in front of a little path that opened into a clearing, the surveillance of which had been confided to me. Nothing before me was moving, nothing as passing through my field of vision except for a few sparrows and a few butterflies chasing one another, with what intention I don't know, although I suspected strongly that they were employing their time more agreeably than I was employing mine. In the direction of the clearing, as in the direction of the path, everything was silent, with the exception of a birch tree that was rustling over my head in the breeze.

"Suddenly, a rumor went up; there were the cries of the beaters, mingled with the barking of dogs. I scarcely had time to pull myself together, put my gun to my shoulder, turning, as usual, to face the little path, than I felt myself lifted up, thrown ten feet into the air, and then fell back, stupidly, into a treacherous little pond that hid black and fetid water beneath a verdant epidermis."

"Ha ha! Bravo!" exclaimed the doctor, who had not thought of interrupting me until then. "At last that's an emotion. Without these little incidents, the pleasure of hunting would be as insipid as so many other pleasures. But to what invisible ballista did you owe that aid, that unexpected and anomalous ascension?"

"Nothing simpler, Doctor. As I put myself on guard, my dog, pursued, not by a young pig, but by a monstrous solitary with a gray beard, had just sought shelter between my legs, and the frightful boar, hot on its heels, with the furious impetus of its charge, had sent me with a single thrust...you know where. That was, in fact, my last prowess of the hunt. Let's quit the woods of Chambord, if you don't mind, and return to my aunt's house."

"Gladly," said the doctor. "I only appreciate hunting for its purely culinary results. But I don't see, as yet, any matter for consultation."

"Wait, Doctor, wait! When I arrived at the house, my dear great-aunt, who was giving dinner to the local authorities that very day, fearing that fatigue might take away my good humor with regard to her guests, first advised me, then asked me, and finally implored me to go to bed and have a rest, in order to recover myself. Believe me, I did not see any necessity; I felt well and alert, as usual, ready to resume hunting right away; I answered for myself and my good humor.

She gave in.

"At five o'clock precisely, we sat down at table.

"Pay attention, Doctor; it's during that very meal that the strange phenomena occurred, the incredible amalgam of dream and reality, about which I'm seeking enlightenment from you.

"Although it was still broad daylight, the dining room, with the curtains and shutters closed, was illuminated splendidly. My dear aunt was proud of her silverware and her crystal, and only the light of lamps and candles could bring out their full gleam.

"For neighbors at table I had two charming women, and of the highest merit, so my aunt assured me. The one on the left, a poorly-conserved quadragenarian, doubtless out of benevolence, did not talk to me about anything but Paris, its usages and fashions, throughout the meal. I'm not sure that she didn't ask me, like a certain character in an English comedy, what age people were in Paris nowadays. Twenty-nine, Madame, neither more nor less.

"The other, the one on my right, perhaps not as young, and more grave in appearance, never ceased bragging about the merits of her husband, a counselor at the prefecture of Blois. He was a man destined one day to occupy the highest employments, if the government understood its own interests; the list rolled on of his bureaucratic and administrative virtues. The lady, doubtless thinking that, because I spent three quarters of the year in Paris, if I cared to take the trouble, I could easily have him appointed sub-prefect, for a start

I had, therefore to sustain the crossfire of my two neighbors, chatting about fashion and administration at the same time. For the moment, I was allowing them to take turns, riposting from time to time with a few elastic and obliging monosyllables applicable to almost any question, as in the game of twenty questions, when I was gripped by a sort of dizziness.

"I affirm to you, Doctor, that although the meal had already been going on for an hour—which, as you know, means in the provinces that it was a third of the way through—and although the wines had already begun to circulate, I had given proof of heroic moderation; I ought, therefore, physically, to have been in a state of perfect calm. However, it seemed to me that a vapor full of glittering reflections had just invaded the room; the lamps and candles had changed into stars; my aunt's silverware was radiant; even my fork, which I was just about to put into my mouth, threw off a flash.

Although somewhat disquieted by that unexpected phantasmagoria, I quickly applied my napkin to my half-closed eyelids. When I took it away again, as if an optical instrument had just been placed in front of each of my eyes, everything around me took on exaggerated proportions. My friends the hunters, the physician, the curé, the tax-collector, the president of the horticultural society, the mayor, his wife, the husband of my right-hand neighbor and the husband of my left-hand neighbor, had the effect on me of as many giants armed with pitchforks, occupied in engulfing quarters of beef and entire military loaves The famous cup of Promachus was nothing by comparison with the immense flagons from which they were ingurgitating gulps the equivalent of a quarter-liter of wine.

"I closed my eyes several times: a movement that appeared to detach those frightful magnifying spectacles. When I opened them again—or, rather, when I succeeded in opening them slightly, for my eyelids were strangely heavy—the table and the guests, the walls, the house, my aunt's guards and my aunt herself, had all disappeared.

I found myself in a cheerful, florid plain, bearing no resemblance to the plains that I had seen previously in the vicinity of Paris or Blois. Here, there were no fields of rye or beets, nothing that suggested agriculture. Thick, grass, bushes, mosses and strange multicolored flowers covered the earth, and there was no evidence anywhere of the presence of humans: no paths traced through the rich grasslands, no Chinese bridges thrown over the streams that were running capriciously through the grass.

"Where was I? I had no idea, and scarcely cared; but I was surely no longer in France, nor in Europe. The birds and the butterflies, clad in the most brilliant colors, the form of certain plants, the intense deep blue sky, and the huge sun with ardent rays, were all suggestive of the Orient, and I gladly resigned myself to the Orient, and even to my solitude, although that was less complete than you might think.

"In order to avoid the direct rays of the sun, I had taken shelter under a beautiful tree with shiny foliage, capriciously shaped, and I was chatting with it. The tree was telling me about the marvels of the beautiful country into which I had just been transported; I was relaxing into the charm of its conversation without being astonished in the slightest by having a tree for an interlocutor, when a slight rumor became audible, which I mistook at first for the sound of the wind.

"'Take care,' the tree said to me, 'there's a big hunt today.'

"And that faint rumor, attributed by me to the breath of the wind, gradually developed, toward *crescendo* and *risforzando*, and soon changing into a frightful racket.

"From all the depths of the forests that served the plain as a girdle, cries, lamentations and howls went up, rising and falling like a resounding wave, mingling with the rolls, blasts and clashes of an infinite number of drums, trumpets and cymbals.

"In the midst of that infernal racket, during which you could not have heard God thunder, would you believe, Doctor, that the thin, soft and discreet voice of my right-hand neighbor and my left-hand neighbor still arrived in my ears distinctly, one talking to me about the theaters of Paris and the other the prefecture of Loir-et-Cher. I replied to them with the same insignificant monosyllables, which said nothing and responded to everything.

"Without my vision being interrupted, as if through a cloud furrowed by lightning, for an instant I glimpsed my aunt's dining room, my friends and our guests; all of them had resumed their accustomed stature and physiognomy, save for the fact that each of them, without exception, had a lower jaw furnished with the tusks of s wild boar. My neighbors seemed quite ridiculous with that borrowed ornament.

Then, in the beat of a wing, the dream transported me again to the other side of the world, into my lush plain and beneath my loquacious tree.

"My solitude, mute at first, then noisy, was considerably populated, not yet with hunters, but with game of large species. Bands of tigers, lions and panthers, their flanks quivering with fear, along with those of deer and gazelles, chased from the forest, were running across the plain in all directions, searching under the rare clumps of palm trees, and even in the tufts of long grass, for a refuge from the invisible but noisy enemy.

"Already, a few of them were prowling around my tree; fear gripped me in my turn. A protective hand was extended toward me through the foliage...yes, Doctor, a white, slender hand; a woman's hand. You're doubtless going to explain by that means how my tree was endowed with the gift of speech: a woman was hidden in it. That's the whole secret! Wrong! For the dreamer, as for the fabulist, don't trees and rocks, as well as animals, all acquire a natural voice? Let's avoid reasoning in the manner of people who are awake, I beg you.

"That woman was the one that, in the adventurous courses of my second life, I rediscovered everywhere, whenever I needed help or good advice. Don't ask me anymore, my dear Doctor; our amours, even those of our dreams, ought to have their modesty and their mysteries...

"Thanks to her, therefore, I was sheltered from any affliction. From the height of my verdant observatory, I then saw appearing from all the points of the forest, a veritable army of hunters. Clad in strange, bizarre costumes, they had heads decorated with clusters of jewels and long plumes, and at first, from a distance, I might have believed that it was a invasion of marvelous birds, but as they gained ground, the birds became humans; those humans, still uttering their clamors, still making their trumpets of war resound, some mounted on horses and some mounted on elephants, all with bows or spears in hand, continued to advance, gradually tightening their circle, in which the panting throng of deer, lions and tigers were soon enclosed, as if in an abattoir.

"A frightful rattle of tom-toms then gave the signal for the carnage. By virtue of one of those sudden transformations, even easier to accomplish in dreams than in the plays performed on our boulevards, I suddenly found myself on a spirited horse, spear in hand, clad like the others in rich cloth, with my head covered by a colossal turban garnished with ostrich feathers. Ashamed of that contest, which made us butchers rather than hunters, I ordered…for, I don't know how, but I had become the chief of those Asiatic hordes…I ordered our ranks to open in order to give our terrible prey a passage toward the mountains; the host of ferocious beasts launched itself in that direction; our hunters followed them.

"For an entire day, without rest or respite, we continued our pursuit, crossing endless spaces, at the end of which limitless horizons opened; those of us on horseback traversed, at a precipitate gallop, solitudes of sand, jungles, forests of baobabs and bamboo; we hunted in the depths of dark valleys, on the snowy summits of blue mountains, in the clouds, even a little above them. Our interminable route was strewn with the remains of tigers and lions.

"When we had nothing more to kill, we stopped near little springs, so full of weeds that we mistook them for fields of water-cress. They were nothing less than the sources of the Ganges.

"We had pitched our tents close by; during the night those springs had overflowed to such an extent that when we awoke, we were prisoners in our turn: prisoners of growling waves that surrounded us.

"Accompanied by a few devoted friends, among whose number was the husband of my right-hand neighbor, the counselor at the prefecture—I ask you, what was that counselor of the prefecture of the Loir-et-Cher doing on the Ganges?—I threw myself into a boat that happened to be floating by; a multitude of aquatic monsters mounted a furious assault upon us; my counselor was cut in two by an enormous caiman...

"In sum, what can I tell you, Doctor? After a long time of ordeals and combats, after having traveled across part of Persia and India, I found myself back in my aunt's house, at her table, from which I had not budged, where I was still continuing, monosyllabically, my conversation with my two neighbors. Once again, that is the point to which I call your attention essentially. I have talked about dreams, but can one call those visions that do not wait for our slumber to surprise us 'dreams'?

"No, I wasn't asleep, since, from time to time, even while chatting with my tree, I inspected our guests, aligned around the table, with my gaze; since the enchantment happened to me without my eyes being completely closed; since I continued to hear the babble of my neighbor to the right and the one to my right; since I replied to them while being carried away by my horse in hot pursuit of tigers and panthers or, manning my boat, tossed by the torrential waves, I had to deal with all the hippopotamuses and crocodiles of the Ganges, while words arrived in my ear such as 'Monsieur, if the Minister knew what my husband is worth...!' and "Monsieur, what is being put on at the Gymnase?'

"One final word, Doctor. How long do you think that my vision, so numerous and so complicated in all its developments, took to unfold? I have been able to calculate its duration almost to the minute. At the moment when it made my debut in that land of mirages, my right-hand neighbor, the one of the prefectoral administration of the Loir-et-Cher, was beginning the dissection of a chicken neck, of which she seemed very fond; when I recovered my wits completely, arriving from China, India and Japan, she had not yet completed her anatomical task. In truth, what is the pretended rapidity of railways, and even the electric telegraph, by comparison with that of dreams?

Now, my friend the Doctor, the floor is yours; it's necessary for you to find me a cause, or a name, for that strange, complex state, if there is one, now that you are sufficiently informed."

My dear Hippocrates collected himself for a few moments, and then spoke.

"Of your two hunts," he told me, "the second was only a hallucinated remembrance of the first; the panthers and the tigers there replaced the boars and the piglets; the woods and clearings of Chambord became jungles and forests of bamboo, where the cries of your beaters made themselves heard, accompanied by the sound of all the eccentric instruments executing a frightful concert in your head by themselves, under the influence of nervous excitement. Your chatty tree, surely, was the same birch with which you had already chatted beside the little path through the brushwood.

"You see that I have listened carefully and retained the details of your dual huntsman's Odyssey. As for the white hand that pierced the foliage, I dare not pronounce...you seem to have made it the object of a mystical cult, but I strongly suspect that at that moment, in front of you, on the table, the hand of one of our neighbors, the one on the left or the one on the right..."

"Doctor, you're blaspheming!"

"All right...! Finally, there's nothing left but the fetid black pool, which, under the wave of your magic wand, became the sacred sources of the Ganges. Far too much honor for it, in truth, as for its frogs and tadpoles, transformed for the same occasion into hippopotamuses and crocodiles. Now, let's get to the serious side of the question.

"A long fatigue, as always happens, was appealing within you for slumber; on the other hand, a cerebral excitation maintained you in a state of wakefulness: hence, two opposed impulses, two opposed efforts, which ended up being confounded. And who knows? Perhaps the candles, and your aunt's silverware and crystal, had something to do with it. You've heard mention of the effects of hypnotism? It's sometimes sufficient to fix one's eyes on a shiny object to provoke a sort of catalepsy, participating by its effects in those produced by the inhalation of an anesthetic..."

"Oh, Doctor! Please, not to many big words! Anyway, I'll bring you back to the principal point: I could hear, and I even replied to, my two neighbors."

"Exactly! During the catalepsy, certain senses, certain organs, are far from having abdicated completely. Read the work of my learned colleague Dr. Puel.[12] I'll summarize, then: your second hunt, your great magical spectacle, is what we call a waking dream, or, more precisely, a *hypnagogic hallucination*."

---

[12] The botanist and physician Timothée Puel (1812-1890), the founder of the *Revue de psychologie expérimentale*, whose pioneering study of "catalepsy" and "hysteria" was published in 1856. If the story really is quasi-autobiographical, however, the "consultation" must surely have taken place in the 1840s, looking back to the author's youth in the 1820s.

"Mercy, Doctor! That's a *hypnagogic* capable of killing a man."

"In any case, 'waking dream' explains the thing sufficiently. In that state, you aren't asleep, but you're subject to a numbing, almost asphyxiating, influence, the cause of which is the swelling of tiny blood vessels in the brain. Be careful, my dear friend, that's a menacing sign of carditis. Perhaps you need a good bleeding…?"

I burst out laughing. "You're distracted, my learned friend…twenty years have gone by since my double hunt; I'd like to think that carditis is no longer to be feared?"

"That's true."

And he laughed too, as wholeheartedly as me. "Come on," he said, cheerfully, "I'm beginning to believe that a glass of water will be sufficient as a cure; I have to prescribe you something: no consultation without prescription."

"Prescribe me to take you to dinner somewhere, Doctor."

The Doctor's Hallucinations

A Moving Terrain. The Danae Delusion.

In accordance with the doctors own indication, we had been occupying a private booth in a small restaurant of the second order, but the first choice; physicians know about that, and in that regard, at least, one can trust their experience and their conscientious observations.

The dinner, in which iced champagne had taken the place of other wines—that was another of the doctor's prescriptions—was approaching its conclusion, and we were beginning to chat with our elbows on the table, when he returned of his own accord to our previous conversation on dreams and visions. Knowing that I kept a journal of my dreams, he asked me whether I had classified them by order—from which I had carefully refrained, great God!

He spoke to me first about "lucid dreams"—*clara somnia*—during which the mind retains all its power of dedication and even invention.

Poets have been known to make verses, and mathematicians to have solved problems during those sorts of dreams, which are also called 'psychic,' the soul enjoying its complete liberty therein, during the complete slumber of the senses. In a contrary order, there are 'hyperesthetic dreams,' in which the senses are solely dominant, and excessively, as if unchained in the absence of the mastery of logic.

"In the great class of hyperesthetics," he told me, "we first distinguish the 'symptomatics,' whose character is not so much passionate as persistent. Hippocrates, and Galen after him, had already called attention to them as providing an excellent diagnostic in maladies, hence the name of symptomatic. In order to inform us, those dreams proceed by the law of contraries. If, during your sleep, my friend, you frequently participate in good meals, if you dream about cooking, feasting and food for three days running, consider yourself warned; your habitual alimentary regime is insufficient, or one of your digestive organs is only fulfilling its functions imperfectly. Thank God, I think that neither you nor I will dream about Pantagruelesque feasts tonight…to your health!...and to mine!"

He held out his glass.

"Your symptomatic dreams, Doctor, are reminiscent of a mirage, which, in the midst of the desert sands, presents water and shade to unfortunates extenuated by thirst and heat."

"Let's not get confused, my dear friend; a mirage is only manifest to open eyes; it's a hallucination, not a dream, and before we arrive at hallucinations, let me take up my theory of dreams again. After the symptomatics come the 'symplegadics';[13] they are disor-

---

[13] I can find no remaining trace of the term *symplégadique*, which I have transcribed straightforwardly into English as symplegadic, having been used as a medical term in France, but it might well have been deployed by Puel and his pioneering contemporaries. On the other hand, it might have been invented by the author, who uses it again later in the present volume. If, of course, he really did consult a physician about the issue, that supposed expert might improvised it on his own account. In any case, the etymology of the term is obvious; it comes from the story of Jason and the Argonauts, who encountered the Symplegades, or Clashing Rocks in the course

dered dreams in which the senses and the imagination collide, in which several dramas are mixed into a single one: complicated, monstrous dreams with neither head nor tail, in which the nightmare rightfully takes its place. But you're right, to the devil with these big words, which even the Greeks, who furnished them, don't understand. For me, what springs evidently from my observations is that in a dream, a man is doubled; the body and the soul are able to isolate themselves from one another, or recombine in conditions quite different from the normal state."

"Bravo, Doctor!" I exclaimed. Now you've arrived at recognizing my theory of *the second life*."

"If it is a theory," he replied, smiling, "it might well, like my theory, lack common sense—but pass for the second life, and even the third, which I'm very far from renouncing, even though I'm a member of the Académie de Médecine."

The dear doctor took a few sips of the wine that I had just poured for him, seemed to abstract himself from his reflections for a few seconds, and then smiled again.

"Since we've come back to this terrain, in exchange for your two hunts, I'll tell you about two odd little accidents of my youth, which, I believe, with a few developments, might furnish two curious chapters for your journal. It's up to you to recognize your property and to classify them as seems good to you."

And immediately, he launched into the first chapter.

---

of their adventure, so-called because they smashed together when anyone tried to pass between them. The English adjective symplegadic does exist in a few commentaries on that story.

"The most audacious traveler," he said, "has never traversed a bolder, stranger, more moving and more stirring route than the one I came to travel one day—yes, a day when I frayed a passage above a dense, compact human crowd that took the place of a parquet: a veritably mosaic of living, grimacing, convulsed heads, rolling terrible eyes and each vociferating louder than the next. On such a path, the most skillful equilibrist wouldn't have been able to take ten paces without stumbling, for along with the heads, arms were agitating, bent and stiff, terminating in closed fists, similar in their movement to the swaying of gastropod tentacles—or, rather, the multiple limbs with which hideous cephalopods are equipped. If, as a poet, you prefer mythological comparisons, imagine a thousand or twelve-hundred heads of Medusa with their serpentine tresses.

"In spite of those heads, those arms, those eyes, those cries and those fists, all of which were menacing me simultaneously," my savant friend went on, "I continued walking, still upright. My feet sank into their bushy tresses, slid over the curve of foreheads, clung on to the angular projections of shoulders, and I, strangely enough, whose nature shares nothing with that of a lion, did not feel for a moment the dread of danger—not even that of the harm I might cause. Tell me, doesn't that have a complete resemblance to a dream?"

"Wasn't it one?"

"No; everything was real in the contact of my feet with those heads and shoulders, and without worrying overmuch about it, I walked there as if on rugged terrain with a few fissures, that's all."

"What, then, Doctor, inspired you to such audacity?"

"Fear, my friend—the fear that sometimes gives birth to heroes. I launched myself across that scabrous route without any other preoccupation than that of flee-ing—and not fleeing a peril, but a simple emotion.

"I was a medical student then; all my studies were marching ahead, and valiantly, I dare say; only operatory science still found me a rebel, in revolt. Twenty or a hundred times I had tried in vain to watch some unim-portant operation. Meanwhile, my pusillanimity threat-ened to ruin my future.

"One morning, I was following the visit to the Hôpital de la Charité when our illustrious professor an-nounced to us for the following day a surgical operation on number 17 *with a new apparatus*. Number 17 was a little man with a grim and harsh physiognomy. That physiognomy did not inspire any compassion in me, and by virtue of its very unpleasantness it suited me.

"I got up at first light, resolved not to weaken this time, to watch the operation, not only in such a way as to get a good view, but in order not to desert my post. I was in the process of keeping my word.

"The Amphitheater of the Charité presented the form of an immense funnel equipped with steps from the top to the bottom of its perimeter. I went down to the bottom of the funnel. When I found myself facing the operating table, so close that I was almost touching it, I sat down on the narrow banquette, toward which con-verged, necessarily, all the steps of the enclosure, soon garnished with numerous students, because of the an-nouncement of the new apparatus.

"Not a single place remained vacant; the last arri-vals were forced to give one another a leg up in order to make use of the window-sills, for want of anything bet-ter; the doors were obstructed by a triple rank of spectators, like the entrance to the orchestra stalls of our theaters on days of grand performances. And I, literally plunged and submerged at the bottom of the funnel, like Cain in the final circle of the Dantean Inferno, got ready, with sweat on my brow, finally to commence my course in human suffering.

"A little door opened facing me. Preceded by the hospital interns, like a consul by his lictors, the professor made his entrance, to the sound of applause. He said a few words about the operation and about the new apparatus, showed the instruments, with a clear and rapid comment on each one. Then two orderlies brought the unfortunate number 17, enveloped in the sad gray overcoat that is the uniform of the place.

"At the sight of him, I shuddered, but without losing courage. However, that physiognomy, which had only inspired an antipathetic sentiment, was ennobled, as at the approach of martyrdom. While he was being stripped of his only garment, the poor fellow paraded over all of us a gaze imprinted with such a dolorous resignation that it seemed to me that the knife prepared for him had just plunged into my chest. He was then laid on a thin mattress; his wrists were drawn toward his feet and secured by solid ligatures...

"I did not see any more. I had already commenced my terrible ascension of the steps; a violent nervous shock had simultaneously shaken within me the organs of intelligence and given incredible strength to those of locomotion. A blind movement impelled me forward, whatever obstacles there might be; I would have confronted a battery of cannons. I could no longer see clearly; I believed that I was traversing a phantasmagorical terrain, that an enchanter had strewn grimacing heads and contorted arms in my path.

"Thus I accomplished that terrible climb, thus I traveled intrepidly that moving route strewn with reefs, and above all with punches—for when I recovered my senses in the street, in the open air, I was bruised. The next day, my legs and my body were black with contusions.

"Such is, my dear friend, the exact story of my odyssey across the great amphitheater of the Hôpital de la Charité in Paris. To enlighten you more fully on the provocative causes of that unusual manner of travel, read *Recherches sur les hallucinations* by Szafkowski, and especially the works of the savant Alfred Maury..."[14]

"My dear Doctor, I prefer to hear your second chapter.

"Good!" he said. "Another glass of champagne to make us forget the amphitheater of the Charité and poor number 17."

After a moment of silence, he continued: "This time, it's no longer a matter of a hospital scene; it's my turn to transport you into a land of enchantment, into the midst of a voluptuous tableau, and even slightly libertine—which might appear strange to you on the part of a grave practitioner like me, but are we not in a private

---

[14] *Recherches sur les hallucinations au point de vue de la psychologie, de l'histoire et de la médecine légale* (1849) by Louis-Rufin Szafkowski. The physician and scholar Alfred Maury (1817-1892) was an important contributor to nineteenth-century exercises in the hypothetical interpretation of dreams, and a significant precursor of Sigmund Freud, although his writings covered a wide range of subjects, including oft-reprinted studies of *Les Fées du moyen-âge* [The Enchantresses of the Middle Ages] (1843) and *La Magie et l'astrologie dans l'antiquité et au moyen-âge* [Magic and Astrology in Antiquity and the Middle Ages] (1864).

booth? The lady at the counter won't know anything about it; furthermore, I'll be brief in my descriptions in order not to put your modesty and mine to too long a proof."

That beginning of the second chapter caused me to prick up my ears. The doctor emptied his glass, filled it again himself, as if distractedly, and, holding it up at eye level, he spoke:

"For you, as for me, it's determined that today will be entirely consecrated to memories of youth. My youth, when I evoke it, seemed to arrive in a direct line from Villemomble, near Paris, where my father had a country house. So, I was at Villemomble, and I was collecting plants in the little wood that surrounds it and is linked to those of Rainey, when the air suddenly seemed to be separated before me into globules absolutely similar to the ones rising from the depths of this glass, except that, instead of rising they were descending. They were descending like a fine granular rain of little transparent yellow pearls.

"That yellow tint was gradually accentuated in its gleam and vivacity; soon, further revived by the warm rays of the summer sun, filling the atmosphere of the wood, the globules began to vibrate, to swirl pell-mell like myriads of midges, and to vanish into a general flamboyance, in the wake of which their golden gleam was attached to all the objects living or inanimate, that surrounded me.

"Around me, nature seemed to be entirely the work of a goldsmith; gold shone on the foliage of the bushes and thickets, as on the grass and the pebbles of the paths; all the flowers were buttercups; the birds had golden eyes and golden plumage; flies and insects were transformed into flying nuggets; one might have thought that the mines of California and Australia had come of their own accord to show themselves above ground; it was a complete Eldorado.

"A few paces away, an immense tree loomed up, as rutilant as the other trees but distinguished among them all by gigantic pods that hung down all the way to the ground. I approached and I opened one of them; to my profound surprise, I found on the satin parchment of the sheath, separated from one another by a light partition, graciously folded up and arranged in rows like haricot beans in their pod...yes, I found...I'll give you a hundred guesses!...women, my dear friend, charming young women!"

"What! Women in pods?" I exclaimed.

"And blondes, of course—more than blondes, since the material of their tresses was pure gold. That is the way things were in the country to which I had been suddenly transported; the women there grow on trees, on trees of the leguminous family, as you've divined; there's no need, moreover, to take the trouble of shelling them.

"As I recoiled, bewildered and confused, almost frightened by the sight of that marvelous discovery, all the pods hanging down toward the ground opened spontaneously, by dehiscence, as we botanists say; the pretty fruits of the enchanted tree, detaching themselves from their envelope, were launched to the right and left, bounding and falling back, like the seeds of the balsam tree when their capsules burst; an army of sylvan nymphs surrounded me, all in a costume that only mythological habitude and great warmth can authorize. Holding hands with one another, some formed groups worthy of antique sculpture, true living tableaux that did not lack golden frames; others performed dances before me, whose choreography the foremost ballet master of the Opéra would not have disavowed. I had never found myself at a similar fête…but enough details."

"Why, Doctor, why? Anyway, this time, you won't deny that this really is a matter of a dream?"

"A dream? No, a poisoning."

I started in my seat. "A poisoning? What? How? In the middle of a wood, when you were only thinking about collecting plants?"

"Exactly. But let's go back a little. In imitation of our skillful novelists and our imperial prosecutors in their speeches, I had to establish the facts first in order to keep your curiosity alert, saving the explanation of the cause for later. Now, in order to discover the cause of the principal, and even unique, event of my second chapter, it's necessary to return to my first chapter, as you'll see…but let's drink! A storyteller, like an orator, has a right to a glass of sugared water, for which champagne can substitute, after all, and even with a certain advantage."

The waiter had just brought a third bottle; I filled the doctor's glass, and he continued.

"Since my famous affair with number 17 in the amphitheater of the Charité, I had been much preoccupied with hallucinations, and, having concluded my medical studies. I chose as the subject of my thesis hallucinations provoked by the ingestion of certain vegetables. I was the first to identify their logical, philosophical and therapeutic development…

"Listen carefully. First, the narcotic substance acts upon the senses, which then react upon the imagination; the latter, violently overexcited, renders to the physical machine the shock that it has received therefrom; it's a reactive shock…a reactive shock, you understand…and then between the two components a sort of entente is established, a harmony, an equilibrium: an order within the very disorder. Hallucinated eyes see externally, as well as in the plastic state, which only exists in our mind, and in the dream state; hence the visions and apparitions, gracious or terrible, the visual tricks that abuse you...but that's my thesis that I'm passing before you, my dear friend, when I only wanted to tell you...what did I want to tell you, then...?"

He put his glass down on the table, after having emptied it in a single draught, and then filled it again, still distractedly.

"Ah! I have it! Well, my dear, not content with making observations and theorizing, I experimented on myself; I sampled opium, datura, mandrake and hashish; I subjected myself to the action of all those powerful anesthetics, mysterious enchantresses, which opened the doors of unknown paradises or frightful infernos by turns...

"When I was on the point of sustaining my doctrines before my judges in the Faculty, in the matter of narcotics, it only remained for me to make the intimate acquaintance of henbane, a wild plant with hairy leaves and yellow flowers striped with purple, perhaps excessively calumniated, in my opinion, for although it makes one pay a little dear for the fêtes it gives, it gives splendid ones, or at least complete.

"Henbane, the henbane with which I had not yet experimented, I had just encountered in the little wood of Villemomble. For love of the art, I had chewed its leaves, its stem and its roots, albeit with precaution—I knew how poisonous the plant was with which I was dealing...

"A quarter of an hour later, I was prey to the delusion…the Danaë delusion! That's the name that the famous Boissier Sauvageot…or Sauvage... gave it.[15] Then, in the wake of my vision of leguminous women, I was seized by a violent headache…that diabolical cephalgia I think I still have..."

The doctor put his hand to his head and searched for the bottle that was already three-quarters empty, but I had caused it to disappear. Evidently, iced champagne was not as inoffensive for him as he had claimed.

He continued his story anyway, mingling it with rather vague reflections.

"As I returned to Villemomble, my gracious houris, who had suddenly changed into aged witches covered in spangles and tinsel, accompanied me as far as the entrance to the village, vociferating insults addressed to me and blasphemies.

"Having arrived at my father's house, I had difficulty recognizing it, so magnificently was it gilded from top to bottom. Inside, everything, furniture and personnel, was glistening under gold; the cook had a golden apron; the manservant was braided with gold on all the seams of his waistcoat; even my father, instead of his fine gray beard, had a long golden beard, which reminded me of the sign of a certain silk-merchant in Paris. I was laid down in golden sheets after being made to take a footbath in liquid gold at forty degrees.

"Finally," continued the dear doctor, whose tongue was thickening increasingly, "…fortunately, I have a

---

[15] François Boissier de Sauvages de Lacroix (1706-1767), a friend of Linnaeus who attempted to compile a classification of diseases modeled on the latter's classification of biological species, carried out early research on mental illness.

solid head...I prescribed myself two grains of lemon-ade...no...two grains of emetic in a pint of lemonade..." He interrupted himself, and said: "Why do you have two heads...? The next day, I could no longer see anything but yellow...dark yellow. The day after, bright yellow, the color of champagne...hang on, where's the bottle?"

"We've drunk enough, Doctor."

"Perhaps you're right." And, after having looked piteously at his empty glass, he turned toward me: "Beware of champagne, my dear friend; it too is a hallucinator."

And my savant doctor did not take long to fall asleep.

Insects and Flowers

I love to see clouds flying in the sky
    And, under a light breeze,
The crowns of forests gently shaken,
The wheat swirling and rolling,
    Like squadrons of war;

I like to see underfoot and in my hand
    The flowers that grow without culture,
And, proud of my conquest, surprising as I go,
Beneath their robe of enamel, alabaster or carmine,
    A few secrets of nature;

Above all I like to dream, to walk, to sit down
    In their brilliant colony;
To contemplate by night the magical censer,
The white campion, only perfumed at dusk,
    A sad symbol of genius;

I like the gilded insects on wild roses,
    Fully armed warriors whose races
Live in iridescent floral ramparts
Agitating azure darts in the sunlight
    And the bronze of their breastplates;

I like seeing them grouped on their silky parquet,
    Having returned from their raids,
Scintillating in the rose where they hold their ban-
quet

As one sees a bouquet sparkle at a ball
    Along with sapphires and emeralds;

As a morning is a whole season for them.
    The troops hasten its looting,
Submitting to fate, changing garrison
When destructive time has strewn the lawn
    With the debris of their wild rose.

No matter! Are there not palaces to choose?
    At midday, on the water is displayed
The flower of the nenuphar, open to leisure
Where each of them can live like a great vizier
    In Oriental splendor;

There, moderating the fire of a dazzling sky
    Beneath the nacre of the corolla,
Murmurs the sound of a caressant stream,
Gliding blue and luminous while rocking them
    In their odorant gondola;
 With their gauzy oars, their amorous flight,
    There, blue damsel-flies,
Beat the air to the profit of the blissful viziers
Animated fans, hovering above them
    With their quivering wings.

Half-intoxicated in their moving palace,
    Reclining on soft ermines,
Inundated by perfumes, I have often seen them
Fall asleep, weary of amorous games, while drink-
ing
    From the golden waves of stamens.

But fate is changing. Sometimes, one morning

The scarab, making furtive war,
Falling upon the nenuphar, avid for booty
Transforms the feast into a field of death
    And makes a meal of the guests.

For all down here have their share of woes
    To gamble is to run to defeat;
Happiness has its term, and cries of pain
Resound in flowers as in cities;
    Death is at every feast.

Lise's Dwelling

Lise M*** had once played an important role among the numerous and pure amours of my early youth. She had quit Paris twenty years before, and I had not seen her since.

One evening, after emerging from a rather copious dinner in the country, near Brunoy, I was walking along the little river Yerres in order to breathe the fresh air, when, to my great surprise, I encountered her, and recognized her immediately, in spite of the long absence.

She had hardly changed: still pretty, although a trifle frail, and a little paler than before. Fearful of being deceived by a close resemblance, I followed her for a minute or two, examining her profile, her gait, her complexion, all the more certain of not being deceived in my inspection because the moon was illuminating the landscape brightly.

Strangely enough, Lise, once so careful in her attire, had renounced the futilities of fashion. Her short, plain costume, devoid of amplitude, seemed to be modeled on the one she had been wearing when we last met, but that very singularity confirmed her identity for me.

I called her name; she turned round, smiled at me, more with the mouth than the gaze, and resumed walking.

"Are you in such a hurry to get away from me, then, Lise?" I said.

Her only response was to increase her pace. I hastened mine, resolved to take advantage of the encounter to find out what had become of her in such a long time.

"You're doubtless married?" I asked her.

She shook her head negatively, continuing to walk straight ahead.

"And what are you doing nowadays? Are you still occupied with embroidery and dressmaking?"

Another shake of the head.

"Do you live around here?"

This time, an affirmative nod, but still nothing other than a movement of the head.

"So your habitual abode is in Brunoy? Where do you live, Lise?"

She raised her arm and indicated a hill rising to our right.

Quitting the bank of the Yerres then, she headed in that direction.

Although she had only taken part in our dialogue thus far by means of gestures, I thought I could accompany her as far as her home; did she not seem to have encouraged me by indicating the route?

The terrain became steep and difficult; Lise only walked more rapidly, and I had trouble keeping up with her. The moon being veiled by a thick cloud, I had difficulty making my way. Finally, we went into a vast enclosure where the paths were hardly less rough than those of the hill. In traversing a somber avenue of green trees, for fear stumbling, I tried several times to take her hand, doubtless only to invite her to serve as my guide, but every time, her hand escaped the grasp of mine.

A fine drizzle began to fall; perhaps she had anticipated that and had thus hastened her pace. I was not put off. Before that menacing rain, she would be constrained to offer me shelter. Having become my hostess, doing me the honors of her lodgings, her mutism would necessarily cease, and I would discover what I wanted to know about her.

Then again, perhaps curiosity was not alone in impelling me in that adventure. Why not admit it frankly? Ideas of old were returning to my heart. Our adolescent amours had almost always remained in the state of sketches, scarcely initiated drafts, with no great crime; could I not think of taking up where I had left off and completing them? Lise had been so young twenty years before!

As we drew closer to her lodgings however, the difficulties of the route increased proportionately. Little pathways intersected on both sides, and I bumped into mounds of earth that seemed to bar the route in parallel lines.

As for Lise, perfectly informed of the topography of the place, having become more active, and lighter, almost airy, one might have thought that she was no longer touching the ground.

Having reached the top, in an uncovered spot, she stopped. I could not perceive any trace of a habitation, though.

"This is my dwelling," said Lise, her tongue suddenly untied. "I've dwelt here for fifteen years."

And in front of her, a large stone rose up.

I was in a cemetery.

Frightened, I started to run, as if I feared that Lise, in her turn, might set off in my pursuit. The gate of the unreal enclosure was solidly bolted. By what means, then, had I been able to penetrate into it? In order to get out, I had recourse to climbing; I went over the wall...

When I returned to Soulins-lez-Brunoy, where I had dined and where I was to stay for a while, after having laughed at my otherworldly air and my clothes, stained at the elbows and knees, I was handed a deck of cards; I had been awaited impatiently to provide a fourth for whist; they had been playing with a dead hand.[16]

At that phrase, I shivered. I recounted my encounter with Lise, and how I had escorted her back to her dwelling. They laughed even louder.

The mistress of the house, a charming woman and a subtle observer, told me that she had noticed, during dessert, that, distracted by a lively conversation, I had washed it down with a certain *rancio* wine, instead of the usual accompaniment of a petty local wine. I had, therefore, had a vision, an inebriation, rancio never producing any others.

I did not give in immediately; I still bore on my elbows and knees the traces of my climb in the cemetery; I showed them as evidence; it was suggested that I had fallen and that I was devoid of common sense.

Everyone was in agreement on the latter point; I ended up falling into line with them.

The next day, however, in the morning, I went to visit the cemetery; the churchwarden let me in. The cemetery was situated on a hill, and I recognized the avenue of green trees, a grove of large thuyas. More than that, I found Lise's grave—not covered by a large stone, it's true, but carefully maintained and decorated with seasonal flowers, thanks to her sister, who still lived locally.

---

[16] In French, the practice known in English as playing whist with a "dummy" is known as playing *avec un mort*, which I have translated quasi-literally for an obvious reason.

The epitaph of the modest tumulus told me that Lise M*** had been resting there for fifteen years.

The Song of the Nightingale

The nightingale sang.

Three philosophers, quite capable, if they could be believed, of interpreting the language of birds, listened in silence and scrupulously noted down each of the modulations.

The three philosophers were Dupont de Nemours, Martin Luther and me.

When the nightingale had finished singing, each gave the text of his transition.

According to Dupont de Nemours, an authority in the matter,[17] but who was then old and suffering, the bird had just intoned a requiem, repeating in all tones: "Brothers, it's necessary to die."

Martin Luther had already had a bone to pick with a nightingale at the time of the Council of Bale; he affirmed that this one had only sung impious and obscene little ditties. He made the sign of the cross several times and then he exorcised the singer, as being none other than the Devil in person.

As for me, through the chirping and twittering, I had distinctly heard the bird declare that he alone was the king of harmony, and that Auber and Rossini could not hold a candle to him.

It is necessary not always to trust translators, much less interpreters.

---

[17] Pierre Samuel du Pont de Nemours (1739-1817) published an alleged dictionary of the language of crows in 1807.

A Little Hand

"No, young man, nothing is lost; there is not a grain of dust, even if it is lifted as high as the clouds or swallowed in the ocean that will not reappear in time. No ray of sunlight has passed without leaving a trace; its luminous trail is effaced, but the blade of grass that it has animated, the butterfly's egg that it has enabled to hatch, and the wave that it has warmed, have conserved it by absorbing it. Even the song of a bird does not resonate, even at night, without exerting its influence on some of the beings of creation.

"There is all the more reason why things ought to happen similarly in the moral order. Not a word has been spoken, believe me, that has not left an echo; our thoughts, even those we have kept to ourselves that which the memory no longer recalls and we believe to be dead forever, are only in lethargy, accumulated with others and atop others, profoundly buried in the inferior layers of the brain like a heap of vain relics, like any icy, inert detritus; then, one day, after many years of silence and forgetfulness, it only requires a sound in the air, the perfume of a flower or the collision of our gaze with the most insignificant object to resuscitate one of them from the depths of those catacombs. That one, once in motion, awakens others, which it draws in its wake. It is an entire sequence of our past existence that is revived, and often harasses us to the point of making our present preoccupations fall silent, overturning our momentary projects and annihilating our greatest resolutions.

"What is necessary for that? I repeat, the slightest little thing, a word in the air, a smudge on a wall, a line in a book, a dream..."

My young man started in his chair, stood up, and looked at me with a gaze full of anxiety.

"You know my story, then?" he said.

"Me? I was philosophizing at hazard..."

"However, a smudge, a book, a dream! A glance cast upon the most insignificant object overturning our projects and our gravest resolutions. Oh, you know!"

"My friend," I said to him, "in the matter of grave things, what I know about you is that scarcely two months ago you left Paris to go to Bordeaux, in order to marry a certain beautiful lady, rich, pretty, charming, even titled: Madame la Baronne de N***; what I know is that before leaving, you wanted to consult me regarding your choice, that I approved; for one thing, you seemed to me to be very smitten, and any objection on my part would have been futile. Today, I will admit, on seeing you again after that two month absence, during which I did not even receive the obligatory announcement, that I have been slightly surprised to hear you talking to me about nothing but political events, the weather, or asking me abstract philosophical questions, in which Madame de N*** could scarcely intervene. What's the matter, then?"

"Alas, Monsieur, it's a matter of someone other than Madame de N***."

"What! A new, sudden, overwhelming amour!"

"No, a forgotten amour, and amour in lethargy, left for dead. But listen to me, please; I owe you a sincere confession of my errors, my cowardice, to which you might give an even more severe name—and you'll understand how I was able to believe in listening to you that I had nothing more to reveal to you. Have you not said, Monsieur, that *nothing is lost?*"

Then he told me his story—a story that seemed to me to be worthy of figuring in this book of dreamers and visionaries.

"I was, therefore, about to marry the Baronne," the young man said. "I had only departed for Bordeaux with that intention. I believe that I loved her; perhaps I did love her. At any rate, we were due to sign the contract the following day.

"As I was walking under the Quinconces, there was a heavy downpour. I took refuge in a reading room. The weather had turned cold; the sudden downpour and the morrow's contract had put a gray fog in my brain. I asked the lady at the counter for something cheerful and distracting, a volume of Charles Monselet, that charming wit, the delicate wisdom that he hides under a burst of laughter...forgive these details, my dear Monsieur, but they're necessary.

"The lady brought me, in its stead, a volume of Sterne, a Frenchman from overseas. 'Here's one,' she said, 'that's said to be as humorous as possible; I'll even recommend Monsieur not to laugh too loudly, because of the other readers that he might disturb.'

"It was *Tristram Shandy*. Although I had known it for a long time, I refrained from refusing it. I opened the volume at random, and from that moment on there was a muted stirring in my head. I seemed to have held that same volume in my hands before. I had the works of Sterne in my bookcase, left incomplete; *Tristram*, the former companion of my excursions and walks must be one of those missing. Where had I lost it? I had no idea. In any case, all the volumes of an edition resemble one another. How could I imagine that, from Paris, my

93

Tristram had been able to end up in Bordeaux, in a reading room in the Place des Quinconces?

"I rejected the idea. I needed to distract myself; however, as I leafed through that book, so cheerful, so humorous, my forehead darkened and my breast swelled. That is because it was not on the text that my eyes had been fixed most attentively: it was on the margin, where, here and there, a few broken lines showed, sometimes in pencil and sometimes in ink, not too much characters as disorderly doodles, made at hazard.

"Why did those incorrect, eccentric lines attract all my attention, and cause a thousand thoughts of old to rise into my mind? It was because they had been traced by a child, and above that stained margin I seemed to see the little hand that had held the pen or the pencil. Don't you find, as I do, my dear Monsieur, that ingenuousness of form and touching grace exist nowhere as much as in a child's handwriting? That hand, that little hand, I saw it, and my heart was increasingly constricted.

"I resumed the inspection of the book from the beginning—for, as I said, I had opened the volume at random, in the middle. One the page before the title page I found words written: *This book belongs to M. Henri de B****, and I recognized Thérèse's handwriting easily. Thérèse, Monsieur, was a young seamstress, my first student amour...

"That volume, which I was holding in my hands, had belonged to me, and it was in Thérèse's abode that I had left it, on the very day when I left her, with the egotistical, cowardly, cruel resolution of never seeing her or her child again; they would both have hindered my career and opposed the possibility that I might make an honorable marriage later. All the honest men in my entourage were in accord on that point.

"Thus, my presentiments, my paternal instinct, had not deceived me: those bizarre, jerky lines, that scribbling, had been traced by the hand of my daughter! Undoubtedly, by inscribing my name at the front of the volume, poor Thérèse had wanted to consecrate my memory in the eyes of the child, and she, the child…who can tell? Confident and credulous, as one is at her age, she might have believed that she was writing to me, and in the margins of the book that had belonged to me she was saying: 'Come back, come back and console my mother!'

"Before the ideas of tenderness, pity and remorse that invaded me, I forgot where I was, and by what people I was surrounded; I burst into sobs.

"The mistress of the establishment might have mistaken them; in fact, she had mistaken them, and in her discreet voice, while tapping me lightly on the shoulder, she said: 'I begged you, Monsieur, not to laugh too loudly.'

"But I turned my eyes full of tears toward her, and she was able to judge the effect produced on me by the joyous adventures of Tristram Shandy and the honest Corporal Trim.

"I drew her to one side. I learned that the book in question, with a few others, had become her property after a seizure carried out six months before at the home of a young seamstress. That seamstress, reduced to the saddest deprivation, had been thrown out of the frightful hovel she occupied on the sixth floor for being unable to pay her rent.

"It seemed to me that all the maledictions of Heaven had just descended upon my head.

"Nevertheless, Monsieur, I don't want to appear to you to be better than I am. I was then too firmly engaged to the Baronne to think of a rupture in our marriage. Were we not to sign our contract the next day? But I was resolved to save the mother of my child from poverty.

"I started my research immediately, and I continued it for several hours, anxious and breathless, tormented by sinister ideas; and along the way I seemed to see a little white hand extended toward the passers-by, imploring alms. That little hand I recognized; it was the same one that had appeared to me on the margins of the book.

"Night fell; my research had been vain.

"I nevertheless presented myself, that evening, at the home of Madame de N***. Could I do otherwise? She scolded me at first, but with an exquisite grace, for my lack of assiduity. A whole day spent apart from her, in Bordeaux, where I did not know anyone, when I had only come for her! What had I done with my time? It was necessary to find a reason; I found one...a false one; she was content with it. She was charming with me, more charming than ever, and she fixed our marriage herself for the Tuesday of the following week.

"I left her, scarcely thinking of anything but the happiness of soon possessing such a wife...

"Note, Monsieur, that I no longer loved Thérèse, and that I had separated from her when her daughter—our daughter—was still confided to the care of a nurse. That child I had scarcely seen. Did I even know that she existed? The lady of the Quinconces had only mentioned a poor seamstress, that was all. Then, I thought about the Baronne, my amour, propriety, the opinion of society—and before that accumulation of such respectable things, my cowardice took hold of me again. I would look for Thérèse, I would furnish her needs, but on the eve of my marriage I had other things to do than run after a former mistress!

"Having returned to my lodgings, those were the honest resolutions with which I was struggling while pacing back and forth in my hotel room. At the moment when I turned from one direction to the other, my gaze went to a certain little object placed on my chest of drawers, almost the only objet in my room that belonged to me. It was a paperweight, a precious and symbolic gift that I had received a few days before from Madame de N***: her hand, her delicate hand modeled by a skillful molder and fitted on a thin marble tablet.

Strangely enough—and which, at first, I could only attribute to the fatigues of my journey, which were troubling my sight—at every change of direction I effected, that hand, that simulacrum of a hand, seemed to shrink little by little, to tighten in all its parts, in its most delicate lineaments. It was soon no more than the hand of a child: still the same one…the one that I had seen extending toward the passers-by in the street; the one that had initially posed on the margin of the book… the little hand!

"I thought I was going mad, or at least becoming enfevered; but I struggled against the obsession. I summoned to my aid the memory of Madame de N***; I closed my eyes; and then, finally, yielding to lassitude and emotion, I fell asleep.

"Then, the vision was succeeded by a dream. What a dream, Monsieur!

"I had fled my room, not without effort, for I had sensed something along my route, some kind of force, opposing me, struggling against my will, retaining me, pulling me backwards...

"Then I found myself, I don't know how, on one of the sandy islands in the Garonne, which the incoming tide had just rendered unapproachable. I rejoiced in that;

I was safe, calm was about to return to me; nothing could any longer trouble my solitude, protected by the rising tide. However, the same tug that had tried to prevent my flight was still sensible.

"It was the little hand, which, detached from its tablet, was suspended from one of the tails of my coat, pulling at it.

"Under the impulsion of fear, thinking that I was warding off a spell, I grabbed it and tore it away...but it seemed to me that it was my heart that I had just torn from my breast.

"It fell to the ground, into a hole hollowed out in the center of the island. After having piously covered it with sand, I knelt down in front of the hole. Oh, don't accuse me, Monsieur, of attaching a ridiculous importance to the wanderings of the mind, but that dream, even after it had ceased, was to have grave consequences for me..."

"I'm not as scornful of dreams as you seem to believe," I replied. "Go on, my young friend..."

He continued:

"For a few moments, I felt relieved, either by the prayer or by the disappearance of the strange object. Having collapsed, I was sitting on the ground, and now, by virtue of the return of my keenly impressionable nature, I fixed my moist eyes on that slight excavation that I had just filled in, the tomb of the dear little hand.

"Suddenly, I saw the sand stir, and the little hand reappeared. Frightened, I made a movement of recoil; it agitated its fingers, but without changing place, as if it had already taken root in the soil.

"A further miracle! At the extremity of each fingers, the nail broadens out like a sort of horny cuff, and from each of those five cuffs another little hand emerges, of which each finger becomes the stem of a new little hand, and all of them, elongating in a cluster, multiply, reproducing themselves five by five, from minute to minute and second to second. Soon the ground is covered by those innumerable little hands, which, accumulated, each at the tip of another, broaden their circle, crawling, ferreting through the long grass and the bushes, searching for me, pursuing me...

"And I, without having the strength to stand up, still recoiling, finally find myself driven back to the shore, between all those little hands, which grasp me, and the rising tide, which threatens to engulf me. 'No, no! My daughter isn't dead! She's appealing to me with all these evocations, with all the voices of my sleep and wakefulness!'

"When I woke up, old sweat inundated me from head to toe. I dared not sleep all night for fear of falling back into a similar dream.

"Scarcely was it daylight than I resumed my search for Thérèse. This time, as if the little hand were guiding me, I went straight to the bailiff who had carried out the seizure. Thérèse, employed in a factory, was living in a village a few leagues from Bordeaux. Immediately, I sent her—without naming myself, of course—all the money I could spare.

"At two o'clock, in was at the Baronne's house.

"Without any further preamble, I told her about my student liaison with a poor Parisian seamstress. The story seemed to amuse her, for she laughed a great deal at it. Of her own accord, however—I should like to render that justice—she engaged me to do something for the poor unfortunate woman, to come to her aid. But when I confessed to her that my formal, unshakable intention, was to cede to Thérèse and her daughter half my fortune, she stopped laughing, and signified to me that she was not a woman to content herself with the residue of my amour.

"What else remains for me to tell you? I saw Thérèse again. When I met her, I gave her the volume of *Tristram Shandy*. 'When Providence is watching,' I told her, 'nothing is lost, neither stray volumes nor the memories of a first tenderness.'

"Today, Monsieur, I'm married, and, not without hesitation, I've made you party to the story. I'm happy; my daughter is a charming child, and the little hand, the cause for me of so many violent emotions, I can cover with my kisses from morning until evening."

A Night in the Woods

Here comes the dusk
Let's go sit down
Near to the strand
We'll be happy
And then we two
    Can dream.

Let's dream, let's dream,
And let's pursue.
The sweet phantoms
With which the woods
Sometimes people
    The crowns.

When, far from noise
The dense darkness
Envelopes us,
Our souls will then
Free of restraint,
    Gallop.

In the far west
Formerly bright.
The sky is dark,
Lake and forest,
All disappear
    In shade.

A shining dot
Vacillating,
Lights in the north
Its subtle fire;
Will it pierce
    The mist?

See, close to it.
Others have lit,
The dark brightens,
It's a signal
Is that polar
    Beacon.

In heaven's face
Two divine eyes
Open and shine
And others still
With lashes gold
    Sparkle;

Under their rays
Visions appear
Of pallid forms
In the valley
Gliding along
    Branches;

Then, traversing
The verdant trees,
Tearing apart.
In the background,
Skeletal, white,
    The moon.

One seems to see
It making move
Enormous arms;
Its silver jets
Are extending,
    Deformed.

But later still
Our gazes will
Change position,
Cast far away,
The specter then
    Effaces.

Then, in its place
In the blue sky
The rounded moon
Blossoms fully
And rejoices all
    The world!

Two large brown eyes
With no lashes
Simulacral
Will shortly come
To pit its face
    With pearl;

Its pallid hue
Its feeble air,
Or taciturn,
Rends nonpareil
That nocturnal

White sun;

Touching pale star
More than naughty,
With heart of stone
You compare to
A famous mime,
　　To Gille

All the sad clowns
And cold rhymers,
The profane troop
Will not triumph!
Tell them your name
　　Diane!

In the Heavens
All is truly
Mystic grandeur
But we should not
Ever set foot
　　On Earth.

Let's dream, let's dream,
And let's pursue.
The sweet phantoms
With which the woods
Sometimes people
　　The crowns.

All falls silent,
Nothing appears
Let's lend an ear
In its furrow

The King Cricket
    Awakes;

It yields a cry
And every squeak
Makes it leap
In search of loot
Ready to sound
    Aubade.

The strident call
Spreads out around
From tuft to tuft;
What fine sweet sounds
What lovely songs
    Beneath!

In the air too
I see from here.
A thousand quarrels
All is peopled
With a winged world
    Of flies.

In their squadrons
The little gnats
Enter the dance
The cicada
Has taken up
    The beat.

And the cousins
And good neighbors
At the sylvan ball

Have trumpeted
And completed
   The band.

Moles and crickets,
And butterflies,
The whole frail troop
Are spiraling
And fluttering.
   Mingling;

But like the swarms,
When I set up
In my pandects
A true account
Of this great ball
   Of flies,

A sudden wind.
In getting up
Closes the door,
And the jumpers
And the flautists,
   Vanish!

It seems as if
For having blown
On every star.
In all the sky
From end to end,
   Veils fall,

A muffled creak
Twists and wrenches

The arid branch,
Beneath a surf,
The little lake
    Empties.

The tree quivers,
The birds all groan
In their dwellings
Near the Islet,
Is it the wave
    That weeps?

Do you not think
That you can hear
Doves over there,
Touching their beaks
And both flapping
    Their wings?

The lake, the woods.
Mingle their sounds;
The hour is sweet;
The nightingale
Suspends its flight,
    And sings!

Song, joy, amour
Have had their turn...
The night will end;
How glad we are
When two of us
    Can dream!

The Cup of Tears

I had passed from one world to the other, perhaps a little belatedly...

When I presented myself before the sovereign judge, he was holding in his hand a shiny metal cup, the contents of which he seemed to be interrogating.

Although I had been named to him, he had scarcely turned his head in my direction, and only to give me a sign to sit down and wait.

Solely preoccupied with his cup, he appeared to have forgotten that I was there, palpitating, full of anguish. The welcome that I was receiving was cold, and scarcely reassuring, as you will understand.

According to my preconceived ideas, once before the supreme arbiter, a sort of judiciary debate ought to be engaged between my good angel and my bad angel, tending to bring out the merit or the unworthiness of my terrestrial life; and my conscience, interrogated, told me that my good angel would have excellent things to say in my favor.

But nothing...nothing? Time was flowing heavily, crushing me with its weight; the silence that reigned around me resembled a threat; the preoccupations of the judge, still fixed on the same object, rendered my thoughts dolorous to the point that, no longer able to stand it, I stood up, and even if the verdict were to reflect my audacity by bringing punishment down on me instantly, I dared to provoke it.

"You think that I've forgotten you, but it's with you, and you alone, that I'm occupied," my judge said to me, in a voice so soft and paternal that my irritation suddenly dissolved into meekness. "You're complaining about a few moments of waiting; I judge that waiting ought to be favorable to you."

He plunged his gaze into the depths of the cup again, and I saw him shake his head with a dissatisfied expression.

"I understand your forbearance, Lord," I exclaimed "You want to give the prayers said for my salvation time to rise from the earth to Heaven; they will be fervent, I hope; numerous, I'm certain. I've taken my precautions in that regard."

"An often impotent means, which cannot suffice on its own to disarm my justice," he murmured.

I emboldened myself then to list a few meritorious actions capable, I thought, of inclining the balance in my favor.

"Equivocal testimony!" the judge responded, without letting me get to the end of my hymn of praise. "Vanity, shame for oneself, and the opinion of society sometimes also extend to the wicked, but this cup that I have here will tell me more about you than you could tell me yourself. It contains the tears shed for you since your exit from the world—not the official, ostentatious tears shed with a great reinforcement of moans in order to disarm malevolence, but the veritable tears of regret shed in your memory in meditation and solitude...

"Thus far," he added, "they're rare; only a few infantile tears...but there are some belated ones, and we'll be patient, as always. If, a year from now, this vase is full...then..."

I looked at the cup. Its dimensions were small…yes, very small. I had left behind me a numerous family, friends, servants, obligated individuals…and yet, I shuddered.

"Oh, my Mother!" I cried. "If you still inhabited the world of the living, the cup would already be overflowing!"

Psylla, The Gold-Eater

A little grass snake, with faded colors, almost effaced, had introduced herself into my home—in order to warm herself by the fire, I suppose, for the north wind was obscuring outside, and frost was obscuring the panes of the casement.

In France, one generally mistrusts all sorts of snakes, inoffensive grass snakes as well as vipers with a mortal bite. Perhaps that mistrust is wisdom, but I once traveled in the Orient and I was imbued there with the idea that a snake brings good luck to a house.

Furthermore, in Sardinia I had seen the ladies of Cagliari lifting up with care and tenderness a gracious little necklace snake,[18] their favorite plaything and their principal ornament, which, one might say, belongs both to their family and their jewel-box. It seemed to me that my newcomer, in spite of her paltry and miserable appearance, must belong to the same species.

I granted her hospitality, therefore, leaving her free to choose whatever refuge seemed good to her. From time to time, in the epoch of intense cold, she came back to warm herself by my hearth. Her coat, duller than ever, came away in patches, and then tatters; that inspired me with a sentiment akin to repugnance, but my pity pleaded in her favor.

---

[18] The common French term for *Natrix natrix*, known in England as a grass snake, is *couleuvre*, often expanded to *couleuvre à collier* [necklace snake].

When spring returned, one beautiful morning, I saw her again; she had made a new skin. What a metamorphosis! Her supple body scintillated in a marvelous network of ocher and dark pink. My boarder was charming thus. Doubtless flattered by the quietly astonished attention I paid to her, in order to enable me also to appreciate her *savoir faire*, she began by slowly unwinding her coils, in which the daylight was reflected by the tiny prismatic facets of her scales, and, with a measured movement full of grace, she went to the threshold of the garden, turning her head occasionally to see whether I was following her.

In fact, I had followed her. Then she wound itself like convolvulus around a slender tree-trunk, reached the higher branches and suspended herself there, swaying; then, allowing herself to slide along the tree, with a rapidity that made me shiver with dread that she might fall and injure itself, she swiftly attained a small stone basin, where she started to swim, her head out of the water, holding her neck curved in the manner of a swan.

The next day we were friends; I had already found a name for her: Psylla.[19]

In the following days, alerted by a slight hissing, I perceived her, sometimes emerging from one of my bookshelves, sometimes from one of the leaves of my parquet. When the weather was favorable we went into the garden together, where she resumed hers customary exercises in suspension and natation; if not, I replaced the flowering ash-tree in which she loved to perch; having become familiar, it was around me that she wound, enlacing my neck in one of her coils and allowing her extremities to hang down over my breast.

---

[19] *Psylla* is the Greek word for flea.

Oh, she really was a necklace snake! But never, in Cagliari, where I had seen so many of them, had one appeared to me so richly rutilant. Her contact caused me an impression that I could not define, and if, raising her pretty head to the level of my face, she looked at me with her little black eyes, illuminated by a spark, I sensed that I was under a strange, fascinating charm, which seemed to be attacking reason itself.

Many other things in her regard astonished me. We had already been living in the same abode for several months, but I could not divine to which corner of the house she retired for the night; I also did not know how and on what she nourished herself. In vain I offered her the tastiest fruits and treats impregnated with honey or sugar; she scarcely brushed them with hers little forked tongue, seemingly only touching them to be obliging and to respond to my good intentions.

Commonly, reptiles—or at least, so I had heard it said—make their meals of heifers' milk. I put at Psylla's disposal a bowl of the purest milk, which only inspired a profound sentiment of repulsion. Hazard soon enabled me to discover, however, that she did not feel the same repugnance for all liquids.

I invited a few friends to dinner; as I was drinking to their health with an excellent red wine from Alicante, Psylla, who had take refuge behind a tapestry when they came in, suddenly emerged from her hiding place, launched herself toward me with an abrupt and rapid movement, coiled round my extended arm and drank avidly from my glass.

Another surprise awaited me.

One morning, I opened the secret drawer where I had carefully deposited a roll of gold coins a long time before, in case of emergency. I did not find my gold in the drawer; I found my necklace snake there, semi-torpid.

At the movement I imparted to the item of furniture, she woke up, uttered a shrill hiss, and fled into the depths of the writing-desk, where a hole communicated with a crack in the wall.

Now I knew the route by which she had introduced herself into the drawer, but I did not know how my gold had departed therefrom.

I thought it was a domestic theft; I kept watch, on the alert. Soon, I acquired the certainty that Psylla ate gold, making her nourishment thereof.

A tradition returned to my memory. In certain countries, it is said, snakes are skillful in discovering treasures. Did they discover them, then, to their own benefit?

Not being rich enough to allow my boarder to persevere in such a diet, I resolved to part from her. But how? The habit of seeing her every day had already projected roots into the depths of my heart. I was obstinate nevertheless in weaning her from all nourishment of that sort, hoping that she would come of her own accord to a more convenient aliment.

A hope deceived twenty times over! Fruits and milk were decidedly antipathetic to her. From day to day I saw her beautiful colors fade; Psylla became languid and paltry again, as in the epoch of misery when she had introduced herself into my dwelling. She no longer even had the strength to raise herself up toward me in order to resume her customary station.

Gradually, my rigor relaxed. My Alicante wine, she was able to drink at her discretion, and under its revivifying influence, her crimson shades reappeared, but her beautiful diamond-shaped yellow patches, discolored and withered, hollowed out and became ulcerated.

I could not see Psylla perish thus before my eyes. The gold that remained to me passed to her; that was the affair of a few weeks.

Then I sold my least useful furniture, and my rarest books. I borrowed. Once filled in, the abyss opened again. Even exhausting my strength in incessant labor, I would not have sufficed for the task quickly enough, nor with sufficiently considerable results. I became a gambler: a determined gambler.

My house became a gambling den. I only lived from then on in the midst of companions equally avid for gain. Some had to satisfy the demands of a deceptive luxury, others to steep hearts numbed by the abuse of pleasures in violent emotions. I had to content the appetites of Psylla, for whom I now seemed to feel nothing but indifference, and even hatred. But did she not keep me riveted beneath her magnetic gaze?

After a few strokes of luck, the game turned against me; it ended up exhausting my last resources. For a month, not a single gold coin shone under my gaze; I only gambled any longer on my word. It was necessary that she do without gold, even if she died of it; what did it matter to me?

Psylla did not perish, however; every day even seemed to add to her splendor and beauty.

It did not take me long to perceive that my companions in gaming were secretly subsidizing her avidity. I felt humiliated; I felt jealous; and my amity for her revived on contact with evil passions.

For her I endured shame; for her I fought.

A rare friend, a true friend, had tried to enlighten me as to my situation; I replied to him with a denial; he reiterated what he said; I spat in his face. We only saw one another again with épées in hand. In the duel, only I was wounded, thank God.

Laid on my bed, with my arm bandaged, I became drowsy. After an hour, on awakening, I felt bitter frissons running through my body; a cold sweat was streaming on my brow. Painfully, I turned my semi-extinct gaze in the direction of my wound. The bandage had been lifted up; a little oval head, oblong and flattened, slid underneath it, was drinking the blood that flowed from it.

I made an effort to stand up, but fell back, breathlessly, on to my bed. And I saw Psylla withdraw herself slowly, weighed down as she was by all the blood that she had just drunk.

What I also saw, which I remarked above all, was that she was then more beautiful than ever. Her plaques of bright crimson had turned to scarlet, and gave her body marvelous reflections.

Were blood and gold indispensable, then, to the blossoming of her complete beauty?

Like a coward. I strove—would you believe it?—to give a favorable meaning to that infamous, abominable crime. In spite of my mental disturbance, I remembered the tale of the ancients that attributed to snakes an innate science of medicine; at Epidaurus, in the temple of Aesculapius, the oracle was rendered by a snake. Is not a snake still the emblem of the healing art today?

Perhaps Psylla had just saved my life.

Should I think about avenging myself on her, of expelling her from my home?

It seemed to me that if I sent her away she would take my happiness with her...

My happiness! Where was it? Poverty was crushing me, and by her fault; repose, study and amity had deserted my abode, and by her fault. Everything in me ought to have revolted against her, speaking to me of ruination, abasement, degradation...

Well, nothing came of it; I was blind; I was mad, or I was going mad, when, one morning, Lalagé came into my home and put her foot on the head of my gold-eater, my blood-drinker.

Today, I wonder whether my adventures with the necklace snake were really only a dream.

China in Paris

As I approached Paris how great was my astonishment! On all sides rose minarets and stout porcelain towers. At the customs barrier, with his feet on the framework of his chair and his hands around his knees, a fat man with a long moustache was sitting, completely bald except for a hank of hair that departed from the middle of his head to fall down his black. He was smoking a short pipe and agitating his head, smiling.

As his entire uniform consisted of a dirty caftan, a frayed silk robe and yellow Oriental slippers, and his only weapon was a wooden sword passed through his belt, I mistook him at first for a residue of the last carnival, an ape in a hired costume, who had not yet been able to recover his official dress. He was occupying the middle of the gateway, and, in view of his corpulence, was an obstacle to my reentry to the city. I tried to slide to his right; he detached one hand from his knees, extended his arm, and thus closed the passage to me. I tried the same maneuver to the left; he extended the other arm.

Thinking that I was only dealing with a drunkard, I took a few steps back, and jammed my hat down over my head, determined to triumph over his resistance. The ape suddenly stood up then and extended both arms at the same time.

He was six feet tall, and his muscular limbs were in perfect proportion to his enormous trunk.

Although he continued to bob his head and smile agreeably, that gave me pause to reflect.

I drew away, darting an investigative glance around me. Still smiling, he recalled me with a gesture full of apparent bonhomie.

"What are you looking for?" he said.

"Clown," I relied, a trifle recklessly. "I'm looking for a customs officer, a policeman, some representative of the authority, who will straighten you out and permit me to go home, to Paris, from which I've been absent for too long."

He opened large—or, rather, gross—eyes, and declared to me that he was simultaneously the guardian of that gate, a customs officer, a policeman, and the personal representative of the Emperor.

As proof, he drew his wooden saber, which he brandished above his head three times. I must render him this justice: he did not strike me; he only wanted to give me a demonstrative evidence of his dignity. I would approve if all police officers were not armed in any other fashion from head to toe.

After having reinstalled himself in his seat, he spoke to me again.

"So, my good friend, we're from Paris?"

"Native born," I replied.

"And we've fixed our dwelling there?"

"Except for the six months I've just spent traveling, I've never left it."

The blissful smile naturally stamped on his face then took on more emphatic proportions; a joyful convulsion made his head, his body and his limbs shake, with movements to the left and right, and forwards and backward-in sum, the veritable evolutions of a *poussah*.[20]

When he had calmed down slightly, he clapped his hands. At that signal, lackeys came running.

"Take this man to the judge," he said to them. "He claims to be Parisian, and doesn't even speak Chinese."

And his automatic laughter seized him again.

Not understanding the adventure at all, unable to divine the meaning of such an accusation, I stood there nonplussed.

The lackeys saluted me with considerable politeness and, after having put me in handcuffs, prepared to take me to the judge. The barrier had just been opened in front of me.

When I had left Paris its physiognomy was already in the process of being modified considerably; its streets were becoming wide and interminable avenues planted with trees, its crossroads gardens and its buildings palaces; however, at the sight of the new changes that had been made to it, I could only utter a single cry of astonishment—but that cry lasted all the way from the barrier to the magistrate's residence.

All the boulevards were reduced to narrow causeways simultaneously practicable for pedestrians and cavaliers, palanquins and carts; their verges presented large fields of lucerne and potatoes, which did not offer a disagreeable sight. The squares were planted with cabbages. One might have thought that all the wasted land was thus being put to use. The current Parisian admin-

---

[20] A *poussah* is an Oriental figurine representing a fat man, weighted in such a way that if it is disturbed, it resumes an upright position of its own accord.

istration had returned to an economic and utilitarian system.

Along my route I only perceived little men with jaundiced complexions and hooded eyelids; through the curtains of palanquins the heads of women emerged, which I seemed to recognize by virtue of having seen their portraits on screens, or their statuettes on shelves. The tall houses of four or five stories, terminated by flat roofs, turned up into points at their extremities, had completely lost their ordinary aspect. They were masked by balconies in sculpted wood, little twisted colonnettes and large masts, at the top of which floated long banners elaborately decorated with green, orange or red dragons and hieroglyphic characters.

The displays of shops were overflowing with silk garments in all colors, bamboo carved in all fashions, pale or dark green vases, boxes of tea, scented candles, musical instruments in the form of tongs or cauldrons and hats in the form of bells. I saw men's shoes there with thick broad soles and women's shoes that one might have mistaken for pipe-stems. Lanterns, suspended everywhere in the shop windows, testified clearly that gas and electric lighting had been renounced, and even street-lights.

How could I believe that I was in Paris?

However, the crowd stationed in our path having forced my guards and me to stop, I thought I recognized a monument painted yellow and blue, which loomed up to my right like a triumphal arch, as the Porte Saint-Denis. Apart from a coating of ocher and indigo, the sculptures representing the victorious Louis XIV had scarcely been modified. The great king only featured there now in the quality of a mandarin. A means had been found of carving him a Chinese hat within the amplitude of his wig. To complete the humiliation, on the platform of his triumphal arch there was a marionette theater, in full activity for the moment—the unique cause of the popular assembly that had blocked our passage.

I understood my situation less and less. The sentiment of places, times, and even that of my own personality, was beginning to escape me completely when we suddenly resumed our march.

"Where am I?" I exclaimed, on entering the judge's residence.

"You're in the house of Hiang-li-lao-kin, literate, decorated with the Peacock Plume and a bright blue button, consequently, a mandarin of the third class," replied the magistrate, whom I found sitting in the middle of his room, a book open in front of him and his box of betel in his hand.

Rapidly, he scanned a piece of paper that the leader of my guards handed to him, and, after having cast a glance of mingled astonishment and pity at me, he said in a soft and almost tender voice: "My brother, what impelled you to take unduly the title of Parisian, which everything seems to forbid you? Of a Parisian you have neither the costume, nor the yellow skin, nor the bald head, nor the oblique eyes. Absent from the summit of your head is the long tress indispensable in order that the Angel of Death can, when the day comes, transport you from the earth to the heavens. What can have got into you, I wonder?"

"Monsieur le juge," I replied, trying to reassemble the little common sense that might remain to me, "I'm a Parisian, a pure-blooded Parisian, born in the Rue Vieille-du-Temple in the Marais. Would you like me to swear to it with my hand raised toward God?"

"Oh, my child, my child, don't blaspheme! In this city, where I've had the honor of sitting as a judge for twenty-five years, in the name of the sublime and revered Tien-Long, the 872nd Emperor, no old Rue du Temple or Marais exists."

"There are two Parises then, a false and a true one!" I cried, with a certain animation that I could not contain. "Do you think you can make me take for Parisians all these apes with which your streets are swarming?"

"Enough, enough, young man," he murmured, with an almost desolate sigh. "I know what I'm dealing with; the case is heard."

He clapped his hands three times, as the man at the customs-barrier had done; my guards came back; their leader was carrying a little open parasol, which he handed to the judge while the latter whispered in his ear. I could not comprehend what purpose the little parasol might serve in a room perfectly shielded against the sun's rays, but I was no longer trying to understand.

My judge having drawn away, after bidding me an adieu full of benevolence with his head and his hand, one of the four guards bowed to me again, profoundly, after which they fastened my handcuffs again and administered a beating to my shoulders—very supportable. I think I ought to declare, as they were only armed with elder rods. Perhaps custom required that one did not emerge from the judge's residence without carrying a more or less durable souvenir of his powers and authority.

We set forth again, going up the straight line of the boulevards. To my great astonishment I saw one, much wider and more spacious than the others, which seemed to have been exonerated, by a special privilege from the cultivation of cabbages and potatoes. On its vast central partition, theaters of every sort were located. In front of the theaters, conjurers, tightrope walkers, tooth-pullers and acrobats were turning and leaping, each one shouting louder than the next. Through the floods of people that inundated its borders, merchants of cakes and fruits were circulating, and sellers of glasses of tea, laden with little fountains, like our licorice-water merchants.

I'm definitely in Paris, I said to myself. *I've already recognized the Porte Saint-Denis, in spite of its Louis XIV in a Chinese hat, and this is certainly the Boulevard du Temple, the infamous boulevard, the delight of the people, whose death-sentence a reckless prefect dared to sign.*[21] *How has it been so promptly resuscitated in its new form?*

I was questioning myself thus when I saw a part of the crowd flow toward us, attracted by the sight of my four guards, my handcuffs, my costume and doubtless also my face. In such a place, no matter how scantly lent it might be to curiosity, one does not pass by easily without making a spectacle.

To the questions that were asked on my account, the leader of my guards responded curtly: "He's a madman."

I was almost of the same opinion. So, remembering that in Paris, human infirmities, physical or mental, only attract mockery and ill-treatment, I prepared myself with resignation; but the worthy folk were not thinking of mistreating me. On the contrary, they all assumed meditative and pitying expressions as they drew nearer,

---

[21] The Boulevard du Temple, nicknamed the Boulevard du Crime because of the concentration of theatres showing popular melodramas, was one of the most regretted victims of Baron Haussmann's drastic remodeling of the city during the Second Empire.

showing me all sorts of marks of interest, offering me by turns tobacco, betel and cakes. Some of them even asked me for my blessing.

On departing from the Boulevard du Temple, the houses continued to present the same aspect of decoration by daubing, perforated wooden shutters, flagpoles, red dragons and multicolored lanterns, except that the shops were much larger and richer, better furnished than anywhere else. From the former Bastille to the former Barrière du Trône, on the long street that had once been the Faubourg Saint-Antoine nothing was any longer to be seen but palaces, pagodas and elegant pavilions. It was the rich quarter, of bankers, high lamas and important mandarins.

One might have thought that Paris, touched in its sleep by the wand of a powerful magician, had suddenly been turned around, like a reptile, placing its head, crowned with luminous carbuncles, where its scaly and somber tail had once extended in the mud.

I only glimpsed the Bois de Vincennes. It had almost conserved its physiognomy of 1860, save that its numerous population of sylvan trees had been replaced by fruit trees, very much in keeping.

We had just turned right, and we arrived at…Charenton.

In the lunatic asylum, which, in the midst of that general upheaval, had only changed its external appearance and not its original purpose, I was received with great evidence of respect and benevolence by the resident authorities. My guards had taken leave of me after reverences and multiple handshakes on either side. My new possessors then took me to a beautiful, well-lighted room. In the said room I found not guards but four orderlies, as polite as everyone else with whom I had had dealings that day.

The compliments of welcome having been exchanged, they seized me bodily, laid me down on my back, and administered a further beating, not with elder rods this time, and not on my shoulders, but on the soles of my feet, with beech-rods. While striking, they assured me of their respectful devotion, affirming that they were only acting thus in my own interest and in accordance with the physicians' prescriptions.

I ought to have thanked them. Evidently, I was mad—no doubt was any longer permissible—and as a curative method, the bastinado here replaced cold showers. I had never had any preference in matters of medical theory, so I let them proceed.

In this Charenton, entirely populated by Chinamen, as Paris was, I was given for a room-mate a seemingly inoffensive maniac, even benign in character, so far as I could judge during the little time I spent with him. He was an eminent literate, very learned, but who got slightly carried away in debate. With regard to a purely grammatical question, he had had the misfortune to kill two academicians, his colleagues, in complete disagreement with them as to the spelling of a word. He was given to me as a companion in order that he could teach me the Chinese language, that being the one thing indispensable to any true child of Paris, the yellow skin and the hooded eyes only being secondary matters.

I ought to say clearly here that, in spite of a few strange facial tics, and his vivacity in matters of orthography, my companion became sympathetic to me at first sight. That impetuous, excitable, manic, insane grammarian certainly had as much common sense and mental lucidity on his own as the man with the wooden saber, the judge with the blue button, my guards, my orderlies, all the Chinamen of Paris and even the medical and administrative authorities of the lunatic asylum, for, thanks to him, I arrived at an understanding of my situation, and the key to the enigma, before which my reason seemed ready to come unhinged, was finally revealed to me.

"Charm of my solitude, perfume of my soul," he said to me, with the excessive politeness that only belongs to the Chinese, "whence comes my good fortune of having you for a companion in this cloudy city of human unreason?"

I then told him how, after a voyage of a few months abroad, I had returned to France, where I had seemed to find everything in its normal condition; the peasants were laboring in their traditions costumes, the inhabitants of the cities likewise and nothing seemed to me to have charged significantly; when, on arriving in Paris people had refused to recognize me as a Parisian, because I did not speak Chinese, did not have a shaven head, a long pigtail, yellow skin and slanting eyes.

My new friend listened to me very attentively, and without allowing any sign of surprise to escape him.

As soon as I had concluded my story, he said: "Nothing is easier to explain. Everything you have seen exists in reality; don't worry, you're no more mad than I am, but you've been asleep."

I made a movement, which he repressed with a gesture, in order to ask me this question: "In what epoch did you undertake your voyage abroad?"

"September 1860."

"Well, you've slept for exactly a hundred years."

"Is that possible?"

"There's nothing astonishing about it. Thanks to the improvement of chloroform, we can now, without any risk to the chloroformed individual, put him to sleep not merely for a century, as in your case, or for two centuries, but in perpetuity."

"So," I said, completely bowled over, "I'm a hundred years older than I thought? But tell me, my dear companion; in spite of its new coating, its chinoiseries, its streamers, its dragons and its potatoes, it really is my dear Paris that I've just traversed?"

"It's Paris itself; you're not mistaken, and your man with the wooden saber and your judge with the blue button were idiots and ignoramuses for not having recognized you as an ancient Parisian, an inhabitant of old Paris, when Paris, like France and the rest of Europe, had not yet submitted, by reason of conquest, to the laws of the Celestial Empire."

"What? France...!"

I could not finish; I was overwhelmed by surprise and dolor at the same time.

"Flower of my life, anemone with sensitive foliage, arm yourself with resignation," he went on. "The events that, before your slumber, had to be accomplished, have been accomplished; you can no longer ignore them now that you are submissive to their consequences. In any case, is not history there to inform you that, toward the end of the year 1889, pushed to the limit by the teasing of the little red gnat, the lion finally woke up?"

"What lion and what gnat?" I asked him, with the air of a man returning from the other world.

"Don't you understand that it's a matter here of China and England, a former petty nation, once very inconvenient even for its allies and its friends? Yes, one day, the Middle Kingdom shook off its ancient antipathy for the impious art of war, woke up with its four hundred million inhabitants, assembled an army of eight million men, constructed a hundred thousand rifled cannons, as many Armstrong guns,[22] and an innumerable quantity of propeller-driven ships—armored frigates—and set forth for the Occident?"

In my turn, I listened with an easily-comprehensible attention. He continued.

"Conquering Europe was the affair of a few years. The liberty and religion of the vanquished countries were, however, respected. Russian democracy, in the process of being organized, had just sent all the old Muscovite nobility to Siberia; Spain was still in its new fervor of Protestantism; Germany was continuing to seek its unity; as for Italy, it had finally found itself under the simultaneously theocratic and republican government of the Pope. Our victorious army let things proceed, and was able to embrace all those states without hindering any of them in its particular development.

"It was not the same for the red gnat; we made England a dependency of Ireland, after having first transported its entire government to Australia, the House of Lords to Botany Bay and the House of Commons to Melbourne. You see, radiance of my eyes, that European equilibrium is henceforth assured!"

"But France, what about France?" I cried.

"As for France," he replied, with that air of indulgent bonhomie that one normally adopts when talking to a spoiled child, "although we had a few petty reproaches

---

[22] The Armstrong gun, which went into mass-production in England in 1855, was a breech-loading field-gun that became extremely fashionable, employed to great effect in the Second Opium War of 1856-60 and the various other Imperial conflicts in which England was involved in the Far East in the 1860s.

to make to her, we were content to occupy her capital and to make it a purely Chinese city."

"Everything is explained now! But why did you do that to poor Paris?"

He lowered his voice suddenly and moved his mouth closer to my ear.

"Paris was too active," he said. "Thanks to that sage measure, France is tranquil, and so is Europe, all of whose people now form a great fraternal and democratic confederation under the protection of China."

When I woke up, I was still holding the evening newspaper in my hand, which announced that the small Anglo-French army fighting in China had just made its triumphant entry to Peking.

The Ibises of Ysamboul

I was dining with two of my friends, a painter and an antiquarian archeologist, but men of merit and worthy of faith, both having visited the banks of the Nile in Egypt, and as far as Nubia.[23]

The conversation had fallen upon incidents attributed to the so-called supernatural order, but which nevertheless had an incontestable reality.

"I witnessed a most extraordinary event of that order," I told them. "One evening last winter there was a party at the home of the celebrated sculptor P***; the weather had suddenly turned to black ice, and, the carriages no longer being able travel, he found himself obliged to set up beds for a few of his guests, even in his studio. I was one of them.

"The studio was full of busts and statues. In the middle of the night, under a ray of moonlight that traversed our improvised dormitory, those of us who were not asleep distinctly saw the statues moving, changing their attitude, is if vexed by staying immobile in the same position. One of them got down casually from its pedestal and sat on it; others walked silently back and

---

[23] Giovanni Belzoni published an account of his discovery of the long-buried temple of Ysamboul in Nubia in 1821, which was widely translated and reprinted thereafter. Saintine might, however, have made the acquaintance of the temple in *Panorama d'Égypte et de Nubie* (1841) by Hector Horeau (1801-1872), which contains numerous illustrations of its treasures; he might even have known Horeau, who lived in Paris.

forth. As for the busts, unable to use the arms and legs that they lacked, they frowned, moved their lips and opened and closed their eyelids. One of our comrades assured us that he had seen one of them yawn as if to unhinge its jaw."

"That's nothing," said my friend G**y**, the painter, who had seen and observed a great deal during his long voyages. "I see nothing in that but purely automatic movements, to which, under certain occult influences, all matter is submissive, marble and plaster as well as the wood of our tables. One day, in Egypt, I witnessed an entirely different spectacle."

The archeologist and I turned our ears in his direction. This is his story.

"Surprised by a sandstorm coming from the Sahara, I took refuge with my Arab guide in a hypogeum hollowed out almost facing the great pyramid. Our horses being frightened by the obscurity, the Arab groped around, collected a few pieces of wood scattered underfoot and set fire to them. As well as light, the fire spread around us an odor of balsamic resin, which was very pleasant, believe me! The hypogeum, I then perceived, had conserved some of its ancient tenants—a rare thing among the hypogea of Egypt. Sarcophagi, almost primitive, devoid of sculpted figures and exterior ornamented, rose up to the right and left in several rows. It was evidently a mortuary depot destined for people of medium condition. Three or four mummies, removed from their cases, scarcely enveloped by a few remains of bandages, were lying on the ground not far away from us.

"'Is it true,' I asked my guide, 'that in circumstances similar to ours, travelers, and even indigenes, have no scruple about burning the inhabitant of the case as well as the case itself?'

"'They become murderers, then,' he replied, 'for these mummies are not dead; thanks to the embalming, they conserve intact both their body and their soul, and before those who know how to contrive it, they even give signs of life from time to time.'

"As I gave the appearance of doubt, he pronounced a few mysterious and incomprehensible words in a loud voice, doubtless the powerful words of the ancient evocation, and a sort of susurrus emerged from all the sarcophagi. The mummies devoid of cases, entirely free in their movements and their actions, began to chat among themselves. I distinctly heard them articulate entire sentences. Unfortunately, they were still speaking the ancient language of three thousand years ago. That would have been good luck for Salt or Champollion, but I was incapable of translating a single word of it. I maintain nevertheless that it is more surprising to hear mummies speaking than to see statues stretching their arms and even jumping and turning somersaults, as any furniture can, including simple night-tables."

"That's still nothing," said the antiquarian archeologist in his turn, and without any preamble, he went on:

"On the extreme frontier of that same Egypt, the true land of marvels, near the cataracts of the Nile, in the foundations of the famous temple of Ysamboul, ten meters under the sand, I discovered a magnificent bas-relief in pink granite, covered with ibises, hawks and other symbolic birds. When, by dint of hard labor, I succeeded in extracting my bas-relief from the cavity that would soon have been its abode for forty centuries, all the granite birds, hawks and ibises, having arrived in the daylight, took off, uttering deafening cries."

My friend the painter and I recognized without hesitation that the ibises of Ysamboul combined within them, to a superior degree, with regard to movement and voice, everything that our statues and mummies had offered.

The Dream of an Inquisitor

Have you ever been an executioner or a "free judge" affiliated to one of those secret societies in which one draws lots for the role of victim or that of murderer? Have you at least dreamed about it?

Personally, I had the opportunity one day—I ought to have said one night—to be a grand inquisitor, the supreme leader of the Santa Hermandad, in the epoch when devout Spain, today reduced to its bullfights, delighted in the moving and splendid spectacle of auto-da-fés.

How did I reach that eminent position, which had certainly never been the target of my ambitious desires? I don't know; but, at any rate, I was presiding over that terrible tribunal when a young woman charged with heresy was brought before me.

It was Lalagé. When I recognized her, I shivered. However, I felt strong enough to dissimulate and constrain myself. I was her judge, not her defender. By trying to save her, I would doom her, and doom myself with her; I had no doubt about that. As best I could, therefore, I remained impassive, at least in appearance.

When the moment came to interrogate her, I asked her questions skillfully enough to inspire responses whose ensemble was favorable to her cause without compromising myself; but the imprudent Lalagé, addressing me with a gaze full of tenderness and surprise, responded to me quite wrongly, in the most annoying fashion.

A brother masked in black and clad in black placed beside me asked her whether she was a Jew, a Protestant or a witch.

"I'm none of those, nor even a Christian," she said. "I'm a poor girl who has committed no crime except perhaps loving my neighbor too much."

And as she said that she turned her moist and imploring eyes toward me; and I, who felt faint, swore to myself, even at the risk of my life, to do everything possible to save her before the sentence was pronounced.

One of the judges proposed to burn her feet first in order to constrain her to confess; a cold sweat inundated my brow. Another opined for the immediate employment of red hot iron pincers. The very marrow of my bones seemed to congeal.

Beside myself, I rose to my feet, resolved to take her defense, but my voice lacked breath and my tongue remained stuck to my palate; I agitated my lips convulsively, in vain; I could not articulate a single word.

My neighbor, the masked monk, hastening to interpret my thought in accordance with his own, declared that my opinion was to employ both the brazier and the pincers at the same time, in order to arrive more rapidly and more surely at the truth.

My pretended proposal was accepted immediately, my zeal was applauded, and the dear innocent creature, suddenly deprived of her clothes, was brutally tipped back on the rack.

The brother tormenters had already prepared their instruments of torture. The cry of rage and despair I uttered then they mistook for the signal ordering them to enter into their functions. They placed the brazier under the poor child's feet; the pincers, sizzling, bit into the flesh of her delicate limbs; an odor of burned flesh spread through the hall...

Lalagé scarcely moaned, but she had not ceased to attach her gaze to me, and that gaze, so profound, so dolorous, in which the bitterness of the reproach could not cause the expression of tenderness to disappear entirely, transpierced me completely, and I might have died if I had not woken up.

For having presided over that session of the Holy Office, I remained in bed for a week, suffering, agitated and feverish.

I am firmly convinced that in the wake of similar dreams there are people who wake up mad, or do not wake up at all. Many deaths solely caused by a dream are attributed to apoplexy.

Prometheus

What is the significance of the punishment inflicted by the master of the gods on the individual who stole from the heavens the celestial fire—which is to say, the flame of knowledge and intelligence—and imparted it to the human species? Why, in our sacred books, is God seen to expel the first man from Eden, only guilty of having tasted the fruits of the tree of knowledge? Why is Lucifer, the angel who bears light, according to ancient tradition, the genius of evil?

I also recall that the ancient sages of India and China forbade the people the knowledge of reading and writing; a prohibition that our old druids, their disciples, did not fail to propagate throughout Celtic Europe.

Are humans only down here in order to admire, and not to know: spectators, not commentators? A big question!

Sitting in my garden, listening to the murmur of my spring—or, rather, not listening to anything, lost in the vagueness of reverie—I have no idea how a mountain suddenly surged forth before me. That mountain was the Caucasus, and on the Caucasus the unfortunate Prometheus was nailed, in the company of his vulture, occupied in gnawing his liver. Hence the train of thought to which I was letting myself go; and I said to myself:

God, however, created humans with all the instincts of sociability, and what social condition can exist without scientific progress? Is it not knowledge that has extracted us from brutishness, and from barbarity? But

perhaps the distance between knowledge and science is
infinite. Let's examine the case...

Is it probable that humans emerged from the hands
of God without the notions of the just and the unjust,
already perverted, like wretches escaping from a prison
camp? I find it repugnant to make humans, in their
origin, idiots or ferocious beasts. No, the savage state is
not a state of nature; barbarity is born of our vices; at
the beginning of the ages a society must have existed of
simple people—ignorant, if you like—but directed by
honest instincts that I would like to believe innate in the
beings of my species.

While I was arguing thus with myself, Prometheus,
his mountain and his vulture had disappeared, giving
way to lush fields strewn with small primitive huts.
Swarms of handsome young men and beautiful young
women, not under the orders of a master but a father,
were devoting themselves to their rustic labor without
any great excess of strength. Humans, not very numerous then, had been able to choose the place of their set-
tlement in a suitable, salubrious terrain on the edge of a
lake or a river, already shaded by fine trees bearing
fruits. I supposed them to be installed in some Oriental
region, the Orient reputedly being the birthplace of society; at any rate, I could see palm leaves serving as cover-
ing for cabins.

Among all the laborers, united by family ties, the
father or ancestor—in sum, the elder of the tribe—was
both chief and judge; he accumulated the three powers n
his person, everything emerged from him, and the book
of the law was only written in his consciousness. People
did without other books then.

It was the patriarchal age, the Golden Age, which,
in order for there to be so much talk of it, must have

been more than a word. But that primitive civilization, scarcely sketched, where no one was able to fathom any other science than that of wellbeing, could only count as the first stage in the progress of humankind.

Once again, the scene before me changed; a surprise that I was able to give myself at will—in that regard, reverie is more accommodating than dreaming.

The population had increased; the families had become populations, and then peoples. The land being unable to occupy so many arms; there had been territorial disputes. War had mingled and disciplined races, bringing in its wake many dolors, but also new ideas of heroism and devotion. Although Jupiter, Moses, the philosophers of India and the Celts had been able to think of it, the law of progress was also the law of God. The need to occupy so many inactive arms had given impetus to commerce, industry and the arts.

There, where I had seen—with my mind's eye—wretched cabins of pastors and cultivators, stood palaces, temples and splendid monuments. Only a few centuries had gone by, and science had removed the stopper from the source of all the forces of nature put in the service of humankind. Humans, in an unlimited expansion of their power, were enthroned in the midst of a paradise of delights that they had made themselves.

The image of that prodigious civilization, which our Occidental civilizations might never attain, then passed before my gaze.

In the midst of a cortege of soldiers clad in brilliant armor, on gilded chariots, young women showed themselves with coiffures laden with rubies, emeralds and diamonds. Between the chariots and the troops, a double row of slaves were shredding flowers or singing, accompanying themselves with harps, not songs of love and triumph, as one might have thought, but tender and plaintive mewls.

Then, beneath an awning sparkling with gems, a shrine rather than a shelter, one could scarcely make out a sort of human appearance, so much was the air obscured by clouds of myrrh and incense.

In its wake marched the college of astrologers and all the other academic societies, extending endlessly as far as the eye could see.

It came to a halt in front of a palace as large as a city; a man, in the prime of life, with a royal ribbon around his head, emerged from beneath the awning, and, with a smiling gesture, dismissed his cortege of soldiers and scholars.

In a vast courtyard, with porticoes of jasper and marble, a platform was set up. There, by his order, fabrics and the most magnificent carpets had been disposed along the steps, as well as his jewelry, his gold, and all his treasures. His favorite slaves, his odalisques and his women took their places there, adding the splendor of their costumes, their ornaments, their youth and their beauty to the spectacle of all those splendors. Soft music was heard; golden cassolettes cast their perfumes into the air; slaves threw flowers, and women smiles. Then the representative of that civilization, the king of that people, the possessor of that palace and those riches, the master of those women and slaves, put his lips to a cup full of delicious wine, and drank: to Oblivion!

And at the same time I saw flames spring up on all sides and mount from step to step. The stage was nothing but a pyre.

That Assyrian, Babylonian, Ninevite civilization had for its ultimate name *Sardanapalus*.[24] After having spent nearly a thousand years attaining the culminating point of human science and glory, it suddenly collapsed, leaving nothing behind but ashes.

Sardanapalus, that sated son of Prometheus, was, like his people, softened, depraved by contact with the sensualities of the body and the mind; he was no longer able to occupy himself with anything but pleasures, touching spectacles, passionate discussions of the arts, cuisine, perfumes and philosophy; his weapons had fallen from his hands, and he no longer had the strength to pick them up, although the enemy was howling at his gates. After having cast a glance around, seeing no one there but poets, scholars and the voluptuous, and voluptuous himself, he had come to savor death in one last illusion.

Looming up before me in the wake of those tableaux, succeeding one another like dazzling flashes, came the towers of Notre-Dame, the Tour Saint-Jacques, the column of the Place Vendôme, the Luxembourg, the legislative Chambre, then the Rue Vivienne, the Rue Saint-Denis, the Boulevard de Sebastopol...in sum, the entire city of Paris, as great as Nineveh, similarly popu-

---

[24] Sardanapalus, the mythical last king of Assyria, who did not exist, seems to have been an invention of the Greek writer Clesias, although that writer's account in only known second-hand via Diodorus Siculus. Sardanapalus was presumably invented as an archetype of decadent opulence, and was thus perfectly designed for adoption as a symbol by the writers of the Romantic Movement and their Decadent offspring. His most famous literary incarnation is in Byron's eponymous tragedy, which became the basis of a French Opera.

lated with scholars, skeptics and Epicureans. I shivered at the mere idea of that analogous connection.

It seemed to me that during my itinerary from Nineveh to Paris, abrupt and rapid as that change of location and time had been, I had seen passing along my route the sinister shadows of Tyr, Sidon, Athens, Rome and Byzantium, all powerful cities that had lain down in their turn on the pyre of Sardanapalus.

Was Paris, my dear Paris, menaced, in the imminent future, with dying like them of a plethora, of an excess of science and material wellbeing, infallible generators of the languor of races and the extinction of the moral sense?

The progressive march of our century frightened me. Our industry seemed to me not so much to multiply our wealth as our artificial needs; I feared that our arts, in perfecting themselves, would succeed in softening even more than charming the present generation. Science—science, above all—with her everyday miracles, caused me more fear than all the rest.

In a final tableau she appeared to me, not, as before, with a book or compasses in hand, but terrible, noisy and formidable; she was a giant sorceress with muscles of steel and a face smudged with coal-dust; around her was accumulated a frightening materiel of bronze and iron, enormous tubes, engines of war and machines even more terrible.

Alas, I said to myself, *has human intelligence any need to arm itself with such means? Steam and railways risk making human beings nothing but incessant travelers, who will soon no longer have any family or fatherland. The human brain is enlarged, but the human heart is desiccated; we are in decadence!*

What means can ward off the peril? A return to the patriarchal era, to the Golden Age? Fourier has thought of that. Although seductive, his phalansterian ideas have been declared utopian and unrealizable. Opposing to the scientific, progressive barbarity that is invading us, the true barbarians, those who have already transfused their vigorous blood into the veins of sickly and decrepit Rome? Today, the Teutons and the Germans have become metaphysicians and philosophers; they could only add to the evil; The Cimbrians and the Scythians are reputed to be the most artful diplomats in Europe... Let us search elsewhere.

But why do we not appeal to the class of people who, among us, have remained closest to nature, to the primitive state, who witness our improvements without understanding them, who oppose to our forward march their routine and immobility: the peasants?

A voice goes up that replies to me: "The peasants? They have conserved their customs of old without the mores of old, the traditions without the virtues; rejected violently, perhaps arbitrarily, to the bottom of your social hierarchy, they have become jealous, envious, full of rancor and covetousness. Besides which, have they not been able to take their place, broadly, without waiting for your appeal? They have done it so well and so wholeheartedly that they will end up invading everything.

"The French nobility has disappeared since it stupidly decided to teach the peasants to read; ignorance protected them so well! They did not suspect their rights then! A narrow paltry, bourgeoisie, which speculates from day to day, which imposes economically the number of dishes that ought to figure on its table, and the number of children that can be permitted, has succeeded them; it has taken their employments, their land, even their titles; but where has that bourgeoisie, high or low, financial or mercantile, been recruiting its ranks for fifty years, and still is, and where will it necessarily recruit tomorrow? Among the peasants, who produce innumerable offspring in swarms and send them to assault the cities. There, they fill in the enormous voids that are made in superior circles; they populate the workshops and the boutiques; from workers they become masters, entrepreneurs, capitalists; from merchants they pass on to become landowners and even castellans. A few are sent to the Chambre to represent their départements. You see that you have nothing more to desire in that direction."

Well, then, I was alarmed too quickly. I'm reassured now; the barbarians have arrived; the transfusion of blood will be operated without violence; progress will find someone to negotiate... Blessed be those barbarians, since we find in them, instead of enemies, compatriots. But it was just in time!

"You don't believe in Providence, then?" the voice went on. "Your peasant parvenus, scarcely uncrushed, cast aside all their good and honest prejudices along with their blouses and satchels, only to take them up again when indefinite progress threatens their shops or their castles; but the cause of which they ought to have been the faithful servants by virtue of their right to ignorance, thank God, can count on other, more constant defenders. Among all people, in all latitudes, since the beginning of the world, that retrograde party, so jeered and so shamed, has always existed, and even counts among its most fervent adherents a large number of sages and the learned. It always will exist, because it is a necessity.

"In mental matters as well as physical mattes, life is movement; movement is flux and reflux, action and reaction, affirmation and negation. Those two contrary principles, which dispute the world, serve mutually as checks and balances; if one disappears the other dies of its excess. A bird needs its two wings, a boat its two oars, a chariot its two wheels, a steam engine its two pistons, a railway its two rails; the opposing part, no matter what side it is on, is the second wing, the second oar, the second wheel, the second piston, the second rail. It completes the machine and gives it, if not thrust, at least the equilibrium that prevents it veering to the right or the left.

"If revolutions are aborted, if a day comes when they turn violently against themselves, it is because, after having broken their second wing, their second oar, they necessarily experience the need to replace it, to bisect the vanquished party in order to create an opposition.

"Since antagonism is one of the essential laws of nature, as of society, since both only arrive at their normal development by means of struggle, refrain in your political debates from hating your adversaries; they are useful to you—indispensable, even. A fortunate modification has taken place among you, in any case; for those furious duels of contrary parties, in which the earth drinks blood, you have substituted struggle by speech, battle by sitting down and standing up; today, in our diets, the projectiles of war, instead of being thrown at the head, are dropped into the ballot box.

"That is better; that is good! On that legal route, progress can advance for a long time yet, without danger to anyone, thanks to the great law of antagonism that moderates it; live in peace, then, and no longer doubt Providence; God, in mingling the two elements of fire, hydrogen and oxygen, has made water, which extinguishes fire; trust in him, let things take their course and reconcile yourself with your two neighbors, whom you have ceased to see because they wounded your moderationism with their two opposed poles, the right and the left."

The voice ceased to make itself heard. Where had it come from? I looked around. I only saw Lalagé. Sitting on the edge of the stream, watching it flow, her head inclined, her legs crossed, her arms extended toward her knees and linking them together, she was meditating, and scarcely seemed to be thinking about me.

"Oh, Lalagé," I said to her, "thank heaven you interrupted me in the fastidious colloquium in social philosophy that I've just been having with myself! Why did I, who was with you a little while ago, smiling at flowers, birds and the sun, suddenly preoccupy myself with the state of modern society, our legislative chambers, our peasants and our railways, all of that in comparison to the Golden Age, Nineveh and Sardanapalus? I remember…it was Prometheus who appeared to me first. But why did I think about Prometheus rather than someone else?"

Lalagé smiled, and pointed to a little daisy, white and pink, on the same grassy mound where we were sitting.

"A little while ago," she said, "you were looking at that little flower, a charming reduction of the large ox-eye daisies of our meadows; an insect with gaudy wing-cases came to settle on it, in order to drink from the cornets of its florets. Do you remember? Then the daisy received a shock, and swayed for some time on its stem; it was a tiny bird—a wren, I think—that had just touched it with its wing—and when the bird flew away, it had the insect in its beak."

I remembered the event perfectly, but could not understand as yet that it might help me to recover the first cause of my great philosophical, political and palingenetic reverie.

Lalagé added: "Then you followed the wren in its flight, and your thoughts, rising above it, went into the upper regions of the air, searching for the bird of prey of which, in its turn, the raider might become the victim; you thought about a kite, and then a vulture; you were led to wonder what mystery of wisdom the ancient tradition contained; the rest followed naturally.

"The drop of water that falls from the rock covers the surface of the lake with spreading ripples, which connect one to another; likewise, the highest human inspirations sometimes have no other primal cause than the cry of a cricket or the sight of a blade of grass; an atom of the air is sufficient to put in motion and cause to radiate in its immense orbit a thought that can simultaneously embrace God, time and space."

For as long as Lalagé spoke, I did not think either of interrogating her again, or even of responding to her. Only one thing preoccupied me, which was the fact that, at that moment, her voice resembled the one that had resounded in my ear during my reverie.

The Flight from Saint Helena

Prometheus had his vulture;
Perhaps Napoléon had worse;
For Hudson-Lowe, his vampire.
Gnawed and tore by turns
His liver and his heart.
                          One day,
Pensive and solitary on his isle,
The Emperor, on raising his eyes
Thinks he saw a somber moving dot
Surge from the utmost depths of the sky.
He seizes his long telescope,
And his eyes moisten with tears
A balloon reflects as far as him
The three glorious colors.

That evening, beneath a starless sky
Everything is asleep, and yet
Hudson-Lowe, still prowling,
In the bay filled with sails,
Smiles at the growling waves·
"Well guarded are those the sea guards,
Especially when, for my part,
I watch!" he says. A light,
Sudden, rapid and pale,
Furrows the cloud; he looks.
In the midst of the obscurity
A globe of oval form is moving,
Skimming the ground near Longwood.

He runs, he crosses the interval…
But the balloon has taken off.
Your terrestrial or naval force
Can do nothing; your prisoner
Is fleeing by air. Hang yourself, jailer!

But who, then, is that Argonaut,
Bold navigator of the air,
Who, so briskly, from that side
Has descended like the lightning?
A young Englishman, an aeronaut,
Sickened by seeing his country
Betray the most sacred rights,
Swore to repair its fault,
Let's say its crime, toward its guest.

On his aerial vessel
For three years, without respite,
He labored, sparing nothing
Of his time or his gold; his task
Was to be able to steer
Securely, in a light skiff.
Was the thing even possible?
There was talk of invincible obstacles.
And yet he brought it to the end.
Will triumphs over all.

During the high crossing
The ex-prisoner, silently
Sensed welling up in his mind
A thousand audacious projects.
In the morning, before him, the earth
Of which his share was denied
Like a military map

Unfurled before his gaze.
He is alone, no gold or army,
The road to success is closed;
Must he resign himself? No!
If he wants to resume his role
Does he not still have his name?
That name from pole to pole
Thunders more loudly than cannon.

In a plain in the Americas
They descend; the inhabitants
Toward the magical globe
Come running breathlessly.

"Strangers, who are you?" asks
An old man, the local chief,
"Among us who recommend you
To holy hospitality?"
"Among you," replies the great man,
"I have never come before,
And yet I am known to all,"
And then he names himself.

But at that resounding name,
Which all repeat, no one
Is excited or astonished.
No one among them knows it.

All glory, all aureole,
Every star has places down here
Where its radiance does not reach.

The young Englishman speaks.
"Sire, these fortunate lands

Surrounded by the Andes,
Have, thanks to desert sands
Uncrossable frontiers
All kings in league and jealous
Can do nothing against you here.
The earth here, doubly fertile
Pours out its gifts incessantly,
The sky is cheerful, mild and clement;
You will find in this refuge
At the same time, security,
Repose and liberty."
But before he has even finished
The Emperor, having bowed his head,
As if under the weight of an insult
Suddenly looks up again.
"I'll be forgotten here," he says.
"Let's return to Saint Helena now.
There, at least, the isle is full
Of my misfortunes and my exile;
There I am great by my torment;
There, I am still Napoléon.
The world watches the sacrifice
And my torturers know my name!"

The Great Discovery of Animules

It is said, and people are generally glad to think, that our souls have already encountered one another in an anterior world, and that some of them have even been paired, giving rise to sympathies that still attract them to one another today and often determine our affections. There is an ancient link, which seeks to renew itself across the centuries, a pleasant habituation inclined to continue from heaven to earth. I would willingly endorse the ideas of poets, and lovers themselves, if reflection, and something even better than reflection had not demonstrated to me that they are vain and puerile.

Petty as it is, our terrestrial globe has not neglected to populate itself adequately. How many human beings, and, in consequence, how many souls, pullulate between its poles? India and China alone furnish six hundred million, before adding Europe, Africa, the Americas, Australia and Oceania to the count. In the midst of such a multitude, dispersed over the surface of the earth, split up and separated to an infinite degree by mountains, deserts and oceans, admit that a meeting of two predestined souls is no more than exceptional. Now, it is the work of a madman to build systems on exceptions.

This cannot happen as imagined. Fortunately, thanks to an unexpected and unlooked-for revelation, I find myself in a position to offer partisans of the ancient dogma something that will take the place of the belief that I have taken away from them, with sufficient compensation, and even some profit.

If our mutual sympathies do not originate so remotely, they are exercised at close range with greater surety, strength and plausibility. Why should souls, like light and perfumes, not have their radiance, or, to put it better, their emanations?

These emanations, these reciprocal attractions, not only attach souls to one another, but also, thanks to another universal law that desires nothing in nature to unite without fecundity, engender by their contact, not a soul—that is the work of God alone—but an *animule*: a more or less viable parcel of soul: *animula vagula, blandula*, as the great Emperor Hadrian once said.[25]

These animules, atoms emanated by our souls, form a sensible atmosphere around us. Our individual soul, or divine guest, partakes more intimately in our joys and dolors, our particular inclinations and personal affections; while assisting in that, our animules have another role to play: they compose the great chain, the great network of general affections. Love of family, that other love, broader but sometimes no less passionate, that makes itself felt by an entire people, which, on a given day, lifts them with the same enthusiastic impulse, evidently flows from them.

There are ideas in the air, it is often said; in the air there are animules, which imprint thousand of souls with the same impulse simultaneously, exciting them and

---

[25] The first stanza of the famous Latin poem that begins with this line, from which Saintine might have derived the inspiration for this story, may be roughly translated as: "Pale, wandering little soul/Guest and companion of my body/Where are you going now/Pallid, rigid and naked/Forsaking the jokes we used to share…."

causing them to palpitate in the magnetic milieu that is their own essence.

"But you have not announced a discovery," it might be objected, "you have given us a hypothesis. Who has demonstrated the existence of these animules? How can you know that they populate the air if, like the air, they are impalpable and invisible?"

As invisible and impalpable as the air: exactly. Listen! Scientists found the means to weigh air a long time ago, to divide it into its elementary components, and yet, in spite of their most complicated optical instruments, they have not been able to obtain any visual perception of it. One day, an intelligent man who was only a scientist in his leisure hours took a piece of card, made a hole in it with the point of a needle, looked through the hole, and saw the air; he saw all the gaseous atoms composing it moving and radiating before him. Well, it was very nearly the same for me with respect to that other supposedly invisible entity, the animule.

Following a long botanical expedition, once evening, having returned home with many plants, aromatic of the most part, and occupying myself with analyzing them by the light of an excellent Carcel lamp,[26] I was astonished to perceive white forms apparently passing under my magnifying glass. I thought it was some reflection of light on the instrument, and set it aside. The forms continued to appear to me, confused at first, then distinct, especially at the borders of my lampshade.

Every great discovery initially causes a distressing hesitation, in which a residue of doubt painfully suppresses the explosion of triumphant joy. Almost fright-

---

[26] Bernard Carcel patented a new kind of oil lamp in 1800, which used a clockwork-driven pump to bring oil to the wick.

ened by my success, I stood up, went outside and headed for the boulevards. Everywhere, in the streets, along the house-fronts, around the gas-lamps and in the brightly-lit display windows of shops, I saw before me those floating animules, whose revelation had until then been only a revelation of my thought. This time, I had them, not under the error-prone lens of a microscope, but in my own line of sight, without any intermediary; I had not even needed to pierce a piece of card. To those who are endowed with the gift of prescience, heaven momentarily grants in the same way the faculty of verifying with their own eyes the calculations of their imagination.

Having become calmer, I observed attentively, and made notes.

These animules, almost diaphanous, presented at their central point a sort of dark patch, indicating the presence of some substance, doubtless borrowed from the air, in whose environment they live; that is their material aspect.

As for their forms, varied according to their different categories, at first sight, they presented the appearance of light shining bubbles of air, with a pearly gleam, surrounding the opaque nucleus I have already mentioned. Not one projected a shadow; on the contrary, the pearly mesh, composed of tiny imperceptible scales, that enveloped their diaphanousness without darkening it, not only amplified luminous radiance but gave off phosphorescent sparks, in all probability electric.

Momentarily, I found in them—regretfully, I confess—the physiognomy of an elongated aerostat floating horizontally. I examined them more attentively. Little silvery oars were beating on their flanks. With their shiny mesh, inflated by air, these oars gave them the appearance of those little feluccas with sails that appear through the morning mists at sunrise in Mediterranean waters.

In the first instance, I had before me the infinitely tiny spectacle of an aerial fleet; in the second, a maritime fleet. But how was it imaginable that these emanations of the soul might be so similar to vulgar machines invented by humans?

Fortunately, at that moment, my eyes, by virtue of an incredible nervous overexcitation, were endowed with the magnifying power of the finest microscopes. My new investigations allowed me to discover semblances of limbs, scarcely protruding from the body, and a conically-shaped and slightly-flattened head sunk between the shoulders—admitting as shoulders the two concave muscular structures between which the head was embedded. An animule of the strongest species, which I was fortunate enough to keep motionless before my gaze or a few seconds, permitted me to rectify my first judgment entirely. The little silvery oars of my feluccas became its slender silky fins, and it breathed air while lifting up, at regular intervals, a membranous partition not unlike the operculum of a fish.

At first I had imagined for my animules a gracious, even mythological form, with wings on their backs, like sylphs or sylphides; I had seen them, in the first place, as balloons, and in the second place, as boats; the turn of the fish had come: I took them for fish, saw their scales, fins and opercula. Was not the air a fluid sufficient for them to be able to live in it and move through it at their ease?

Now that I was no longer thinking of dressing them in a form according to my fancy, in truth, I found them very fine as they were: alert, graceful and charming. I ended up concluding that they were, in every detail, that which they ought to be.

It remained for me to study their habits and inclinations.

The majority swirled in swarms around certain individuals, especially young women and children; they enveloped them like an animate cloud, allowing themselves to be drawn along by the movement that the latter impart to the ambient air; they crossed the road with them, pausing where they paused.

On occasion, however, some of those little atomistic souls broke ranks and allowed themselves to be drawn into the orbit of another company. Sometimes, encountering one another as if unexpectedly, they made an abrupt movement of separation, which I attributed to an antipathetic influence; but every truth is proved by its antithesis, and if antipathy has its effects among the animules, by the same virtue, sympathy must make itself felt—as I was not long in observing, in the most convincing fashion.

I saw several of them, belonging to different swarms, show themselves two by two, drawing apart and drawing closer by turns, as birds traveling together do, and when they drew closer, their pearly mesh shone more brightly on the two sides that made contact, and they interconnected like a shower of sparks.

Experimenting in the busy street, I could hardly expect to verify the fact, but I do not doubt that, in the right circumstances, two entire groups might be combined by mutual fusion. These groups cannot be content to be thus confused for a few seconds; they accompany, and alternately escort the two individuals from which they have emanated. The latter may not have met yet, but they are already subject to the influence of the magnetic atmosphere that surrounds them; they sense one another and seek one another, without being aware of the invisible magnet that is attracting them to one another. When they finally establish a relationship, the sympathetic effects are immediately manifest, creating, in proportion to their strength and vivacity, those furious spontaneous infatuations that so often have no other rationale, which fade away as quickly as they have come, or the calmer, more rational sentiment of progressive affections, ardent love-affairs and long friendships.

Does this mean that all human beings are equally liable to experience or to communicate these sympathetic impulses? The opposite is easy to demonstrate.

A man walking two paces in front of me was only escorted by a few animules. These, although apparently weak and, I dare say, unhealthy, left his company to mingle with other swarms, but they came back to him hastily, and always alone. I overtook the man in order to inspect his physiognomy; he had a fixed stare, thin lips and a harsh expression—and grey hair to boot. He had to be an old misanthropic bachelor.

I also made many other observations that it would take too long to report; but one that I ought not to pass over in silence is the truly remarkable incident that crowned my experiments.

I was continuing my investigations in the open street, in the corners of squares, in front of cafés and shops—everywhere that a bright enough light permitted my eyes to take advantage of the singular clarity of vision with which I was endowed at that moment—when I suddenly noticed a liveliness, an extraordinary coming-and-going, in my animules. They were no longer arrayed as exactly around certain individuals; all of them, as if obedient to a general commotion, were allowing themselves to be borne along by the same current, into the same whirlwind, like a blizzard of snow blown by a storm-wind—and yet the air was calm, and there was not a cloud moving in the sky.

Without losing its force, this emigration took on a more regular appearance; it was as if invisible leaders had established order and discipline in the ranks, and among these ranks thus aligned I never once perceived the antipathetic somersaults that had previously been possible. Our animules went along the Rue de Richelieu, in such great numbers that the majority were lost in the shade, and even in the darkness, of the upper floors.

Suddenly, as if to give me the power to observe them even at those heights, and in their various directions, all Paris lit up from the bottom to the top of its houses and palaces. Then I was able to see them emerging from every window, descending from every balcony and even from every attic, in order to join the great procession.

On turning into the boulevards, I perceived that the Parisian population, hurled outside by innumerable waves, was filling and cluttering the sidewalks, experiencing that evening an impulse and an agitation entirely similar to that of my animules.

That same Saturday, the 25th of June in the year 1859, when my great discovery should have received its consecration, the news had just arrived by telegraph of the important victory won by the Franco-Sardinian army on the banks of the Mincio.

The victory of Solferino was that of good,[27] which serves to prove the role that the animules play in great

---

[27] The crushing defeat of the Austrian army at Solferino was the military high point of the Second Empire; Saintine could

popular emotions, whose explosive spontaneity has never before been explained.

Since that day, it has not been given to me to renew my experiments—which, at any rate, have not yet been contested by anyone.

---

not know, when he wrote the story, that the vital stimulus it provided to the unification of Germany under Prussian domination would pave the way for the revenge of the Franco-Prussian War of 1870, which smashed and humiliated the Empire in question. Amour, of course, often has similar eventual results on an individual level.

On the Pedestal

If I addressed myself to a young woman, she did not seem to have heard me. Most of the time one might have thought that my dancing partners simply took me for an instrument of the dance, so little did they seem to care, save for the hands and the feet, what my person was worth.

In the houses I frequented assiduously, people observed in my regard, at the most, the rules of the most vulgar politeness. If it was a matter of a dinner, I infallibly occupied the bottom end of the table, near the service door, exposed to air currents and spills.

If invited to a musical soirée, relegated to the back, standing on tiptoe, I was in the antechamber rather that the drawing room, without a chair to sit on, and the singer's finest flourishes did not reach me, any more than the refreshments.

At a play, the seat reserved for me in the box was always the "impossible" one, from which one cannot see anything and cannot hear very much, except for the noises in the corridor and the chatter of the usherettes. Before the end, whether it was a comedy or a drama, I was sometimes casually sent to ask the coachman to be ready. The denouement they promised to relate to me at the first opportunity.

And yet, there was a certain atmosphere of benevolence around me, in which I felt that I was living pleasantly—but I was a simple student then, and all I had was the allowance that my father gave me. I could not aspire as yet to high consideration.

Too soon I had the unhappiness of seeing fortune address a first, untimely smile to me—a smile of mourning; also too soon, perhaps, I declared myself to be a poet. I published a pink volume entitled *April Flowers*, which a great newspaper eulogized in a review. Well, in spite of my surplus of ease and my pink volume, if anyone had as much benevolence for me as before, they scarcely gave me any more evidence of respect.

I was irritated by that; what did I need to do, then, to mount the metaphorical pedestal, and no longer to figure within the circle of my friends—I had no hopes beyond that—as just anyone, but as *someone*?

I published a second volume—yellow, this time. The same welcome, the same causal attitude.

My irritation turned to frenzy...

Finally, one day, after having received an almost ceremonious invitation card from Madame C***, I presented myself at her house. Contrary to habit, the valet de chambre proclaimed my name loudly, and both battens of the drawing room door opened wide.

The announcement made, the men stood up, and the women inclined their heads in salute, turning in my direction. I was beginning to count for something, then?

The good welcome was not to stop there. Madame C*** came toward me and indicated a large armchair to me near the fireplace, from which she had just expelled the previous occupant with a gesture. Slightly confused by such a reception, to which I was far from being accustomed, I wanted at first to decline that distinction; she insisted, with a kind of authority. I gave in.

At dinner, I was seated next to her, to her right, and yet a few high notabilities of finance and administration were distributed around the table. My hostess, I had every reason to think, placed litterateurs well above capitalists and functionaries in her esteem. I thought nevertheless that I ought to show modesty by asking her to what I owed such an honor. Doubtless detracted by the thousand and one preoccupations of the mistress of a house, she only responded with a few inconsequential and scarcely articulate words, but in which there was certainly mention of my age.

What, I ask you, had my age to do with it?

The conversation having become general as it warmed up, emboldened by the position I had been given, I did not hesitate to involve myself in it. People listened to me in an almost admiring silence, and then applauded enthusiastically—and while applauding, murmured a few words *mezza voce*, in which my age was again brought into play. That was puzzling; although still young, I had did not have any pretention of passing for a phenomenon of precocity.

No matter! I had mounted the pedestal. Flattered—very flattered—no longer to be anyone, but someone, astonished nevertheless to have been magnified so rapidly in public opinion, reassuring myself in thinking that I was neither a minister not the administrator of a railway company. My social position and my wealth had remained the same, so those eulogies, those attentions and that respect, after which I had sighed for so long, were addressed to me and me alone: to my individual merit, as a litterateur, as a poet, to my pink book and my yellow book, now appreciated as they deserved to be!

In the evening there was a reception, and a semblance of an orchestra improvised in a corner of the large drawing room allowed it to be perceived that youth would have its part in the festivities.

On entering, the invited guests, after having saluted the masters of the house, came to incline before me. I was increasingly flattered; my pride, recovered from the initial surprise, had had time to sit down squarely in its aplomb; I was no longer astonished by anything, except to hear all the newcomers talking to me about their respect and veneration. The simple word "admiration" appeared to me to be sufficient.

Soon, a few groups of young women spread out in the drawing room, which they embalmed with their youth, and caused to flourish with their beauty. Among them I distinguished one that I had preferred to all others for a long time. She perceived me, came toward me and, after a semi-reverence, with a graceful swan-like movement that caused the spiral of her blonde hair to rise and descend, she offered me…her forehead to kiss.

The imprudent girl! But no one in the assembly seemed to attach the slightest importance to that unqualifiable action, which ought to have caused an enormous scandal.

I don't know why I felt less triumphant. I was experiencing certain symptoms of anxiety. The idea of inviting one of those pretty young persons for the next quadrille did not occur to me, and, Madame C*** having presented me at that moment with a card for whist, I had no hesitation in taking it.

While the violins scraped their first chords and the dancers, passing close to my armchair, made the magnetic swish of their gauzy robes audible, I did not experience any other sensation than a very marked chill in the legs, an effect of the robes and the air current that they had just established.

Before going to take my place at the card table, I approached the mantelpiece. I raised my head. There was a mirror in front of me...

Horror! I scarcely recognized myself.

White, sparse hair was spaced like arid brushwood over my jaundiced cranium, as shiny as ivory; my bistre face, covered with a network of scaly mesh, was furrowed by numerous and profound wrinkles; my eyes, in which the gleam of the gaze was still sparkling, were sunk in their bony orbits, circled with scarlet...

All was revealed; I was no longer anything but an old man. I was eighty years old!

Those attentions, those homages of which I had been the object were not addressed to my mind, nor to my merit, but to my age—and that repeated word had not enabled me to understand. In me, it was not so much my personal value that was being honored as the mere fact of being alive.

Yes, there is good reason to honor the old; they represent ancestry, experience and wisdom; but if they are truly wise, can they draw any vanity from respect and praise that are only sounding their funeral knell?

In giving me the armchair near the fire, in placing me to her right, had not my hostess said to me clearly: "You're neither the richest, nor the noblest, nor the most important of my guests, but the oldest; I'm honoring you because you're soon going to die."

And her guests, after having listened to me with so much benevolence, and the late arrivals in coming to incline before me, and the beautiful young woman offering me her forehead, had all come to address the same mortuary compliment to me.

Precipitated from the height of my pride, how I regretted the good times of my youth, when everyone

166

treated me with such scant regard, when I occupied the bottom end of the table, the antechamber during concerts, and the impossible seat at the play: the thrice-blessed time when no young woman would have been audacious enough to offer me her forehead to kiss!

Old Goethe, when Bettina Brentano,[28] murmuring a few words of amour, went to sleep on your knees, you too were proud on your pedestal, you, the Olympian poet, the scholar, the immortal! But the shrewd Bettina knew full well that your pedestal was the stone of the sepulcher, and her passionate words could be summarized thus:

"I admire you, I love you, because you are great, and if I dare to proclaim it out loud, it's because you will soon die."

---

[28] Bettina Brentano's friendship with the aged Goethe begun in 1907, when she was in her early twenties; it ended abruptly when his wife objected to it. Shortly thereafter she married the Romanic poet Achim von Arnim; she was a significant figure in the Romantic Movement herself; marriage put an end to that for two decades, but she went on to greater success in the 1830s when she was widowed; she published an account of her correspondence with Goethe in 1835.

The Three Lights

(Another Night in the Woods)

Night has fallen
Blackening the clouds,
Blackening the woods;
One can scarcely hear
Far away in the plain
Confused voices.
In a few cottages
Lights are shining,
Uncertain reflections;
Soon the noises cease,
The gleams disappear;
All is silent, asleep;
The plain is tranquil
The shadow still,
The hamlet mute.

Indolently,
The god of repose
Hovers in the air,
And pours in silence
Shadows and poppies.

Vainly I listen;
The echoes of the road
Are silent;
A solitary dreamer,
In vain to the sky,

In vain to the earth,
I bear my gaze;
Everywhere darkness...
Funereal thoughts
Chill my spirits;
By a secret fear
I feel surprised;
Already I regret
Daylight and Paris.

But in nature,
Something reassures us,
Something distracts us,
My terror flies away
I have, in the forest,
Seen the firefly
And its bright fire
In the dark night,
Populating the verdure
With sparkling stars.

Of that mild prodigy,
God makes use, I think,
In these cheerful woods,
To aid, in the shadows,
The chaste amours
Of countless insects,
Which, in the maze
Of the new grass,
Without the prompt help
Of a faithful beacon,
Would always go astray
Losing their way,
Doubtless missing

Their rendezvous
So brief and so sweet.

Austere philosopher,
Protect your reason.
Yes, in this grass
There is love, and pleasure
When the season comes;
Even among flowers
There is seeking, amour;
Everywhere lovers,
The fecund race
In the air, in water,
To the utmost depths
Of our old world,
Populating the round
With all the elements,
Seeking, enchaining,
Easily destroying
Your vain arguments.
I believe in dryads;
I believe in naiads;
I believe in fiction!
I glory therein:
Can illusory wealth,
Not be charming?
It is good to believe,
It is sweet to love!

But swift, unexpected,
God, what clarity,
From on high descended,
Discovers to my sight
An enchanted world!

Before me, all changes;
A fortunate mixture
Of shadow and light,
Of a strange prestige
Charms this abode.

The time of enchantment
And sylphiry[29]
Are recalled to me;
By magical sounds
The air is troubled;
With fantastic beings
The fields are filled.
Laughing phantoms,
Amorous sylphs,
Vaporous follets,
Undines and gnomes,
Wander beneath the crowns
Of these shady woods;
Their numerous swarms
Spread out everywhere;
They rise and descend
Along the branches,
Then others launch forth,
Plunging underwater,
And lightly swing
From the heads of reeds;
Suddenly growing,
Mingling, bounding,
Abruptly vacillating...

---

[29] The original text's *syphirie* must be a misprint of *sylphirie*,
the realm of elemental spirits.

The heavens darken,
Shadow swallows everything
Like a vain dream.

From my reverie,
Too soon deflowered,
I emerge astonished,
A poor tributary
Of a limited world,
In sum, to the earth

I have returned;
For the mad moon
From the sky dislodged,
With its silvery face
Hides the light of dawn;
Of the firefly
The beacon is extinct,
The shadow, which grips me
Leaves me confused,
Afflicted by fear;
I can see nothing more.

I tremble, I listen...
A muffled rumble
Has suddenly
Shaken the path,
Doubtless a storm.

But a flash of light
Suddenly colors
The saddened wood.
In the sky, the dawn
Cannot be born yet;

Is it a meteor,
A brilliant product,
Of the fires of summer,
A subaltern star,
Borne in the air?
No, it's the lantern,
Gray, dirty and dull
Of a muddy fool.

Of my three lights,
I think at present
In consulting myself
That the first couple,
The moon and glow-worm
(Forgive the blasphemy!)
Have at least the price
For my surprised eyes,
With which the third,
The dull and gray light,
Such a wan alarm,
Troubled my mind.

But the bumpkin passes,
I soar through space
Uttering cries;
I find a place there,
I give thanks to heaven,
And return to Paris.

Timothée Jerry's Five Rungs

In spite of my smiling lips and my properly con-
formed limbs, I inspired nothing in the friends of my
family during my early infancy but a sort of horror; they
saw nothing in me but an abortion, a cast-off of creation,
a monster outside the natural and normal order of humankind. Not only was I born deaf, dumb and blind, but
an obstinate engorgement of the olfactory organs was to
nullify for me, for several years, the senses of smell and
taste.

I only possessed that of touch, in fact; but touch is
an exquisite sense, the very seat of sensibility, the only
sense that, to some degree, can substitute for the others. I
was not unhappy, at any rate. If the absence of the other
faculties prevented my thought from developing and participating in certain exterior enjoyments, highly prized
by those who already know them, it also prevented the
penetration of those external enemies, anxieties, and all
the thousand painful incidents of life of which childhood
is itself a tributary.

Isolated, enclosed in my own personality, my mind
floating in the void, living without knowing what life is,
I abandoned myself without fear and without reserve to
the impressions that my unique sense could give me.

The wind that blew, the vivifying gusts of warmth
that departed from the hearth, a gentle hand that was
placed on my forehead or rummaged through my hair,
the caresses of my mother and those of my sisters—and
God knows how prodigal they were!—created for me a

wellbeing of the soul and the body, beyond which I did not anticipate anything.

My three guardian angels watched over me with the instinct of the heart, the surest of instincts; my hand never encountered anything but soft surfaces, cool in summer and warm in winter, which imprinted in my nerves agreeable rather than sharp stimulations. They were my games and my celebrations.

"That's not living," you might say, "that's vegetating!"

Let us not argue about words; granted, I was a plant rather than a human being, but a plant endowed with movement and sensation—a very happy plant, I assure you.

I do not know which prince of the house of Bourbon, gripped by madness at certain hours, believed that he then became a simple bush, and no longer had any other needs than those of vegetables of his species. How bitterly that plant must have regretted waking up to find that he was a prince!

The gift of smell and that of taste arrived later, but, preceding one another, they arrived almost together.

In the early days, that double source of unknown emotions, coming to mingle their two currents with that of my habitual impressions, rendered me prey to perplexities that were often painful. So many shocks and changes succeeding one another alternately, imposed on my intelligence, still inert, a labor of appreciation and comparison from which it was hardly capable of obtaining any advantage. I do not know whether or not those new impressions were entering me through the sensible surfaces of my body, whether their origin was internal or external. Furthermore, with regard to those questions, as well as many others, I am scarcely any further forward today, even thought I have been able to consult learned individuals on the subject, whose contradictory opinions I shall refrain from reproducing, having no intention of producing a treatise on odors and tastes.

What I will mention is that the ineffable wellbeing that resulted later from their alliance with touch, the fortunate modifications that those new guests brought to my existence when I finally succeeded in enjoying their benefits placidly, without giving any thought to their analysis.

The sense of smell developed precious faculties within me, among others that of perceiving objects at a distance.

Once, when one of my guardian angels came to visit me, being unable to see or hear her, nothing alerted me to her presence; it was only given to me to recognize her at close range, by making contact with her. Now, I touched her at a distance; I recognized her by the perfume that impregnated my atmosphere as she approached.

Every person in the house, every object making up its furniture, had its distinct odor for me; however faint it might be, I was able to appreciate it, in its various gradations, with enough certainty to walk freely in my bedroom or the other rooms of the apartment, nostrils open, measuring the distance that separated me from one item of furniture and brought me closer to another, so subtle was the sense of smell that I had acquired.

Among scents there was one that I preferred to all others, which was that of carnations. Why? My mother also preferred it, and her handkerchief and clothing bore the evidence of that preference. Was it a simple conformity of tastes between the two of us? No; I would like to believe that I loved certain odors because of the love I felt for the individuals that they recalled in my mind. It was thus that I placed, immediately after carnation in my esteem—or rather, my affection—iris and verbena, the favorite perfumes of my sisters. That would tend to prove that, taking advantage of my recent conquests, my heart had developed along with my intelligence of things.

It happened that, one morning in spring, my mother came to me with a bouquet of violets in her belt. I remained cold and anxious under her caresses; I seemed to be in the arms of a stranger. She understood that, and did not make the same mistake again.

The sense of taste had added at least as much to my wellbeing as the sense of smell.

In the same way that the external air, of which I had once requested only that it refresh my hot brow, now arrived both cool and balsamic—for we lived in the country—nourishment, which had previously only satisfied a need, became a pleasure: a scarcely delicate pleasure, some might say, refined in their own delicacy, for whom it is easy to talk, but supreme, imperious and multiple for a poor adolescent condemned until that moment to the repugnant absorption of insipid, earthy substances, a medicament against hunger, and that alone.

How times have changed! Now, when nourishment reaches the poor disinherited creature, he senses it coming in advance, his mouth watering at the flavorsome odor that it exhales; and his hands reach out to encounter it! Did that enjoyment, coarse according to you, not satisfy by itself the three faculties of sensation that had been accorded to me, I won't say by miserly, but prodigal and beneficent nature?

Blind, deaf and dumb...doubtless, yes, I was still that; but does one regret the things one has not known, that one has not desired?

After my meals, taken *en famille*, and during which I chatted pleasantly with my mother and my sisters purely by means of handclasps and kisses, I was served a little good wine mixed with water. So great was my sensibility that I felt suddenly transported into an ideal world, my own real world; how could I know any other when sound and color, everything that was not touch, smell and taste, escaped my appreciation? No matter! Surrounded by attentions and tenderness, which I thought would never end, ignorant of evil, mistrustful neither of humans nor of Providence, it seemed to me that life and happiness were the same thing.

Alas, until then I had been living in a dream; I was about to wake up.

One day, two hands were placed on my brow, two unknown, dry, cold and rough hands. I pushed them away with horror; my movements were mastered by force; my eyelids were parted, and I sensed an agonizing pain, accompanied by a jet of light.

I would not have wanted to glimpse that redoubtable clarity again for anything in the world. I firmly believed that it alone had been the cause of my suffering. A blindfold was put over my eyes; I was very glad of that. I understood, vaguely, that it was protecting me from its return.

Nevertheless, I had seen, for a second, perhaps only a twentieth of a second—no matter, I had seen! That was enough to bring disturbance to my mind. I wondered what the menacing sign was that, amid violence, had suddenly appeared to me other than by means of thought.

That night, a dream designed before me a phantom in the form of a flash; frightened, I leapt out of bed; soft hands and beloved scents calmed me down.

After a time, my blindfold was removed, with the blinds and shutters closed; they only wanted to introduce me into the fourth world, the world of light, gradually, taking all necessary precautions. Thus, I passed progressively from black obscurity to gray obscurity, from semi-shadow to dubious clarity.

When I succeeded in distinguishing objects clearly, what I initially experienced was a complete disenchantment. Around me, the furniture and the wallpaper, which I thought I knew so well by virtue of touch, no longer had the form that I had supposed; their contrasting colors, especially the reflections of various metals, wounded by sight. I thought I could reach them by extending my hand, but my hand only attained empty space; my relationships with my habitual surroundings were suddenly broken and rendered discordant.

A much more painful disillusionment! A memory forever dolorous! Three women stood before me, their faces contracted by emotion, their arms half-extended...

Those women frightened me. Their features seemed to be grimacing menacingly. I recoiled from them with all the signs of mistrust, and the first gaze that I addressed to them was one of panic.

It was my mother; it was my sisters!

Fortunately, I was not deceived by the sentiment of surprise full of bitterness that responded to my gaze. I drew nearer to them; before my hands had interrogated their features, the emanations of their three perfumes had revealed everything to me, and I dissolved in tears.

What I could not comprehend then, which threw me into a profound dejection, was that my mother was neither the most beautiful nor the youngest of the three.

Don't forget that I knew nothing about the family, about age or aging, and the person I loved more than anything, because I had found her close to me incessantly, because my life had been spent in her arms, had bistre skin and pale lips: she was old! At least, she appeared so to me, beside two young faces radiant with all the splendor of their twenty years.

Until then, in the midst of the chaos of my confused ideas, I had only recognized as immutable the principle that the woman who exhales the sweetest odor, and whom one loves the most, ought to be superior to all others. Scarcely were my eyes open than they checked and destroyed the previous day's enchantments.

Such was my first and sad experience of vision.

Then came the moment when, in bright morning sunlight, stripped of its veils and shackles, as I had been of mine, my window was wide open to my gaze.

If one has never been deprived of the gift of sight, or even if it arrives when one already possesses the sense of hearing, one does not know, and cannot know, what impressions are produced by sunlight, the extent of the horizon, the depth of the sky, in the midst of an inflexible silence that nothing troubles. To plunge through the infinity of celestial things and not to hear the sounds of the earth or a human voice, the song of a bird, the chime of a bell, the rustle of foliage or the murmur of a stream or an insect, is a spectacle that grips you less by its grandeur than its severity. It does not charm you; it overwhelms you.

I stood there, immobile, struck by amazement. Gradually, an anxious and nervous irritation took possession of me; space, like a bottomless gulf, appealed to me; it seemed that I was about to fall into it, invincibly; I had vertigo—a hallucinatory, dazzling vertigo. Quitting the window-sill, I hurled myself backwards with a cry of distress, and my hands clutched the garments of my guardian angels, demanding protection from them.

Protection against what? Against the light of the sun, against the clouds, against the immensity of the sky.

In the following days, I was put in a carriage; we visited the surrounding countryside, of which I only knew as yet the scent of its mown grass and the penetrating effluvia of its fir-woods. We went as far as the nearby town; there I saw populous streets, shops, bazaars, houses of every size, some of them—the churches—higher than the trees. My sisters watched my face, during our excursion, for signs of admiration, or at least astonishment, but I did not admire anything and astonishment was only manifest in me in the surly form of a profound humiliation. Only my mother, perhaps, understood the reason.

Previously, I had thought myself the center of a world apart, a narrowly circumscribed world in which everything collaborated with my personal satisfactions. Now, I ceased to think that. The earth was so large, the sky so high! More than that, had I not seen a host of people similar to me, coming and going, living and moving of their own volition? I was scarcely able to count that multitude. Then again, among that crowd, beggars clad in rags had appeared to me, and cripples dragging themselves along on their crutches...

My beautiful dream was effaced forever, to give way to the lugubrious tableau of human miseries...

It was easiest for me to shake off that sadness, which became habitual, when I was alone, walking in our garden—a large garden, almost a park. There, I was sometimes able to reconstruct my former wellbeing; I let my eyelids fall; I strove to forget the sun; I tried to make the trees and plants play the same role that the cherished furniture of the house had once played in my regard; I no longer wanted any guides but the senses of smell and touch; the fruits that I picked seemed more flavorsome to me that way. But I sometimes went astray, becoming entangled in thorn-bushes or making other encounters even more unexpected.

Once, I thought I was being watched. The air brought me an aroma that I knew. Ashamed of being discovered in the midst of that puerility, I opened my eyes. No one was there—except, a few feet away, a beautiful plant with red flowers and leaves tapering to a point. That plant had my mother's scent! It was a carnation. I had not seen one yet, and I fell to my knees before it, delightedly.

And yet, the sentiment of love that I had consecrated to it, which had been my life, my soul, my sole interior light for such a long time, gradually weakened from day to day; I transported it elsewhere, further away, underneath; I became curious, demanding, avid for emotions and new relationships; without paying any heed to the anxieties that I might cause, I needed other scents and other faces around me.

By dint of exercising my sight, I had first learned to measure distances, to compare and judge them. Soon I elevated myself as far as the intelligent appreciation of color and form. Finally, passionate admiration came to me for everything that was, or seemed to me to be, beautiful. My admiration, it is true, was addressed less to the beauties of creation as to the creature itself.

If I encountered young and pretty women during walks or in the houses that we frequented, my gaze was inflamed, and sudden ardors made me tremble. A species of savage suddenly cast into the midst of that society full on conventions and delicacies, I went straight to the young women and, reverting to my old system of experimentation, boldly seized them by the hand or the arm, uttering the raucous sigh of a deaf-mute.

A few revolted; others, kind souls, more touched by my infirmity than my demonstrations, had mercy on my youth, smiled, and did not withdraw their hand. Well—how imperiously our first ideas act upon us!—it happened that I sometimes let go of one of those merciful beauties, drawing away from her abruptly. Why? Because the essence that perfumed her hair or her handkerchief was not one of those that had the gift of charming me.

Colors also exercised a prestigious power over my imagination now. It was sufficient for a woman to be wearing a blue or pink dress immediately to set my heart ablaze. The next day, if her costume was not the same, my amour was extinguished as if the wind had snuffed it out.

The story of my infatuations of that era would be both ridiculous and lamentable. I felt jealous, to the point of violence, and hatred. Other young men, my rivals, possessed a marvelous faculty that I envied them, which had been refused to me. It was sufficient for them to open their mouth and move their lips to stimulate or divert our charmers by turns; I only had gesture, which I abused strangely and brutally. I had become an object of aversion for everyone. The houses to which people had deigned to admit me, out of regard for my family, closed their doors to me. Once again I was reduced to the socie-

ty of my mother and my sisters; it was no longer sufficient for me, and I had no hesitation in allowing them to
divine the immense ennui that tortured me in their company.

That was what the sense of sight had added to my
happiness! Daylight, had I asked to know you?

Finally, the last seed of organic life that nature had
deposited in me along with the others, but which was
still dormant, was awakened by an unknown charlatan.

I reached the last rung of the ladder.

The first sign that I perceived excited me less than
the first jet of light had done. I had had a kind of confused sentiment of it in advance. However, the sound of
voices, noises from outside, the rumble of carriages,
seemed to be shouting and bounding in my head; one
day when there was a great storm, I fainted and fell face
down on the ground....

Let us abridge these futile details. When my adapt-
able ears had become accustomed to all those discord-
ances, when I felt that I was fully in possession of the
sense of hearing, I was then able to measure, fearfully,
the distance and the obstacles that seemed to separate me
from its positive results.

I could hear, yes, but without understanding; articulate speech was only to come to me after sustained, incessant efforts.

Touch, taste and smell, those elite senses, had manifested themselves in me of their own accord, each of
them adding to the sum of my wellbeing, without demanding anything in return. Preceded by pain, sight had
marked the second era—the fatal era—of my existence;
it had precipitated me from the height of my mysterious
felicities, but at least it had not constrained me to associate myself by my efforts with the harm that it was going

to do me. It was entirely different with the last arrival; by what rude labor did it not pay me for my complete degradation!

I was already a man, and it was necessary for me to become a child again, to learn to stammer words, to learn to read, to learn to think. I devoted entire years to it. I allowed myself to be caught by the deceitful lures of study; I had transferred to it all the impetuousness of my nature. Fashioned by speech, I provoked to discussion the men most renowned for the intelligence and knowledge; I wanted to know all books and all systems of thought...

That was my undoing.

Men and books! What one affirmed to me was belied by the other, with convincing evidence on either side; the world of ideas had no foundation but hypothesis: certainty did not exist anywhere; the first and holiest education that I had received from my mother disappeared in the midst of a poisonous fog.

I read—in Plutarch, I believe—that a certain Xenocrates wanted to fit young boys with iron ear-muffs in order to prevent them from hearing anything that was said around them.

Why had no one applied Xenocrates' iron ear-muffs to me?

Passion had entered into me via the eyes; it had rendered me miserable, ingrate, full of envy and hatred; corruption entered into me via the ears; I doubted everything: truth, virtue and myself. My heart withered, my mind disenchanted, I wondered them whether it was human destiny to descend thus into the abyss as one ran the complete gamut of the senses, and I darted a tearful glance of regret at the beautiful paradise of ignorance that had closed forever behind me.

I shall summarize. Three senses were sufficient for my perfect felicity; Heaven only imparted the other two to me as a gift of its wrath.

You wanted to know my story; may you profit from it—but I am not hopeful about that.

Thus Timothée Jerry, the illustrious misanthrope, recounted to us the various phases of his exceptional life. O dreamers, my brothers, we who, in our ardent anticipations, have loudly announced, after this terrestrial life, better worlds in which a multitude of further senses will be added to those we already possess, can we subscribe to the restricted number that the philosopher regretted so bitterly having extended?

The ingrate has forgotten that three guardian angels stood watch at the gates of his paradise, to supply everything that he lacked.

And yet, what if he has told the truth about one point? What if every key added to the keyboard of the senses only serves to render increasingly discordant notes? Take care! Involuntarily, doubt seizes me in my turn. To see too much, to know too much, and to foresee too much also has it dangers. Between our excessive measure and Timothée Jerry's restrictive measure, a reasonable and sufficient median must exist.

Who knows? Perhaps what God has done he has done well; perhaps, in order to raise ourselves to unknown heights, the five rungs of the ladder that he has given us, of which Jerry was unable to make good employment, are enough.

I Become a Barbel

What a pleasant pastime angling is! It does not preclude reveries, or even dreaming.

While fishing one day, I dreamed that I was a fish: not a monster of the seas but a simple freshwater fish, neither too big nor too small, equally distant from the small fry and the bigwigs of the fluvial aristocracy. I figured, in the quality of a barbel, in the worthy bourgeoisie of our rivers.[30]

I am able to judge, therefore, how false the majority of our proverbs are. "A happy as a fish in water," people say. I was not happy; not enough is known about what the life of a fish is like: a life of incessant torments and anxieties. I had to defend myself from birds of prey, which cleave the air in order to snatch us out of the water; pike, which cleave the water in order to devour us within it; and humans—especially those frightful humans, supposedly the mildest and inoffensive of heir species, who nevertheless think of nothing but murder, and only live for murder. More often than not, do they not make war out of idleness, for pleasure rather than need? And to lure us into their trap, the barbarians, they bloody the waters, they transpierce the bodies of poor innocent worms through the middle of the body, whose employment down here is to preserve them from infec-

---

[30] The French *barbillon*, which I have translate as *barbel*, does not refer to exactly the same range of species as the English term, although it is similarly derived from the "barbs" (projections) to either side of a fish's mouth.

tion and plague. Anglers are the most ferocious of all beings!

As a barbel, of course, I reasoned with the logic of a barbel.

As I was fulminating my anathema beneath the surface of the water, I perceived one of those frightful anglers sitting on the bank of the Marne with his instrument of death in hand. He had a terrible face. Involuntarily, however, an unreflective attraction—I will say more, a sentiment of sympathy—caused me to draw nearer to the bank in order to contemplate him at closer range. On the way, distracted by my contemplation, I snapped up, somewhat at hazard, whatever the current presented to me on the way...

Strangely enough, I was the fisherman, then almost asleep. A slight shock woke me up; my line was taut; the feathered float plunged; I tugged my line mechanically, on the end of which was wriggling...a barbel!

There was a moment of disorder in my mind. Was I the victim? Was I the executioner? Without agitating the question any longer, still conserving within me the sentiment of a fish, I hastened to free the captive and to throw it back into the river.

Since that inconceivable dream, in which I figured at both extremities of my line, the flesh of the barbel has become antipathetic to me.

The Victims' Ball

Among my dreams I have some of a light nature, cheerful, and even grotesque; those easily allow themselves to be guided by a residue of will, and procure what is known as smiling sleep; but I have others that are restive, violent and terrible, which bear me away through catacombs into charnel houses, amid the dead, terrors and funereal apparitions.

This time, I was at a ball, a court ball. By virtue of what was then an exceptional favor, alongside the highest nobility in the kingdom, the bourgeoisie had its representatives there, and the people too. The ballrooms were vast, numerous and splendidly illuminated; light was reflected on all sides, glinting in the gold, in the crustal, in the mirrors, in the diamonds of duchesses as in the silk dresses of the bourgeois ladies, and even the fake jewels of the women of the people.

However, some sort of gray vapor was floating in the atmosphere of the fête; at times, the glare of the chandeliers seemed to be dulled, and the faces, previously expansive, were contracted by an anxious thought.

Suddenly, outside, drums were beaten in the fields; rifle-fire resonated in a simultaneous fusillade; inside the halls, where the agitation was great, a kind of electric shock was communicated to everyone; everyone ran toward the main entrance door; the orchestras of the ball played the prelude to a triumphal welcoming march; an immense clamor went up; *the King* had just been announced.

King Louis XVI was giving his hand to his wife, whose benevolent air, grace and beauty were admired; she was smiling, and her smile was reproduced, fixed on the faces of everyone at whom she gazed. Behind her, head slightly inclined, Princesse Élisabeth advanced, another grace, perhaps less seductive, but incomparably serene; then in their wake, a few great lords of their intimate company, among whom the Princes of the Blood did not figure, being absent from France for the moment. At the idea of that absence, a few faces in the crowd became irritated, as if before a threat.

Among those who were forming a hedge for the passage of the royal cortege were great magistrates, general tax-farmers, and even scholars—Bailly, Lavoisier, Lamoignon de Malesherbes and a hundred others. The litterateur Cazotte, after having mingled with them briefly, had retreated into the bay of a window, and there, sad and somber, tears in his eyes, he abandoned himself to the bitterness of his prophetic visions.[31]

The King opened the ball with Madame la Princesse de Lamballe; the Queen chose Monsieur de Malesherbes for her dancing partner. The orchestra played the tune of the latest quadrille—which went back to la Trénitz,[32] it is

---

[31] The critic Jean-François La Harpe commented wryly in an essay published in 1803 how amazed the guests at one of Fanny de Beauharnais' salons would have been if the self-styled Illuminatus Jacques Cazotte had told them, in 1788, where they would all be in five years' time. The comment was often repeated as if it were a statement that Cazotte had indeed done that.

[32] "La Trénitz" or "La Trénis" was a formation in a quadrille named after the dancing-master Pierre Trénitz (1765-1825), who arrived in Paris in 1795; a relentless promoter of "social dancing," he reached the height of his fame during the Consu-

true, for there had been no dancing in France for some years. So, in spite of the zeal of the musicians, their lack of habitude was betrayed by the weakness of the execution, by the lack of unison; sharp and shrill notes escaped the flutes and violins; a dull and plaintive bass served to accompany their liveliest symphonies.

By virtue of a circumstance no less bizarre, the grayish vapor condensed in the halls, thickened gradually. The light of the chandeliers and candles decreased in proportion. A strange pallor extended over the faces of all the dancers, who were only exchanging a few words between them, in low voices, and scarcely stammered. They continued dancing, however.

Then it happened that during an *avant-deux*, one of the dancers began to tremble, and her head, rolling from her shoulders, fell on to the parquet. There was a movement of stupor in the assembly at the time, but it passed quickly. The dance was resumed, and at each figure, whether in one hall or the other, an "oh!" was heard: an exclamation, sometimes a mockery or a witticism; it was a head falling.

Soon, people ended up no longer paying attention to it.

A moment came when the accident was reproduced, during Their Majesties' quadrille; the King himself....

Then, pale as they were, the faces became living; in the orchestra, the flutes uttered something akin to sobs; the violins scraped a *De profundis*; the candles revived momentarily, but their wan light, similar to that of fireworks, was a veritably apocalyptic illumination. Then everything fell into almost complete obscurity.

---

late. The reference underlines the fact that everyone at the ball is dead.

191

Subsequently, such a large number of heads fell at the same time that the dancers, embarrassed, stumbled over them and sent them rolling this way and that. From time to time, a lamentable voice, *vox ingens*, resounded in the direction of the door, announcing that the carriage of Monsieur the Comte de ***, that of Monsieur le Marquis de ***, or whoever, was waiting in the vestibule, and the sound of wheels shook the edifice dully; and those whose names had been pronounced searched for their heads, picked them up from under the banquettes or some corner, and the shaven head, bleeding between the shoulders, descended the staircase thus in order to return to his carriage.

Their carriage was the guillotine tumbrel.

Soon, the ball, breaking with all measure, only resembled a tumult, an infernal dance; all the ranks mingled, but in order to fight, with imprecations and cries of rage.

Heads continued to roll on the parquet; people made use of them then as projectiles of war; then others, less bellicose, imagined using them in a game of bowls. For want of the dance, it was necessary to create a distraction.

An hours later, they were no longer waiting for them to fall; those of nobles and the bourgeois, like those of the populace, were demanded, designated for the blade; each party, and each fraction of a party, took possession of the blade by turns; it was a contest of ferocious beasts, an orgy, a feast of blood; people plunged their hands and feet into the blood, smeared themselves with it, drank it, got drunk on it, spat it in one another's faces...

Still nestled against his window, the worthy Cazotte, Cazotte the illuminatus, got up; he tried to speak; as he had predicted the Revolution, and had designated its principal victims in advance, perhaps he wanted to announce the time of its duration; in spite of all his efforts, however, it was impossible for him to articulate a single word. The cause of his mutism was that his head had already joined those of many others without him perceiving it, because he was so distracted.

A thick, opaque red cloud had extended over that place of desolation; the musicians had broken their instruments while defending themselves against men armed with pikes; a smoky torch had replaced all the illuminations of the ball; the voice that had made the sinister summons resound a hour before, resonated again, and among the names of the victims I thought I heard my own pronounced...

I woke up while putting my hand to my neck.

It was broad daylight, which helped to dissipate the last shivering impressions of that hideous dream. I wondered then whence it had come, to what sinister, fatal cause I ought to attribute it.

In a glass of water on my night-table there was a magnificent tea-rose...

I know everything that people say about the asphyxiating emanations of flowers and the danger of keeping them enclosed with oneself, especially during the night; but how, in truth, could I believe that that magnificent rose, so gracious in appearance, which my pretty neighbor had given me the day before, could have given birth to such monstrosities in my brain? No, no...I looked elsewhere.

Next to the glass of water containing the rose I saw a pile of volumes, placed there by my domestic that morning without my knowledge. They were Lamartine's

Girondins,[33] which a friend, greatly impressed by the work, had sent me without prior notice. The work had something of the historically somber nature of my dream...the epoch and the characters were the same... That coincidence struck me. But a book only speaks under the gaze; it does not produce sounds or emanations that can reveal to us the subject with which it deals or the mysteries it contains...

However, why should I not revert to the supposition that, during the annihilation of the senses brought by slumber, our soul, in its flight, can launch itself freely into the distance, or, circumscribing its flight, ferret around us? Why should not my voyager, scanning the book, even without opening it, thanks to its magnetic power, have taken cognizance of Lamartine's *Girondins* before me, and, charged with the impressions of its reading, communicated them to me in return?

How many things are revealed to us thus, for which we do honor to our perspicacity! Decidedly, I shall stop at that explanation of the phenomenon; it is sufficient for me. I much prefer it to the one that had just denounced my beautiful tea-rose as the cause of that frightful nightmare.

---

[33] The eight volumes of Alphonse de Lamartine's *Histoire des Girondins* were published in 1847, not long before the 1848 Revolution, after which Lamartine was appointed the interim president of the Second Republic but came a poor last in the subsequent election.

Another Solomon

I dreamed; I was a King, a despot King, in Asia;
My people, on their knees, bowed down before me;
For them, I was hope, terror and the law;
      The law, that was my fantasy.
      Had Solomon, in Jerusalem,
Had more limitless powers than mine?
Like him, I was sage, and had a harem,
Furnished like his with three hundred Shulamites,
      For sages, that is sufficient.
      But it is necessary to fear slackness;
      On the advice of that counsel of wisdom,
      I made war…to my advantage.
I assembled soldiers, I passed them in review;
      There were enough; thanks to my generals,
      Skillful men, I became a hero;
Everything succeeded for me, even my blunders.
      I was not a simple conqueror,
I was a legislator, a legislator sublime.
And like Solomon, a unanimous voice
      Awarded me the name of the Great.
That was good. However, my anxious thought
Wanted more; and in that regard I often saw again,
Solomon, the great king, was also a great poet
      I tried it, and with my first attempts
        In two bounds I surpassed him.
      My people acclaimed me a prophet.
      The entire world confirms my success.
I am Solomon the Second, King-poet, great man,

And a thousand ambassadors from China and Rome,
France and Japan, come morning and evening,
        To perfume me with blasts of the censer.
I shall become a god if I don't take care!

But I am wise, and look into the depths of my heart
                What do I see there? New needs
            There is something I still lack.
            Do I aspire to apotheosis?
No, what I desire is not to have as much
Of what is overabundant. Suddenly I cry;
        "Dethrone me, my God, I beg of you;
My renown, my treasures, my wives, my grandeur,
            Take it all back, ambassadors as well
            Forever let my power crumble;
My heart remains empty in the bosom of my splendor
Make me that unknown being in the crowd,
Neither too high nor too low, a model citizen
            Content with a medium estate.
            Let my existence go by
With a few friends, not friends of the court;
Instead of my palace, give me for an abode
A simple small house enclosed by a hedge,
With green shutters, and shade all around;
Instead of my harem let me have a family,
A wife—just one—and with her a daughter...
Books in the house, flowers in the garden,
Silence outside, and that is all!"
O marvel!
                Scarcely have I said it than suddenly.
                God has granted it to me, for I wake up.

Saint Babylas' Day

Gérard de Nerval—poor Gérard!—inspired by some German poet whose name escapes me, recounts to us the sufferings of a poor vagabond during a cold New Year's Eve.[34] I shall try to tell you a true story just as lamentable as his tale, in which he is fatally mingled himself, and whose denouement seems to have imitated his imitation.

Let us enter into the matter directly.

In the latter days of January,[35] in Paris, when a cold north wind was blowing, a man is wandering along the boulevards at the late hour when all the heaters are throwing their spectators out, saturated with musical or dramatic emotions, delighted or dissatisfied....

In the midst of that crowd, which suddenly envelops him, he parades a fearful covert gaze around. A few known faces are offered to him, illuminated by the lanterns of the numerous cafés that are giving the great city its last joyful illumination. Dare he approach them, and extend his hand to them?

No, the unfortunate man responds to himself, after examining his sordid garments; the hand that he holds out they would have the right to mistake for that of a

---

[34] As the narrator remembers later in the story, the story that Gérard de Nerval translated as "La Nuit du nouvel an d'un malheureux" (1830 in the reincarnated *Mercure de France*) is by Jean-Paul Richter.

[35] In the Roman Church, the feast of Saint Babylas is January 24.

197

beggar. If, however, after long years of absence, he has returned to Paris, exhausted by poverty and fatigue, is it to flee those he has known, those he has loved?

This time, he dares not respond.

Since the morning he has bent trying to affirm himself in a great resolution; twenty times he has returned to the faubourg, his native faubourg, and twenty times he has remained on the road, increasingly seized by shame the closer he approaches his goal. Fearing he gaze of neighbors, the curious and passers-by during the day, he wanted to wait until evening; in the evening, the lights of shops frightened him, as much as that of day.

Scarcely an hour ago, in the depths of a dirty little street, he found a sordid tavern, and took refuge there. He had no hesitation in presenting himself therein; had he not had the habit of frequenting such places for a long time? To give himself courage, he drank, and he drank until his last sou. But the courage did not come. He had so little money left!

Now, night is advancing, the day is about to end; will he dare tomorrow what he did not dare today? Today, however, more than any other day, might be the day of his pardon: it is his feast day, the day of his birth!

At that idea, a host of memories rise up in his heart: memories of youth, of joy and wellbeing, which moisten his already-gray beard with tears. Sitting on a bench on the boulevard, he recalls his happiness of old, trampled underfoot: his amour, so true, so sincere on either side, and yet betrayed and disdained by him.

The only son of two good people by whom he was adored, he had received, in a second-rate boarding school, an education far above what they possessed themselves; not that they wanted to make him an advocate or a physician; they simply hoped, when the time came, to associate him with their little business—but the ambitious young man had thought he saw a more glorious morning appear to him on a fourth floor, in the studio of one of his friends, a painter. He wanted to be a painter and become famous, although he had few notions of design and none at all of color.

Desolate at his resolution, his parents had opposed it at first, and then yielded without being convinced; but they told themselves that by working for a few years more, they could still manage to assure him enough to live on. Babylas—his name was Babylas, and he had carefully refrained from repudiating his patron; a slightly strange forename that obscured the vulgarity of his family name, and would more easily stick in the memory of the public and aid his celebrity—had therefore been able to abandon himself to his artistic vocation. And his neighbors, the comrades of his class, and the inhabitants of the quarter did not take long to recognize him as a veritable artist, less by virtue of his works—he had not had the time to produce any—than his beard, which had grown more quickly than his talent, and whose disorder was a good omen.

It goes without saying that the two good people, his mother and father, were the first to fall in line with that advantageous opinion.

But art has its impulsions, which are not easy to repress; there is always a little of the artisan in the artist; the life of the studio leads directly to the life of the brasserie and the estaminet. Art also has other demands, when one wants to take it seriously; if one studies both the figure and landscapes, how can one avoid excursions to Fontainebleau and acquaintance with female models, who are rarely model women? In brief, the good people became alarmed. They only saw one way of preventing the moral decline of their cherished child, and that was to find him a wife.

The daughter of one of their fellow merchants seemed to them to have all the desirable advantages: a pretty face, a suitable dowry, the habit of selling, and magnificent handwriting—which, in petty commerce, is not an advantage to be disdained. Our artist, however, opposed a formal refusal to the proposition, not because he had made a vow of celibacy but because *he loved someone else!* That was the great argument, the only one with which he supported his refusal.

After a further attempt at authority, a *coup d'état*, the suppression of the budget, the good parents, not feeling strong enough to maintain their immutable will any longer, consulted one another. They sought information. By an unexpected hazard, their son's only beloved turned out to be an honest girl, a simple seamstress, having neither the dowry nor, doubtless, the beautiful handwriting of the other, but, in sum, good and laborious.

One evening, at dinner time, the young man, when he returned to the parental home, found the dining room more brightly illuminated than usual and four places set instead of three. As he expressed his surprise, a door opened and the mysterious guest arrived; it was the young seamstress.

"Boy," said the excellent father, suffocating with the joy that he was about to give him, "it's Saint Babylas' Day in a fortnight. Flowers are rare in that epoch, but it's this pretty darling here that we're counting on to give you your festival bouquet. So, the marriage is a fortnight hence!"

They cried out, they laughed, they wept, they embraced. At the end of the meal—a veritable betrothal feast—all four of them exchanged these words mutually:

"My daughter!"

"My wife!"

"My husband!"

"My Babylas!"

Babylas felt that he was the most fortunate of men.

There are men whom good fortune renders sad. Babylas was probably one of them. The next day, a cloud darkened his brow; he shook his head and thought he was rid of it. But on the following day, and as the days of the fortnight went by, his anxious and pensive expression increased. On January 23, both the eve of his birthday and the eve of his marriage, he fell into a sort of prostration and depression.

What could be the cause of it?

It was, once again, the unfortunate result of the demands of art.

Does a self-respecting artist have the right to become the father of a family? Let him beware! If the duties of paternity and the affections of the household exercise too great an empire over him, he is no longer anything but a bourgeois, a cretin, an individual forever unworthy of holding a brush.

Such was the terrible thought that, for nearly a fortnight, had been curbing and paling the young painter's brow, and that thought was fortified by another, more terrible still.

He was conscious of the fact—he did not hide it from himself—that his talent scarcely surpassed that of his companions in the studio; he only had, as yet, the style of the master, not his own, and without his individual originality, what is a painter? What is a painter who needs to sign his paintings with his name and forenames in order to make it known that they are his?

Now, that originality, that special, distinctive ca-chet, how can it be acquired? Is it by always drawing the same tree at Arbonne or Barbizon? By seeking inspira-tion, either in the studio or in the Louvre, with the same models as all the others?

No, he said to himself, *if a few artists have made a great name for themselves in our time, they have been to seek it in a new milieu. Thus, Marilhat and Descamps have sought it in the Orient, others in Algeria; with the same aim, Biat did not hesitate to confront the white bears of the glacial seas and the savage inhabitants of Patagonia. Well, I also have a conquest to make: a splendid, luxuriant conquest reserved for me alone, glimpsed by me alone, in the stories of a missionary to Cochinchina. But how can I visit Cochinchina with a wife and children?*

His last day as a bachelor concluded, when Babylas went to his room to go to bed, he saw, carefully laid out on a chair, the black suit and the white cravat that he was to put on the next morning in order to go to the church...the white cravat! Like a notary! A frisson gripped him. What would his comrades at the studio say?

He could not close an eye. The excitement that had taken possession of him, to which insomnia added, took on such proportions that he posed himself a double ques-tion resolutely:

Should I renounce traveling, and in consequence painting, or my marriage to Hélène? Should I immolate my glory to my amour, or my amour to my glory?

After a struggle full of hesitations, anguish and mental torture, Hélène was sacrificed.

He leapt out of bed; he wrote to his mother and his fiancée. An hour later, he climbed into a railway carriage.

Where was he going? To Cochinchina, of course.

But if art has its demands, positive, material life has its own, which are far more imperious. To begin with, Babylas had to moderate his course toward Indochina in order to subsidize the expenses of travel, accommodation, food and drink. He made portraits bearing little resemblance to their models—true artists take little account of such details—and even painted signs, initially for shops and then for taverns. The following year he was in Persia, occupied with photography: a dubious means of creating a style of his own, but photography brought in much more than sign-panting. In spite of his resources, he was only advancing very slowly toward his goal, visiting new countries but always regretting France, trying new amours without ceasing to think about Hélène. What became of him thereafter? How do I know? Did he know himself?

Driven less by curiosity than necessity, he traveled all countries, except Cochinchina, exercising all professions there, except that of painter. Then, after having been a café waiter and a street porter in California and married a brown woman in one of the Malaysian islands, tormented by remorse, crushed by poverty and prey to a frightful nostalgia, he found no other means of repatriation than signing on with a merchant ship in the capacity of a sailor, which he deserted as soon as it touched the coast of France.

From his long voyages undertaken to satisfy the exigencies of art, he only brought back, after ten years of suffering and exile, a constitution ruined and an imagination brutalized by the abuse of that dangerous consoler, strong liquor.

While the poor vagabond was equivocating, seated on an icy boulevard bench, with his eyes full of tears, the laughing phantoms of his youth, and after them the somber years of exile, passed before his eyes in mourning dress, with foreheads covered in ash; everything around him had become solitude. Not one light was burning in the cafés, even through badly-jointed shutters; only the gas-lamps along the sidewalks were resplendent in the void and the silence, like the prodigious stars that rise over the desert.

It was now too late to go knock on the door of the house in the faubourg. His sad reflections added to his sufferings of very sort; for he was hungry, he was cold, and there was no hope of shelter or a morsel of bread, and it was Saint Babylas' Day, his feast-day, his birthday!

As a consequence of the cold, in spite of his suffering, he was overtaken by an irresistible need to sleep...perhaps to die! Where would be the harm? More than once the thought of suicide had come to him. If his death might arrive thus, gently, of its own accord...!

His eyes were already beginning to close, numbness was already overtaking his limbs...and there was a sound of footsteps.

"What are you doing there, my good man?" said a policeman, appearing suddenly. "It's a cold night and it's not good to sleep in the cold. Come on, go home!"

Go home? Whose home? Whose? Where is his home, that deserter, that Bohemian, that beggar?

He got up, effortfully, his joints creaking; as he traversed the macadam, hardened by frost, it seemed to him that needles were plunging into the flesh of his feet.

Then he walked straight ahead, at random, without knowing where he was going, without being conscious of any goal to be attained.

After some time, he found himself at an intersection of the narrow, miry little streets that one still encountered a few years ago in the vicinity of the Hôtel de Ville. In front of him opened a sort of cul-de-sac, barred at its extremity by a lateral street raised fifteen feet above the ground. He stopped, his strength and his patience exhausted.

This time he would not wait for sleep to return—his slumber might be interrupted again by an importunate; it was of death that he was resolved to demand sleep, repose and wellbeing.

To his right there was a stone stairway, step and massive, linking the cul-de-sac to the street. By the vacillating light of one of the last street-lanterns in Paris, stirred by the wind, he glimpsed along that stairway an iron grille sunk into the wall in front of a broad ventilation shaft, formed by bars sufficiently solid to retain a man suspended a few feet from the ground.

He untied his cravat, crossed the first steps...and recoiled fearfully. Horror! He had just bumped into a confused rigid mass. The upright body of a man was hooked on to the grille.

The place was taken.

Two o'clock chimed upon a nearby clock. Under the double stroke of the hammer, griped by fear, he fled, and then stopped, and looked to the right and the left. He was in a large square. Facing him, looming up in its simple and correct gravity, was the edifice of the Hôtel de Ville. He recognized it; he knew where he was; he had not been conscious of it until then. To his right was the river...

For the moment, however, his ideas of death had given way to others. He marched toward a street opening to his left, turning his back on the river. That quarter was the one in which Hélène had lived, where she might still perhaps live. Before dying, he wanted to see again the house where, every morning and evening for two years, he had taken care to tighten the amorous bonds that he had broken so abruptly.

Of Hélène's house, he only found the debris. Like so many other houses in Paris, it was in the process of disappearing, in the cause of public utility.

His heart broke, and from that broken heart an exclamation escaped: "Hélène, dear Hélène, where are you? Where are you living now?"

Then, in the middle of the mass of rubble, and sticking out above it, he saw an object of initially-inexplicable form, but to which he was all too soon able to attach a meaning. It was a cross: a cross of black wood, such as is ordinarily seen on the graves of poor people.

Before that cross the unfortunate knelt down, and wept, sobbing.

"Hélène, I shall not take long to join you, to implore you to pardon me, but I ought not to die without addressing a final adieu to my father's house."

Hunger, thirst, cold and fatigue were no longer making him feel their tortures; an immense mental dolor, remorse, had replaced everything. However, his march toward the faubourg was lurching and tottering; visions invaded his brain; there were scintillations and flashes in his eyes; the paving stones seemed to be colliding beneath his steps.

Finally, he arrived.

His father's house, the house where he was born, he found standing. A little light was burning in the entresol; his parents habitually slept there. They were still alive, then! That was a relief and a consolation for his heart. Several times, he kissed the lock of that humble house, on which his mother's hand had so often posed, and, seized by surprise, he perceived that the little light that had illuminated the entresol had disappeared, and was now shining on the ground floor; and he saw the door opening slowly in front of him...

Should he not have thought of it? By virtue of a marvelous revelation, his mother alerted to his presence, had come to welcome him.

Bowing his head, ready to cry for mercy, he took a few steps forward; but he did not see anyone in the shop.

Only the little light had come to meet him.

After having leapt here and there around him like a will-o'-the-wisp, it went up the stairs that led to the entresol, seemingly inviting him to follow it. He allowed himself to be guided by it. Was he capable by then of rationalizing his impressions?

The entresol, deserted, hung from top to bottom with funeral drapes, only presented the appearance of a catafalque.

He understood; his parents were where Hélène was. He searched avidly with his eyes for something that might aid him to accomplish his resolution to die...but everything had fallen back into darkness.

The will-o'-the-wisp was now fluttering along a corridor leading to one last room: the one that he had once inhabited. It was from that room that he had departed on the twenty-fourth of January ten years before, to the day.

Well, that room had been witness to his fault; it would be that of his expiation.

He goes in. Still preceding him, the will-o'-the-wisp has reignited a lamp placed on an item of furniture near a bed. In the bed, a man is lying asleep, his features slightly contracted.

He is a young man, only twenty-three or twenty-four years of age. To his profound amazement, in that young man, with the unalloyed brown hair, the abundant beard and the fresh complexion, with smooth rosy cheeks, Babylas recognizes himself.

It's him! Himself, such as he was in the epoch of his good years. He has appealed to his youth, and behold! his youth has appeared to him!

The sleeper made a movement then, opening his eyes partly. For an instant—an instant as rapid as lightning—their gazes were able to meet; thereafter, only a single occupant remained in the room. The false Babylas had disappeared.

Which one was the true one?

The true one was the young man still lying in his bed, who was rubbing his eyes with his clenched fists; he was the dreamer; the other was only the dream.

It was only in a dream that the artist had deserted the paternal house, taking away with him the happiness of a young woman; it was in a dream that he had traveled the world, that he had married the brown woman, that he had abandoned himself to drunkenness and ideas of suicide.

Dawn was breaking. Still frightened by his nocturnal visions, Babylas—the true Babylas, still not knowing which side the error was on and which side the truth, not knowing whether he was waking up in Paris or in the metropolis of the Sunday Islands, with sweat in his brow, his gaze troubled—examined a strange, disparate object placed beside him, which the crepuscular rays only illuminated vaguely as yet. Suddenly, he uttered an exclamation...an exclamation of joy.

That strange object, in which Babylas searched for a form, a reason for being, was a white cravat on a black suit.

"God be praised!" he cried. "It was only a dream! But the experience of those ten years of ordeals and poverty will profit me! Dear Hélène!"

That dream, conceived almost in the same conditions as many other dreams, whose final twist recalls the one that Gérard de Nerval borrowed from Jean-Paul Richter—the name comes back to me now—is recommended by a curious double fact. Firstly, therefore, Gérard de Nerval wrote "Nuit du nouvel an d'un malheureux," a story that seems to have been borrowed from his own story, and which Babylas, without knowing it, appropriated the denouement; and then...

But for the second fact, which you might already have anticipated, it seems appropriate to us to go to the Mairie, where, that same day—Saint Babylas' Day, 24 January 1855; remember that date!—our fiancés, accompanied by their witnesses, their parents and a few friends, were waiting for the arrival of the municipal officer.

While waiting, Hélène was thinking about Babylas, and Babylas was thinking about Hélène, and also about his terrible dream. He had already recounted it to his father and his two witnesses, and he was still preoccupied with it, when, in a group placed nearby, people started talking animatedly about an event accomplished that same night in one of the winding and muddy streets of the Hôtel de Vile quarter, the Rue de la Lanterne.

There was mention of a man found hanging from a grille above a stone stairway. In the opinion of the experts who had been consulted, his death must have occurred between one and two o'clock in the morning.

At that story, Babylas was stupefied, bowled over. What! During the night of the twenty-fourth of January, when he had not budged from his bed, by virtue of the power of the dream, he had encountered the body, already chilled by death, of the charming and unfortunate poet for whom all Paris seemed to be wearing mourning the next day.

Certainly, that is a striking fact, which tends to prove that a dream can be complicated by second sight and magnetic lucidity. I have had occasion to encounter Monsieur Babylas, or rather Jules N***—for he has now renounced painting and the name Babylas; I know one of his witnesses, his intimate confidant, very well; both have affirmed to me on their honor the entire veracity of the dream, and I have no reason to doubt their good faith.

One detail might find its place here regarding the interesting poet for whom dreaming was living, who abused dreams and ended up disappearing into the abysm of ideality that he had hollowed out, as if to forearm us—we other dreamers!—against his excesses. The best things have their dangers; the sweetest perfumes can become poisons.

Doubts have been raised as to whether his end, so abrupt and so premature, was the consequence of a murder or a suicide. This is what I can say about it:

In the autumn that preceded his death, I had occasion to spend an entire day with him at Montmorency. He had shown there an amicable and rather cheerful nature; I had perceived, however, that, although shored up on the one hand by a fine and subtle mind, and on the other by a knowledge that did not lack breadth, his reason easily became unsteady between those two supports, like a bell too easily set in motion by any gust of wind. Without thinking ill of life, he appeared rather disposed to finish with it, not out of disgust, but simply out of curiosity, to know what might come after it.

Two months later, in January 1855, I met him at the home of Victor L***, then our common editor, for whom he had undertaken a work entitled *Les Nuits de Paris*,[36] which had perhaps caused him to contract the habit of incessant nocturnal strolls. That day, as he took out his handkerchief, I saw a piece of cord fall out of his pocket.

"What's that?" I asked him.

"It's Marguerite de Valois' garter," he replied, gravely.

I can conclude therefrom that a fatal idea was already preoccupying him, and that he did not need anyone to push him from the other direction. Poor Gérard!

---

[36] In 1852 Gérard de Nerval had already published *Les Nuits d'Octobre*, a collection of essays describing Paris at night; a similar collection, published as *Promenades et Souvenirs*, appears to have been in progress when he died; the title quoted by Saintine might have been its intended title, echoing the title of Restif de La Bretonne's famous documentary novel based on his nocturnal wanderings. The date of Gérard de Nerval's death is officially recorded as 26 January, but dreams tend to be careless of anachronisms.

The Paradise of Flowers

The Graf von Zoellern, a native of Germany, to which his turn of mind still linked him, was a little, slightly hunchbacked man, something of a joker, very knowledgeable, loquacious and methodical, and full of audacity in his theories. Having devoted himself to botany for only two years, he already claimed to be revolutionizing it from top to bottom—which gave rise to spirited debates between him and my savant doctor.

According to the latter, the Graf von Zoellern's mind, knowledge and imagination—which he did not deny—were, like his personality and the first letter of his name, formed in a zigzag fashion. As for me, the little man's eccentricities and audacious ideas did not displease me, any more than my eyes were offended by seeing his right shoulder positioned more highly than his left.

One evening, when there was to be a table-turning session at my house, and I was counting on the presence of Monsieur Marcillet and his faithful Alexis,[37] the Graf and the doctor were the first to arrive—an alacrity which, I confess, astonished me on the doctor's part; I

---

[37] The famous "somnambule" Alexis Didier (1826-1886), usually known by his first name alone, and his "magnetizer" Jean-Bon Marcillet (1798-?), were a famous double act between 1842 and 1855, performing at séances all over Europe; they once had a famous confrontation with the great stage magician Robert-Houdin, who attempted to expose them as frauds.

strongly suspected him of having only come in the capacity of critic, opponent and spoilsport.

Having a few orders to give, I left them alone for a moment. When I came back, Zoellern was already in mid-argument, proving, or claiming to prove, to his eternal antagonist that plants and animals not only manifested certain points of analogy and parallelism but a complete correspondence of structure and organization. That was, he said, a commonplace that was not even worth discussing. Plato and Empedocles had sufficiently elucidated the question twenty-two or twenty-three centuries ago, so he did not know why Geoffroy Saint-Hilaire, in the philosophical system of *L'Unité de l'Être*,[38] had not boldly commenced his zoological series with the most minimal of vegetables, to continue as far as humankind.

"Come on, Doctor, let's reason it out. Taking the animal as the highest degree of the scale, what are its principal functions? It breathes, it absorbs, it digests, it reproduces itself. Doesn't a plant do as much?

"Its leaves, veritable lungs, pump from the atmosphere the oxygen that will modify its sap, transforming it in the cambium, like our venous and arterial blood. But I don't intend to give you a lesson in vegetable physiology. You know as well as I do that the assimilation of absorbed gases produces in plants, as in us, hydrogen, carbon dioxide, alkaline salts, calcium and magnesium phosphates, even nitrogen, which was thought until recently to be reserved to the animal kingdom. Liquids and solids similarly collaborate in developing their strength

---

[38] Étienne Geoffroy Saint-Hilaire did not publish a book with this title, but was involved in a famous debate at the Académie des Sciences in 1830 with Georges Cuvier regarding the unity of composition of all organic beings.

and furnishing their alimentation. Thus, plants nourish themselves, just like you and me. Look at enormous oaks and tropical trees, so tall, so stout and so sturdy; their cuisine is as good as ours!

"I agree that oaks are more vigorous, and even generally more upright than us," said the doctor, with a certain malicious intent. "I also agree, wholeheartedly, that vegetables and animals have a few points of resemblance between them in their constitutive elements—but animals can move. Do you hear, Monsieur le Comte? They can move!"

"Not all, Doctor, not all! By no means! The polyp in its coral sheath, the oyster and the barnacle, fixed upon their rocks, and many others—are not they animals, although they remain in place?" Zoellern winked in my direction and added: "Besides, plants—notably trees—have their own kind of locomotion. Once freed from the bonds that chain them to the soil, they have been seen to come and go, leap and caper, just as well as the most agile of quadrupeds."

The doctor opened his eyes wide. "What trees do that?" he said. "Pray name the trees in question, Monsieur le Comte."

"Only mentioning the most well-known, I cite the elm, the oak, the fir, the walnut—when they are transformed into tables, of course…into turning tables."

The dear doctor burst out laughing, got to his feet, articulated "Zigzag! Zigzag!" two or three times between his teeth, and started striding back and forth across the room in the manner of a man refusing to prolong a conversation.

I did not like to see it terminated thus; I picked it up at the point where it had been abandoned. That diabolical little man had the gift of amusing me royally. I

214

smiled at the notion that before my guests were treated to a table-dance that evening, Zoellern's idea might serve up, by way of accompaniment, a new theory on the much-debated subject. Unfortunately, he did not have any fully-formed opinion on that subject, so he came back very quickly to his plant-animals.

Zoellern was planning a new classification, a new nomenclature, in which he would include, pell-mell, fish and certain aquatic plants, which respire like them by means of veritable gills, and rise above the water like them to dive back into it by means of something akin to an air-bladder.

He found surprising analogies between reptiles and creepers or climbing plants; between vegetable and animal parasites. The family of rodents ought, in his view, be augmented by those plants that hollow out stone or wood—and he told me about a thousand other intentions that, if they sometimes lacked reason and logic, at least testified to the ingenuity of his mind and the activity of his imagination.

In the meantime, the doctor continued to stride back and forth across my floor in every direction. Soon, wearying of his stroll, and perhaps even more so of the silence that he had imposed on himself, he abruptly returned to us and, with his eyes flaming and his arms cross over his chest, he interrupted Zoellern in mid-sentence.

"Wretch!" he cried. "Is it chaos that you're pretending to systematize, then? There exists between vegetables and animals one unbridgeable line of demarcation:

sensitivity. Vegetables grow, they live, I grant you—but *sed non sentiunt*, as the great Linnaeus said."[39]

"The great Linnaeus would be a donkey today," Zoellern retorted.

On hearing this blasphemy, I got up abruptly to protest, but on reflexion, I sat down again. I was curious to know how the little man would justify his enormity.

He did not give an inch. Without respite, arguing against the *non sentiunt*, he maintained tenaciously that all vegetable species bestirred themselves, not automatically, but purely by virtue of a sentiment of self-defense and self-preservation. He cited the means employed by the whole great family of mimosas to protect themselves from an impact or the violence of a storm; those by which the *Dionaea*[40] traps an insect that wishes to live at its expense; the gyratory movements of the sainfoin; the evolutions of stamens toward pistils, and the modest quiverings of pistils at the approach of stamens—clear evidence of will, an aspiration toward a goal, sensation. How many animals of an inferior order seem to be endowed with less activity and rationality!

"Any wisely-calculated action is evidence of thought, and no thought can be conceived other than under a sensitive influence. By what right to you refuse an intellectual life to plants, since they know the emotions of love and the joys of maternity?

"As for their purely physical sensitivity, in spite of the *non sentiunt*, has your great Linnaeus observed that after the fatigues of the day they recuperate their strength

---

[39] This oft-quoted Latin assertion regarding the insensibility of plants seems to have been initially credited to Pope Gregory I, who held that position from 590 until 604 A.D.
[40] The Venus fly-trap.

by means of sleep? Monsieur Buffon himself, one day when he had forgotten to put his cuffs on, was prepared to admit that a plant resembles a dormant animal. The animal has woken up, doctor, it has woken up! After the scientific works by Borelli and Sébastien Vaillant on vegetal sensitivity, Jean de Gorter was the first to credit vital irritability to plants as well as animals.[41] Jean Lups of Moscow and the Comte del Covolo of Florence established the proof of it.[42] You can see that Russians, Germany and Italians are in accord in preaching that doctrine. The illustrious Charles Bonnet, a Swiss this time, and the Englishman Adanson have steered their research in the same direction and added further supporting evidence to the demonstration of this great verity.[43] But that

---

[41] Giovani Borelli (1608-1679), better known as the "father of biomechanics" (the study of animal movement), was the first microscopist to study the opening and closing of plant stomata. Sébastien Vaillant (1669-1722) worked for many years at the Jardin des Plantes, and published a notable discourse on flowers in 1718. Jean de Gorter (1689-1762), a follower of Herman Boerhaave, contended, along with the British anatomist Francis Glisson, that there was a vital force operating in both animals and plants independently of the soul and nervous system, which was responsible for movement.

[42] Jean Lups (1667-1732) was actually a Dutch arms dealer who supplied weapons to Russia, but he was named as "Jean Lups of Moscow" in a history of medicine published in 1815; the reference in question was slavishly copied by several other 19th-century reference books, one of which Saintine must have seen. The "Comte del Covolo", however, seems to have only one significant mention, in Gall and Spurzheim's monumental work on the anatomy of the brain (1810-19), which founded the science of phrenology.

[43] Charles Bonnet (1720-1793) published a book in 1754 which did indeed credit plants with sensibility and powers of

217

congress of sages lacked a Frenchman; the good Desfontaines has arrived, who has demonstrated in an *ad hoc* memoir that plants enjoy a real life.[44] I therefore have against you, doctor, European science in its entirety. But don't be so impatient! Let me finish...

"Do not plants, like us, need air and light? Do they not have their periods of growth, sometimes so risky; their diseases, so similar to ours; their hemorrhages of sap, like our hemorrhages of blood (pardon the pleonasm); chlorosis and phthisis? Frostbite, sunburn, wounds, asphyxia, even poisoning; everything that threatens our life puts theirs in danger; and, strangely enough—a further point of concordance between plants and animals—the same remedies are employed for their cure: iron sulphate for chlorosis, bleeding for plethoras; and moxas,[45] incisions and amputations!

"All these maladies that they have in common with us, plants feel if they are suffering from them, and they do suffer from them, since they die of them."

Thus spoke the Graf.

Truly, one would no longer dare to pluck a rose or have one's grass mown.

The audacious little man was not about to stop there. Moving from induction to induction, he came to

---

discernment. Michel Adanson (1727-1806) was not an Englishman but a Frenchman of Scottish descent who produced a system of classification markedly different from that of Linnaeus, which lost out in competition with the latter.

[44] René Desfontaines (1750-1833) worked at the Jardin des Plantes before becoming director of the Musée National d'Histoire Naturelle.

[45] Moxa (mugwort) was and is extensively used in connection with acupuncture to warm the skin before insertion of the needles.

pose this question, which made the doctor and me start on the spot: "Why should plants not have souls?"

I protested; the doctor made no reply, but he drummed his fingers on his snuff-box, murmuring: "Zig-zag, zigzag!"

"The idea is not mine," Zoellern hastened to add. "It was originated by Thales—one of the seven sages of Greece, gentlemen, as one contemporary member of the Académie des Sciences put it—but it has had its parti-sans a long time after that. Leibniz, who is also known as the great Leibniz, in his essay on *Theodicy*, was not afraid to propose that the divine seeds destined to be-come human souls, pre-exist in organic substances, where they are first subjected to a kind of apprentice-ship. Malebranche and Bayle seem to be marching along the same road and, nearer to our own day, one even counts a physician among the declared partisans of that opinion—do you hear that, doctor? The physician Dédu, who was only on the faculty of Montpellier, it is true, has written a very curious book on the souls of plants."[46]

"Zigzag! Zigzag!" muttered the doctor.

"That's on the part of Europe," the Graf continued. "As for the Orient, no one there doubts the doctrine, generally professed throughout the Far East." He stroked

---

[46] *De l'ame des plantes, de leur naissance, de leur nourriture et de leur progrez* [sic] (1682) is signed "N. Dedu [*sic*], docteur en medicine de la Faculté de Montpellier", hence the narrator's slightly dismissive remark. Dedu must have been a botanist of some reputation, however, because he also co-authored a book on plant anatomy with the much more famous Nehemiah Grew and Robert Boyle in 1685. Nicolas Male-branche (1638-1715) and Pierre Bayle (1647-1706) were among the rationalist philosophers who pioneered the Enlight-enment.

his chin, and continued: "I recently had the good fortune to discuss the question with the Japanese and Siamese ambassadors, who were both passing thorough Paris. The former spoke at length about a certain god Fottey,[47] whose breath is sufficient to give a soul to the most vulgar of plants; the latter affirmed that, in his country, the theory of souls, applied to vegetables, is so well-recognized that no one there mutilates a tree without expiating the sacrilege by an act of contrition, and no one there pulls up a culinary herb without addressing a mental prayer to the soul thus condemned to displacement." As if in parentheses, Zoellern added: "Take note that these beliefs are not mine."

"I'm glad to hear it," the doctor put in.

"No, in this respect, I still envelop myself in philosophical doubt: do plants have soul, or don't they? A weighty question, gentlemen, a weighty question!"

For my part, what can I say? However bizarre it might be, this animation of all organic substances, no longer forming any but one single complex being, moved by the same laws and marching by a thousand roads toward the same goal, was beginning to impress me. God alone knew whether it was impossible—and who among us can put limits to the great and mysterious theology of nature?

Then, within myself, I returned to my turning tables. Why should not the spirit or demon, which could so implausibly become invisible guest of the table, simply be the soul of the tree that had furnished it? I decided to

---

[47] This name is idiosyncratic to Saintine, but is probably an expansion of Fo (the Chinese character representing Buddha); Fo-Ti is the name attributed to a herb employed in traditional Chinese medicine.

interrogate that vegetal soul that very evening, demanding that it yield its secret to me. What a discovery, if I could clarify a question so hotly debated, and finally provide, dogmatically, an explanation of the phenomenon!

On the stroke of nine, almost all my guests arrived. I immediately ordered that the table be brought in—a table in which I had particular confidence, the most impressionable, the most alert and the chattiest of all my tables.

As often happens on such occasions, in spite of the chain of fingers obstinately fixed upon it, the table did not budge.

The dear doctor was radiant, and sniffed pinches of tobacco one after another, with the attitude and gestures of an insolent victor. The Graf von Zoellern voiced the idea that the presence of a skeptical unbeliever is sometimes sufficient to abort the operation completely. I had every reason to believe that the little man had hoped to have his habitual contradictor massacred in the midst of a popular uprising.

I ordered that the tea should be served on the same table. The doctor, who was now playing the leading role, criticized my imprudence. "What if it starts to dance a saraband at the moment when it's least expected?" he said. "Watch out for the Chinese porcelain!"

Zoellern called him an atheist.

Fortunately, Monsieur Marcillet and Monsieur Alexis had just made their entrance into the drawing-room. There was no longer any topic of conversation but magnetism.

The doctor rubbed his hands; he was counting on a disappointment in that regard as in the other. To get in ahead of the others, he hastened to propose a card game to Alexis—who, with his eyes blindfolded, named his cards before touching them, taking the trick, then read the contents of pockets, counting up the sums of money to be found therein, in gold, silver or copper, and finished up by telling him that he had dined that day on vegetable soup, fillet steak with olives and sole *normande*.

"How do you know that?" asked the doctor, somewhat nonplussed.

"By means of your restaurant bill, which is still in your waistcoat pocket."

Zoellern rubbed his hands in his turn. He begged the magnetizer to put him to sleep right away; he had an urgent voyage to make.

After a few conscientiously-administered passes, he did indeed go to sleep, and so obviously that some time went by before he was even able to reply to the questions addressed to him.

Finally, he released a sigh, and his lips moved.

"The moment has arrived," said Monsieur Marcillet—and he resumed the interrogation. "Can you hear me now?"

"They have one!" replied the magnetized man.

"You don't understand. Do you know who is speaking to you at this moment?"

"The god Fottey, honored in Japan and throughout the Indian archipelago."

Monsieur Marcillet recommenced his passes, and interrogated him further. "Where are you?"

"In the *paradise of flowers*."

The magnetizer paused, looked at us with a slightly disconcerted expression, turned to the gallery and said: "Gentlemen, I think I ought to warn you that dreams sometimes interfere unduly with magnetic influences. I don't think the subject is in a perfect state of lucidity. Let's try, without jarring him too much, to put him back on the right path...

"According to you, then, flowers have a paradise?"

"Why not, since they have one?"

"One what?"

"A soul! Is it not just, then, that like us, they have their places of recompense and punishment?"

At the point, there was a slight murmur in the assembly, in the midst of which I distinctly made out a certain *zigzag!* and the tapping of a finger on a snuffbox.

Monsieur Marcillet continued, with perfect condescension: "Are you quite sure, Monsieur, that you're not mistaken?"

"How could I be mistaken? At this very moment, thanks to the benevolent intervention of the Japanese ambassador, the divine Fottey has opened the abode of floral felicity to my curiosity. In spite of Thales, Leibniz, Malebranche and Monsieur Dédu, I doubted—I repent of it! Now I see, I am forced to believe! Oh, what spectacles! What perfumes!"

"Come on, let's try to divert the course of these ideas..."

"Shut up!" the sleeper shouted at him, in an imperious tone. "Stop disturbing me in my delight!"

The magnetizer made as if to wake him up; I stopped him, and on my request, he consented to put me in fluidic communication with the patient.

Zoellern continued talking almost without interruption; he described what he could see, or what he thought he could see, with such precision that I was unable to suspect the slightest trickery in his narration, utterly strange and utterly supernatural as it seemed; his mind, his knowledge and his imagination alone would not have been sufficient for such an improvisation.

The circle tightened around the visionary; with a gesture to the doctor, I indicated a vacant spot next to me.

"Zigzag!" he replied, drawing away in order to pour himself a cup of tea.

I noticed nevertheless that he had sat down at the end of the table nearest to us, with his ear turned in our direction.

The Paradise of Flowers, created by Fottey, the god of vegetation, in one of the Maldive Islands, had its eastern part divided into a series of little parallel valleys. These valleys, separated from one another by gentle slopes from the top of which fell sheets of water, forming cascades on either side, blossomed in the midst of a warm atmosphere; humid vapors, colored pink, blue and violet by the sunlight, filled them with the radiance of rainbows; the inhabitants of the location lacked nothing, either in the way of gentle sunlight or balsamic dew—but I shall not dwell on that paradisal poetry, with which the sleeper perhaps overindulged himself.

To get back to purely topographical matters, all the squares of this great chessboard were occupied by plants assembled without any classificatory order, having no other link between them than their virtuous qualities and the kinds of services rendered by them to human society.

Pell-mell, in the cheerful part of the garden that had been consecrated to them, the first to display themselves to the visitor's eye were the Nutritious Plants: wheat, maize, rice, and then the numerous family of legumes—green beans, broad beans, peas, lentils—all elegantly sporting their pretty caps on their heads.

Also found in the Paradise of Flowers were the benevolent plants that ease suffering and sometimes even render life to the sick. Zoellern therefore visited the Valley of Medicinal Plants.

He was greatly astonished to find an extremely restricted number there; cassia and senna did not figure there at all; and, as if the magnetic fluid had added a stimulant to his natural malice, he credited to the god Fottey the explanatory opinion that the marvelous virtues of so many plants formerly praised as universal panaceas but rejected today to the ranks of harmful herbs, had never profited anyone but messieurs the physicians, either in Europe or Asia, all of them beings charlatans.

As a faithful reporter of the séance, I am obliged to declare that at that moment, my dear doctor noisily sniffed another pinch of tobacco and poured himself a second cup of tea.

Continuing his narration along with his route, the Graf went through the Valley of Industrial Plants, textile or tinctorial. Cotton, hemp, flax, madder, the indigo plant and a thousand others of similar importance seemed to form up in ranks to either side of his path, in order to be inspected by him.

On mounds reminiscent of altars, silphium,[48] sesame and the lotus, so dear to the ancient priests of Egypt and the Brahmins of India; vervein, the *herba sacra* that served to purify the temples of Jupiter and Apollo; the

---

[48] *Silphium* was in such great demand in the ancient world that it was driven to extinction, perhaps due to overgrazing by cattle to whose meat it was supposed to impart a special virtue. It is generally thought to have been a kind of giant fennel.

mistletoe of the druids of Gaul and Germany; persea,[49] the subject of so many pious commentaries; the acacia, the ultimate mystical tree; the rose of Jericho, symbol of death and resurrection, and a whole series of holy herbs no less worthy of veneration, displayed themselves surrounded by the attributes of various ancient and modern cults. God as he was, Fottey bowed down as he passed them by; Zoellern was obliged to do the same, but he reserved his admiration and his surges of enthusiasm for the joyous Valley of Beautiful Plants.

More sensual or less hypocritical than the Occident, the Orient has made plastic beauty a virtue. Beautiful women, even if they are former fisherwomen, enter authoritatively into the paradises of Mohammed and Brahma, and are elevated by right to the rank of houris or apsaras. It is the same for beautiful plants in the paradise of the god Fottey.

When that magnificent vegetable, the pride of floral creation, MacDonald's cactus,[50] whose corolla, as large as a grape-gatherer's basket, displays its long silver petals implanted in a golden calyx, with its style standing up like an ivory column surmounted by a purple feather; then the great Aristolochia, the Gustavia, the Victoria Regia, the Nelumbium and the magnolia presented themselves on the shores of his isle,[51] did he say to them:

---

[49] The best-known member of the genus *Persea* is the avocado.

[50] "Mrs. MacDonald's Cactus" is one of the many names given in the 19th century to the species now classified as *Selenicereus grandiflorus*, more usually known as the night-blooming cactus, or Queen of the Night.

[51] *Aristolochia* is the birthwort genues; *Gustavia superba* is also known as the Heaven lotus; *Victoria regia* (or *regina*) was the name originally given by John Lindley in 1837 to the

"Where do you come from? What good have you done?"
No; he said to them: "Come in."

And after them, when the other royal flowers of every climate and every country, the lily of Japan, the Tigridias of Mexico, the Strelitizia of the Cape,[52] the orchids of Central America, the hollyhocks of Syria, the Agapanthus of Africa, all the way to the peonies of Siberia, offered themselves to him, similarly recognizing the right of their beauty, he opened his door again and breathed on them to give them a soul.

And, thinking about our European gardens—even the winter gardens in Paris, London and The Hague—Zoellern told himself that to compare them with that luxuriant valley would be to compare the Societé d'Acclimation's aquarium to the vast Ocean.

And yet, although dazzled by the spectacle unfolding before his eyes, he thought he noticed, especially among the royal species, certain irregularities of form, certain abnormal accidents that he was astonished to find associated with so many perfections.

He did not hesitate to impart these critical observations to his divine guide. The latter smiling, immediately refuted them. What Zoellern suspected to be deplorable irregularities were no more than further perfections, additional organs accorded by Brahma to the inhabitants of this blissful abode.

In the paradise of the Maldives, flowers can move and detach themselves from the earthy, which scarcely

---

water lily nowadays known as *Victoria amazonica*; *Nelumbium speciousum* is the "sacred lotus"
[52] *Tigridia pavonia* is the most commonly-cultivated species of "tiger flower"; *Strelizias* are sometimes known as "bird-of-paradise flowers".

retains them, their roots being formed like birds' feet; they can walk, hopping from one place to another; better still, they have wings, pretty white, blue or variegated wings, depending on the color of their petals or stems, and which, when folded up, become almost undetectable by eye. With a single flight, they can cross the borders of their respective valleys if it pleases them to visit one another.

The good Fottey uttered a cry then; that cry, repeated by a thousand echoes, ran from valley to valley, soon filling the whole island with a clamor.

Zoellern thought he was prey to vertigo. A unanimous, spontaneous movement was manifest in the plain and along the slopes where, until then, ranked by size, all those floral marvels had stood motionless. The plain, the hills and the sky itself seemed to quiver before his eyes. Breathless, gripped by anguish, almost terrified, he witnessed a spectacle that it has not been given to any man down here either to see or to imagine.

Confusing their colors and their perfumes, the flowers of the splendid valley crossed paths in every direction, flying through the air by means of beating wings. Hurrying from adjacent valleys through the damp dust of cascades, appearing over the crests of hills, they mingled together and, all together, whirled about as if at play— but without Fottey's preliminary warning, the Graf would certainly have been able to believe that a furious storm had just descended upon that abode of enchantments.

Now, he saw them slowing down in their flight, breaking up the vortex, gliding, and then descending with fluttering wings to settle on the earth again.

After a few moments' rest, some started walking in groups; those were generally the largest, and the most remarkable in their forms and colors. Zoellern took note of their precious attitude and ladylike gait; during the promenade, with a perfect art of coquetry, they showed off their large petals in such a way as to make their varied hues stand out, while maintaining their leaves in good order and correctly angled.

Other flowers had landed beside little lakes formed at the bottom of hills; they bathed their roots therein, doubtless to refresh their tints or straighten their stems, slightly fatigued by the heat of the day.

On the edges of these same little lakes, aquatic plants had naturally chosen their domiciles. Like their terrestrial sisters, they could detach their roots from the soil, draw away from the bank and, moreover, tour their lagoons by swimming. To the foremost, the benign god of vegetation had given wings; for others he had determined that their lower leaves were prolonged in the form of oars; those oars were adequate to sustain them above water, so that they could move around with their stems straight and their corollas spread out.

Butterflies are admitted to the Paradise of Flowers, for flowers and butterflies can scarcely live without one another; but, attached to the soil or some rocky projection, they are captive, their wings paralyzed, unable to take part in all that celebratory movement, and it is the flowers that, contrary to the established order here, fly to meet them, make their choice, caressing them or neglecting them according to their whim.

The Paradise of Flowers is the butterflies' Inferno.

Zoellern then asked the god Fottey how that attractive sympathy could have arisen between two species of beings that seemed, at least on earth, to belong to entirely different races.

"By virtue of a great harmonic reason, of which you cannot take account in your backward Europe," Fottey replied, "the transmigration of souls. According to the laws of metempsychosis, the soul of a flower, after its time of proof, passes into the body of a butterfly, or some other insect—a fly or a beetle. That ought to suffice to make you understand the secret attraction than brings these various species together."

The Graf dared to follow up his question. "And what becomes of a butterfly's soul?"

"It passes into the body of a sparrow or an animal of similarly scant importance—but not alone, however, for it requires three butterfly souls to form that of a flycatcher, as it requires three flower souls to form that of a butterfly, and so on; the souls of three flycatchers or wrens form the soul of a wood-pigeon; and always three by three, always progressing in strength and intelligence, they thus climb the scale of beings, step by step, until a myriad of souls of every sort, newly purified by the breath of a god, eventually form the soul of a human being, the only one created immortal."

Delighted with these cosmogonic confidences, Zoellern collected them carefully, promising himself firmly to propagate them for the instruction of poor Europe, so backward.

While chatting, the god and the voyager advanced toward the most elevated regions of the isle. The latter was astonished to see that the valleys and hills that had been so cool and cheerful a little while ago were succeeded by steep, sterile mountains, from which no springs emerged, and where their feet sank into the sand.

His astonishment was further increased on encountering in this wild terrain the flowers most highly esteemed among us—not only camellias, balsamines[53] and tulips irreproachable in color and form, but the most beautiful roses in the world: the tea rose, the king's rose, the rose with a hundred leaves.

Why were they not in the Valley of Beautiful Plants, where their place seemed to be established by right? He submitted this question to the master.

"We're in the region of expiation," Fottey replied. "Once, tulips and camellias possessed both beauty and perfume; they became too proud. I took their perfume away to give it to the violet and the reseda, humbler plants whose modesty deserved recompense."

"But what about the rose?" Zoellern interjected. "The rose, regarded by us as the queen of flowers?"

"A title usurped! Her royalty is nothing but a lie; neither her beauty nor her perfumes belong to her; the whole is nothing but a work of art and cunning. Born a simple flower of the fields and woods, her natural grace brightened the bushes in spring that her coralline fruits decorated in autumn; ambition took possession of her; she has had her paradise on earth, where she was fêted by everyone; now, in this arid and stony ground, she is expiating her mendacious success; this is her punishment. But misfortune purifies; subjected to this dolorous proof, the rose will recover her primitive state, with her five petals, which make her sparkle in the morning mist, and her original scent, naively sweet, with which she should have been content. Brought back then to the laws of her nature, from which the industry of humans has

---

[53] "Balsamines" was one of the common names given to flowers of the genus *Impatiens*, also known as jewelweeds and touch-me-nots. The one most familiar in Britain is the Busy Lizzie.

distanced her so far, along with her pistils and stamens she will recover her soul, for doubled flowers do not have one, and love and maternal cares will easily make her forget her fraudulent triumphs."

Slightly mortified by the regime inflicted on these flowers, which he loved most particularly, Graf von Zoellern continued to follow his guide as far as a chain of black and angular rocks that crowned the peaks of the mountain.

Scarcely had they reached them than a suffocating heat and acrid, caustic and nauseating vapors, by which Fottey seemed not to be affected at all, overtook them. As for the voyager, he only had time to plunge a rapid glance over the depths of the opposite slope, where sulphurous and bituminous gulfs yawned.

In the profound darkness, he thought he glimpsed a few vegetable forms, spectral in appearance, so shriveled, corroded and withered that no plant buried for ten years in a collector's herbarium could ever have presented a more sickly and wretched appearance.

The uncultivated, sterile place where they had just encountered the roses, balsamines, tulips and others was only a purgatory; this was an inferno. To this had been relegated the venomous plants and the magical plants, those that had aided the operations of witchcraft or the accomplishment of crimes. There too were found plants accused of exciting the human imagination and stirring up deceptive sensualities, at the expense of health, dignity and reason.

Of these latter, Fottey only named three: the opium poppy, which has already killed two million people in China; Indian hemp, with which the Indians manufacture their bhang and the Turks and Arabs their hashish, which lightens their mod, intoxicates and decimates them; and finally absinthe, as deadly as the other two, and in the process of cretinizing Europe.

Our friend Zoellern, did not have to beg him to come down again from those heights...

At this point our sleeper brought his narration to a close, and after a few moments of silence, we heard him murmur in a low voice: "Adieu, good and excellent Fottey... The isle is retreating before me... We're doubling Cape Comorin... Adieu, Maldive Sea!... Here's Europe!... Here's Paris!... Wake me up, Monsieur Marcillet."

Monsieur Marcillet made the regulation passes.

When Zoellern opened his eyes again, he did not retain any memory of what he had seen and heard in the Paradise of Flowers.

"Well," I said to the doctor, "the séance must have interested you more than any other. It featured a magnetic dream, which I believe you have not yet classified in your scientific theory?"

"Zigzag! Zigzag! Zigzag!" he replied, loudly this time, drumming more forcefully than ever on his snuffbox.

My Funeral

Next to my bed stood the dear doctor, his eye on the second hand of his watch and his hand on the artery, counting the pulsations, becoming slower and weaker. I had felt his interrogative fingers climbing along my arm. Making an effort to lift an eyelid, I saw him, his brow furrowed, as if self-absorbed, making a negative sign with his head; then I heard ill-contained sobs in the room...

It's all over, I said to myself, and I lost consciousness.

In fact, it was all over; I had just died.

How is it that, a moment later, standing by the window, my hand on my elbow, I was contemplating that motionless, rigid thing extended beneath the bedclothes, repeating to myself: "It's all over." And, if not perfectly calm, at least without a very keen emotion, I remained a witness to all the cares, henceforth futile, lavished by the man who was with me—or rather, the part of me that Xavier de Maistre designates by a vulgar name.[54]

I do not pretend to make it understood here that the mysterious individual who was standing, upright and attentive, in a corner of the mortuary chamber was the soul of the deceased; let us not play with such big words. But I had lived in him as I was now living in me; I was

---

[54] The previously-mentioned Xavier de Maistre notoriously contrasted the *âme* [soul] not with the *corps* [body], as conventional parlance has it, but the *bête* [beast].

234

not his soul but what the ancients would have called his simulacrum.

On examining myself, I had every reason to convince myself of it; I had retained the form, the exact appearance of the other. I much prefer that appellation— the *other*—which is, moreover, that of Plato, to that of Monsieur de Maistre, which is truly unsuitable. The *beast*—pooh!

So, I was standing there, while the required duties were rendered to my body. Saddened by the spectacle— for one cannot live the same life together for such a long time without an emotion of regret seizing you at the moment of separation—I left the room, coming and going through the house without my footfalls making the slightest sound on the parquet and in the corridors.

My domestics were already pocketing a host of small objects that had belonged to me. Perhaps, not confident in my testimentary dispositions, they were only thinking of conserving a few pious souvenirs of their master.

I let them do it and, moved by a slightly hasty sentiment of curiosity, I went out into the street, without having the need, thanks to my present immateriality, for the doors to be opened to let me through.

The weather was fine that day; the sky was blue, the sun shining brightly, and, which astonished me nevertheless, the entire Parisian population had its habitual physiognomy. Everyone was going about his business, attending to duties or pleasures. One might have thought that nothing extraordinary had happened. However, I was dead.

It is true that the evening newspapers had not yet been able to inform the public of the fact.

I went to visit a few of my friends: a dangerous proof, as nothing could reveal my presence to them. It was spying of the first order. Like the sun and the population of Paris, I found them in the middle of their everyday occupations, neither more cheerful not sadder than the day before. Doubtless they had not received the fatal notification.

The next day, the horizon was somber, the sun scarcely showed itself, the wind seemed to be moaning at the street corners, and a few drops of rain were dotting the pavement. That day, Paris really had put on an appropriate appearance—at least, I thought so. The pedestrians were walking at a slower pace, with a more meditative attitude; I noticed that many of them were dressed in black, or wearing crepe around their hat.

The papers have spread the news, I said to myself. *Not just the evening papers but the morning papers.*

And as I spoke, I saw someone unfold his paper, integrate it, and strike it sharply with his hand, addressing an expression of reproach toward Heaven.

I had no doubt about it; I had before me one of those unknown friends who take more account of us, of our works and of our glory, than our most intimate friends, subject to being embittered by the frequentation of a superiority that diminishes them. And I was approaching that excellent man, that noble heart, when I heard him exclaim: "Down again!"

I had time to cast an eye over his newspaper; it did not bear the somber frame of disastrous days, and yet...

Going past the theater posters, I stopped by virtue of a residue of habit. Not one theater had closed for the day, and yet...

At a mechanical pace, with a pitiful expression, I had resumed the route to my abode when, suddenly, a scene was presented to me capable of compensating me amply for all the petty disappointments inflicted on my vanity as a man deceased.

Black, black, long, long, dense, innumerable, silent, standing in the roadway, cluttering the sidewalk, overflowing all the way to the coaching entrances, blocking the route to carriages, agitating with movements similar to those of the sea, the crowd was everywhere, filling everything from one end of the street to the other, from the top of the house to the bottom: the courtyard, the stairs and the rooms!

A magnificent funeral carriage, harnessed to six horses caparisoned in black and silver, was waiting at the door.

My surprise was great, I declare; I had a sort of suffocation of modesty.

My modesty was about to suffer an entirely different proof!

The cortege set forth, and I perceived a multitude of policemen charged with maintaining order round it; a company of soldiers headed by a band with veiled drums opened the march, closed at the rear by a squadron of the municipal guard in dress uniform.

And, wondering what could have earned me, a poet, those military honors, I was reduced to responding— setting modesty aside this time—that it was, after all, a matter of national mourning.

When the funeral carriage passed in front of me, a new astonishment! Not only was an enormous laurel wreath mingled with golden leaves surmounting it, but decorations of every sort, French and foreign, constellating one of the extremities of the mortuary cloth.

For a moment I thought it was an error; I thought that the magnificent convoy, destined for some high dignitary, mistaking the address, had come to collect me by mistake. But people were saying close to me that all those honorary distinctions had been granted when the news of my imminent demise had spread. In any case, my monogram was resplendent on the panels of the principal vehicle, as on all the others.

I had not yet reached the end of my surprises.

One striking fact penetrated me with the greatest emotion of pride in revealing to me the role I had played, unknown to myself, in contemporary literature: the four cordons of the carriage were being held by Lamartine, Émile Augier, on behalf of dramatic literature, by the permanent secretary of the Académie Française, and the president of the Société des Gens de Lettres. The most eminent men in the sciences, the arts, and my former colleagues, the best known writers in all genres, had not disdained to mingle with the crowd, black, black, long, long, dense, innumerable and silent, that was moving slowly in its wake.

And the sky, still gray, also seemed to have put on its mourning dress, and meditation inclined all heads, as the chromatic notes of brass instruments mingled dolorously with the dull rolls of the muffled drums.

At every minute, newcomers were swelling the cortege. Moving reflexively, I did likewise; I mingled with it. After all, did I have to worry about the figure I was about to present? More fortunate than Charles V, thanks to my invisibility, I was able to witness my convoy without the necessity of any dissimulation.

When we emerged on to the boulevard an immense multitude was garnishing the verges; the shops and cafés were masked by platforms overloaded with spectators; at the windows and on the balconies, gracious feminine groups showed themselves in full mourning dress, and at the approach of the dead man, all the women threw flowers, all the men took off their hats, and I returned their salutes—which had perhaps never happened to any other deceased person—so troubled did I feel.

In the midst of my disturbance, however, I thought I remarked a kind of little red ball bouncing around the carriage. On looking harder, I discovered in that ball a semblance of hands, feet and a small flat head, a sort of fungal excrescence, all scarcely interrupting the spherical shape.

It was a kind of little red man, a deformed dwarf. What was he doing there? He continued to roll, bouncing alongside and in front if the carriage. Now I heard him uttering strident cries and burst of mocking laughter, which did not trouble the general meditation at all.

I don't know why I thought of the hired insulters of ancient Rome, attacking illustrious men during triumphal ceremonies. I was astonished that he was being allowed to execute his grotesque capers between the feet of the horses, at the risk of causing them to stumble, but no one paid any attention to him. Perhaps, he was invisible, like me, and only I could see and hear him.

For an hour the cortege continued to advance, and then traversed the least populated, as well as the least aristocratic part of the boulevard. Necessarily, the platforms had disappeared and the balconies were far from presenting the same groups of graciously weeping women. No rain of flowers was any longer falling from the widows. Heads were still bowed, but, distracted by the capers and cries of the enraged dwarf, I neglected to respond to the salutes.

Exhausted by heat or fatigue, a few of my own kind, dragging their feet, were now only following the escort at a distance; a few others had abandoned it entirely. As we approached the popular quarters, the desertions became more frequent. There are people who only like to show themselves before spectators worthy of them.

Soon, the cloud extended over our heads like a gray awning suddenly darkened; a shower fell, which diminished the number of witnesses further. The military music of brass instruments and drums had ceased, and the funeral carriage, I remarked, with amazement, was now only harnessed to four horses.

I was searching for the cause of that when I perceived the little red man mounted on one of the missing horses and pulling the other along by the bridle, taking them away while making his diabolical laughter resound more loudly than ever.

He seemed to have grown by three feet.

The policemen and the illustrious cordon-bearers maintained their posts, and if the tail of the procession, still imposing, no longer seemed, as it had before, black, black, long, long, dense, innumerable and silent, I was able to think that only the indifferent, the curious and the idlers, so easily drawn into the current of crowds, had detached themselves from it, and that it been enriched by all that it had lost.

But I remained all the more surprised by the disappearance of part of the team in harness because we had just quit the line of the boulevards and were climbing an abrupt, stony slope furrowed by ruts and ridges, where the carriage threatened to become stuck or to break. It was forced to interrupt its progress several times.

During one of those pauses, the accursed dwarf came back, and not only unhitched two more horses, but also, climbing on to the funereal carriage, with extravagant grimaces and contortions, shook the large laurel wreath so violently that all of its golden foliage was dispersed to the winds.

An impotent witness of those sacrilegious actions, I could not say how much time went by in the meantime; when I looked around again, the route, increasingly steep and pitted, resembled a deserted heath; the cortege, singularly thinned out, had been liberated from its severe bearing; many hats had been replaced in their habitual place; people were marching here and there on the verges, in groups, almost disbanded, chatting about various maters.

I went to the head of the column...woe!

The laurel wreath, the French and foreign decorations, the panels of the carriage, the plumes of the horses, the policemen, the permanent secretary of the Académie, the president of the Societé des Gens de Lettres, the members of so many scholarly and literary societies, the elevated fraction of the cortege, its pomp, its glorification, had all disappeared, as if by black magic. There only remained, when the gates of the great necropolis finally opened before us, in order to escort the *other*, the faithful, those obstinate to the last.

There, I must admit, my disenchantment was followed by a moment of tender emotion.

My old friends, those whom death had scythed down first—and they were numerous—ran to meet me, welcoming me with transports of joy. They celebrated my arrival; but, while greeting them gladly, I thought of other loved ones that I was leaving behind me, and, at that memory, my eyes filled with tears. They, who doubtless no longer precipitated in human weaknesses, mocked me for my otherworldly sensibility.

"We believe that you're weeping for yourself!" they said to me. In order to make me ashamed, they laughed and in response to their noisy laughter, which only the dead could hear, a host of tombs opened, and further laughter emerged.

The cemetery appeared to me to be quite merry that evening.

However, while yielding to the renewal of old affections, I remembered the *other* and the last duties that I had to fulfill in his regard. I would not be sorry, moreover, to hear the speeches, necessarily apologetic, that were about to be pronounced over us.

I took my leave of my old friends then; but night had fallen completely; the sky was black; I seemed to be walking through clouds, and I was wandering at hazard, impotent to get my bearings, when I felt someone touch my shoulder. I turned round, and recognized, thanks to the gleam in his eyes, which were shining in the middle of his ruddy face like a pair of carbuncles, the frightful little red man.

"They're waiting for you," he said, the sound of his voice like a cracked bell. "Follow me."

I followed him.

At the end of a somber winding path lined by yews, trimmed in the fashion of the hedges of Versailles, stood a large square building, whose corners disappeared under large swathes of ivy. A small projection in the form of a hemicycle, decorated with a double row of short fluted columns, led to an iron door with two battens, on the fronton of which was the inscription: SILENTUM SEDES.[55]

---

[55] Usually rendered *sedes silentum*: literally, silent abode, or silent seat [of judgment], and often used as a euphemistic way of referring to the Underworld, or Hell.

The dwarf, who had now attained near-normal height, and whose flamboyant eyes had substituted for a lantern during our march, rapped on the door five times, and his folded finger was sufficient to reproduce the sound of iron on iron five times over. I shivered; I had a presentiment of seething unexpected, of which I had not come in search.

In fact, the door opened, and I found myself in a sort of temple illuminated at intervals by torches attached to bare pilasters of the purest Ionic style and the most severe simplicity. A mosaic with a black background, on which sentences in Greek, Latin, Hebrew and Syriac could be read, covered the floor of the building. In front of me, a number of statues, larger than natural size, formed two distinct groups.

Where was I? My anxious eyes searched the parts of the edifice plunged in darkness, looking for the *other* and what remained of our cortege; I discovered nothing there suggestive of speeches to be pronounced or a funeral ceremony—nothing except for five little coffins of unequal size lined up on little trestles as the foot of a stone platform, which I had initially mistaken for ornaments in relief added to the mosaic.

Seemingly in a great hurry, the former dwarf was occupied in placing placards in front of each of those little coffins. Returning then in my direction and leaning toward my ear, he whispered to me, this time in a voice like little bells: "Patience; your judges are deliberating!"

My judges? I saw nothing but statues. I had thought that I was in a museum, but I was before a tribunal, the Tribunal of the Silent. Was that not the exact translation of *silentum sedes*?

I thought of old Egypt judging its dead; the Minos, Aeacus and Rhadamanthus of the Greek Hades returned

243

to my memory. I thought I recognized them in the three tall bronze effigies sitting in curule chairs, in interrogative attitudes, occupying the upper part of the platform.

As if the Underworld of our day had adopted the jury system, twelve tall men of marble, chosen from all times and all countries, composing the second group, seemed to be assisting them in their functions. Costumed in the Greek or Roman style, they were holding lyres or scrolls of paper—also in marble, of course—which did not prevent a few of them being coiffed in ample wigs in the style of Louis XIV. The silence and their immobility impressed me in a singular fashion.

The only being endowed with movement in that enclosure, which was solemn to the point of rigidity, was the dwarf, the red man, the man with the ardent eyes. Incessantly going back and forth, from one statue to another, sometimes with a skip or uttering a little mocking cry, he appeared to me to be linking those grave individuals together, whose thinking was not betrayed by any external sign. He might rightly have passed for the clerk of that supreme court.

Seeing him shifting, stirring and agitating thus, I felt less displeasure toward him, and beckoned to him; he immediately came running, saluting me with the most gracious grimace

"Who is being judged here?" I asked him.

"You, Master," he replied. "That is to say your, literary merit. It's a matter of assigning you the place that is due to you in this necropolis of the arts."

I breathed more freely. However, what could be expected from those judges of bronze and those jurors of marble? They could scarcely allow their sensibility to be led astray into the deceptive evasions of attenuating circumstances; but I counted on their justice; I recalled the splendid, popular, universal ovation of which I had been the hero that same morning, and the memory was sufficient to reassure me.

"If that's what happening," I said, "if it's me with whom the tribunal is presently occupied, what do those five little coffins contain?"

"You! At least, your spirit, split into as many parts as the different genres you have cultivated."

He showed me the inscriptions placed at the head of each of the little black boxes, and I read the titles: *Poetry; History; Philosophy; Theater; Fiction.*

I was astonished at first; then, after reflection, I found that manner of procedure both methodical and ingenious, and I was applauding that division internally, which could only bring out more vividly the glory of an encyclopedic genius like mine, when the red man, who had already returned to his post, shouted in his hoarse voice: "Listen! Listen!"

And, in the midst of the profound silence that had only been interrupted momentarily by the few words that we had exchanged, I head the marmoreal lyre of the twelve jurors render a flat and confused chord, more strange than harmonious.

Then the president of the tribunal, bronze as he was, stood up; the muscles of his face agitated with a visible effort; several times, his lips parted and closed again without any sound being emitted. Finally, he succeeded in articulating a single curt monosyllable: "Psi!"

Immediately, the torches were extinguished; obscurity reigned everywhere, with the exception of the place where the red man was standing, whose eyes projected a wan light over the five unequal boxes, which men—of flesh and blood this time—clad in mourning transported outside.

Composing alone their entire cortege, I marched again after the *other*, thus fragmented, thinking dazedly about that verdict, as brief as it was enigmatic, the significance of which escaped me completely.

Having passed the hedges of green trees, I searched with my eyes or the funeral carriage; there was no funeral carriage there, but a kind of omnibus, into which a host of little coffins was already in the process of being loaded.

Then, a shrill voice that I thought I recognized, cried: "To the common grave!"

And whip in hand, uttering bursts of sinister laughter, the abominable dwarf leapt on to the seat...

At that unexpected, illogical denouement, however, my emotion was such that I suddenly woke up.

Eyes wide open, I found myself at home, in my room, in my bed. The dear doctor, his right hand still placed on my artery, had not ceased to consult the second hand of his watch. Seeing me smile at him, he replaced it in his fob pocket, saying: "Inoffensive, insignificant fever; you'll be on your feet tomorrow."

"How long have I been asleep, doctor?"

"Two minutes twenty-five seconds...agitated sleep...where are you coming from?"

"Oh, my friend, it's a long story, perhaps prophetic. I've just died, died and been resuscitated; I've traversed all Paris in triumph, with policemen, beautiful women at the windows, marching in my own procession in company with all our illustrious men, and a little scarlet dwarf; I've appeared before judges of bronze and a jury of marble..."

"That's good," he said, interrupting me. "Don't talk too much."

"Just one more word, doctor. What does *psi* signify?"

"*Psi*? If I'm not mistaken, it's simply a letter of the Greek alphabet—the penultimate one, the one that precedes omega."[56]

"I understand!" I exclaimed. "In not evaluating me absolutely the last, doubtless they thought they were being indulgent...it's an infamy! I'll appeal!"

"Come on, calm down. Continue taking a spoonful of your potion every hour. You can tell me your dream tomorrow."

---

[56] *La Second Vie* was published long before *psi* was adopted by "parapsychologists" as a designation for psychic force.

A Shadow's Dream

Life is but the dream of a shadow
(Pindar *Pythian Ode* VIII, verse 138)

I have seen on high what ought to have been down below, and down below what seemed to me ought to figure on high; I have seen negation and affirmation change roles mutually and by amicable agreement; truth and lies jump on to one another's shoulders and dominate by turns, as in a game of leap-frog; I have seen wretched and noxious pygmies whom no one could vanquish and powerful and honorable kings disappear in a breath; I have seen councils of sages consecrate iniquity, and light adore darkness; I have seen dogmatic reason lead to the absurd as easily as blind faith; I have seen liberty, as soon as it could spread its wings, fly straight toward despotism, and despotism stumble as every step on its immutable foundations. And in the midst of those contradictions, those struggles, those derailments of everything, I have wondered whether human beings were really made in that fashion, and whether I was not dreaming with eyes open.

Perhaps, behind that dream of terrestrial existence, there is our real life! In this instance, for me, doubt is far from having its usual bitterness.

"Human life is a dream"—an old saying, less metaphorical than it seems, I am beginning to be convinced.

We believe we are alive, but we are dreaming, and God is testing us in our sleep.

During that sleep, does it not happen many a time that we see a crack in the heavens open and another, more luminous earth appear to us? Illusion, we say; reality, we ought to say. It is our true world that is being shown to us in one of our lightning-flashes of lucidity.

Yes, one day, soon, we shall hear a great signal departing from on high and, all together, we will wake up. Where? Who can tell? Why not in the sun? If, of course, there is still a sun.

Does the celestial fatherland that we are about to reenter have any need to be surrounded by the millions of stars and so many other futile heavenly bodies with which we have overloaded our sky? Can space itself not be resplendent? What is the point of a lamp in the abode of light? If we are to wake up, it will be in order to transformed in nature, sensation and intelligence. The day will come when we shall plunge back again fully into absolute, eternal verity, God, Justice and Consciousness. It will be necessary to recover the habitude of it. Someday, we shall have to shake off the human dream before reestablishing normal and real existence.

But, I wonder, during that communal sleep, will the companions of my terrestrial exile have been pursuing the same aims as me? I fear that it might not be the case. Along a thousand different roads, each of us will have pursuing his own chimeras, and casting his soap-bubbles to the wind....

What! Were those beautiful stories that I thought I had learned, first in schools and then in books, nothing but fictions of my imagination? What! Were Napoléon, Caesar and Alexander invented by me? But if Napoléon did not exist, has Monsieur Thiers not written twenty stout volumes on the Consulate and the Empire? In fact, how could I have imagined that there was a writer capable of taking sixteen thousand pages of impressions, and twenty years of his life, to recount the history of ten years in the life of another man? Aberrations of the dream!

Well, what was I thinking? Necessarily, since everything around me is illusion, mirage and phantasmagoria, Monsieur Thiers has not existed any more than the pretended Napoléon, any more than the other pretended sleepers in whose company I imagined that I was dreaming.

So, this terrestrial world on which I think I sense myself living, only belongs to me, is only populated by me, or phantoms evoked by me. But then, all the imperfections of this world, all the insensate contradictions that I reproach with so much bitterness, I have created! Could I ever have thought of having such a deregulation of imagination?

In the same way, the women I have loved, and who have loved me, deceived by turns, and perhaps all together, were simply born of my dreams.

It might be that on this pretended earth of living beings, only one woman has really existed for me: Lalagé, my sweet phantom!

O Lalagé, it is not sufficient that you come to visit me from time to time in the midst of my dreams. Enough crazy visions! Wake me up! Wake me up!

Lalagé

Et fugit ad salices...
Dulce ridentem Lalagen amabo.
(Horace.)[57]

There is a shadow, a phantom, a woman,
Who always marches in my footsteps;
If I am sad, she hastens, although my soul
Escapes first, alas!
Then I hear her lavishing in whispers
Good advice, without my requesting it,
Of which I often do not take advantage.

Indulgent, like a mother,
Ever various and ever charming,
Once, when my amours
Broke the ephemeral weave,
Revealing herself to me in all her beauty,
Coquettish, yet modest, her grace,
To reaffirm my disenchanted heart,
Of absent amour she took the place;
Then, her hand in mine, we went together
Far, far away, without changing space,
To the beautiful land of visions,

---

[57] The compound quotation translates approximately as "Running to the willows...[quoted from Virgil, the runner in the original being Galatea], I will love the sweetly laughing Lalage."

Where reality is effaced,
Where, under a sky without shadows and
menace,
Illusions flourish.

Today, when amour scarcely importunes me,
As charming as of old
Although graver and more severe
She can still distract me
With pleasures, less keen but as sweet, I think;
She charms me, she enlightens me,
And it is through her eyes that I see.

In her is all my science,
My reason and my consciousness;
I am convinced, however
That something is lacking her: an atom, smoke,
Life! Oh, Lalagé, if you had been alive
How much I would have loved you!

The Journal of my Dreams

I. Advice to Travelers

Among all peoples, in all epochs, dreaming has played a great role in the history of humankind. Ancient religions saw it as the revelatory indicator of future events, as witness the oracles of Dodona and Delphi; the cult of Hecate, with her temples serving as hostelries for sleepers, its evocations, and its famous formula: *Bombo! Mormo! Gorgo! b*elonging to India and Egypt as well as Greece.

Even today, do not all our essays in religious reno-vation—mysticism, illuminism, Swedenborgism, spiritism, magnetism—call upon dream or reverie, pushed as far as exaltation, to put us in direct communi-cation with higher powers?

As for history, properly speaking, it is as full of dreams as our ancient classical tragedies; from history they skip to tradition, from tradition to the common-place; the people still have a full and entire faith in them, and the opinion of the people ought to count in an epoch when everything is determined by a majority vote.

I am a dreamer, I love dreamers, and I firmly be-lieve that they have contributed a great deal to the pro-gress of the metaphysical sciences, and even to the geo-graphical sciences.

If I had the honor of bearing a name carrying au-thority in the various Academies of Europe, I would like to compose a book, a synthetic and chronological book presenting the tableau of all the inventions and great discoveries due to dreams, commencing with that of Christopher Columbus.

To him, fine calculations have been attributed after the fact, and he died with the conviction that he had only reached the Indies in a westerly direction, without suspecting the new world he had discovered; but that new world had appeared to him twenty times over in his dreams, and he had gone to search for it where he had dreamed it.

I too have traveled, I have traveled as much as Columbus, as much as Cook, Vancouver, Dampier, Vaillant and Dumont-Durville; I have crossed the Great Ocean, the archipelagoes of the Indies and Polynesia; I have been to the ends of the earth and further still…in dream, I mean.

In my excursions, I have glimpsed in the middle of the immense solitudes of the Pacific, a vast continent unknown to everyone; in central Africa it has revealed to me a interior sea with numerous islands, populated by men with magnificent indigo blue skin. We already have brown, black, white, red, yellow and olive; the collection lacks blue men. Wiser than Columbus, I have contented myself with seeing them in dream without going to search for them, not judging that a new world, or a new human species, even of blue men, is worth leaving home for, if one is comfortable there, with a cool head and warm feet.

Furthermore, all my discoveries in that genre are inscribed, in chronological order, in the journal of my dreams, which I shall make it a duty to communicate to those voyagers who might the tempted to go and discover my discoveries.

That journal, from which I have extracted the majority of the incidents of the Second Life recounted in this volume, is far from being exhausted. I have only collected therefrom what seems to me to have some consequence and some significance. The rest, even including my long haul voyages, scarcely presents anything but rapid visions, remaining in the state of enigmas, frames that lack pictures, dreams abruptly interrupted…by the fog, as used to be said in ancient telegraphy.

Today, however, in reopening that same journal, I believe I have found a few curious things there. I am gathering them here in the fashion of Miscellanies, refraining from giving them more importance and development than they merit.

II. A New Wandering Jew

I was fatigued by a wellbeing—dare I say a happiness?—that had already lasted for several years; by an amour that, while decreasing day by day, seemed not to want to end up being extinguished.

An angel, luminous from head to toe, doubtless the angel of voyages, for he had three pairs of wings, appeared to me and said: "Wish!"

"The monotony of my existence is killing me," I replied. "Without deepening, the circle of my acquaintances is becoming narrower every day; my heart is emptying drop by drop, like a spring whose waters are during up. I have sought happiness in one place: error! Change is one of the conditions of humanity; humans are born nomads, everything proves it. The human heart needs, not to settle down, but to alight momentarily. A day spent in the midst of the same preoccupations as those of the previous day, in the same places, with the same people, adds nothing to our life; it is only a repetition, the print of a picture already familiar, on which the gaze pauses with indifference, and soon with distaste. What I wish, ardently, is that each of my days should be a life apart, distinct from the one that preceded it, a stage, a halt in my great life, with no suture with the rest."

The angel took me in his arms, carried me through space, and I fell asleep to the sound of his wings.

In the morning, when I woke up, I had a new horizon before me, and also before me, a new and charming face that was smiling at me. All the hours of my day went by in the midst of surprises and delights.

It was the same with the following days; and every evening, in the expectation of a pleasant awakening the following day, I blessed my good angel, who had extracted me from the miserable existence that I was leading before his coming.

At one of my stations, it happened that I found myself ten times happier than usual. We were camping in I know not what corner of the globe, in Circassia, I think, or perhaps in Peru, in Lima; the women of Lima are so pretty! The sky, the landscape, the flowers, the birds, the nourishing products of the soil, and above all the young hostess charged with doing me the honors of her dwelling, had delighted me to the extent that it seemed to me that several days could go by without fear of satiety.

When I mentioned that to my guide, he replied: "March! March! Change is one of the conditions of humanity."

From that moment on, the short duration of my happiness took away its value in advance. Did I have time to savor and appreciate it? Did I even have time to conserve the trace of it in my memory? Chaos ensued in my mind, and my heart resembled one of those gulfs to whose surface nothing that they engulf ever returns.

We still had to travel in that fashion many countries, known or unknown, but those new pleasures that awaited me, I already regretted before possessing them. I would have liked to liberate myself, but close by, I heard a cruel, ironic voice, murmuring: "March! March! The human heart needs, not to settle down, but to alight momentarily."

Soon, those pleasures, incessantly renascent, incessantly varied, became increasingly odious to me by virtue of their very variety. Rather death than that mutilated existence, in which nothing was linked by memory, nothing affirmed by habit!

With my hands joined, I fell to my knees before my guide, begging him to restore my life of old, so mild and calm in its monotony, so full of the same amour, accumulated since all my efforts to annihilate it.

But he, my bad angel, my tormenter, repeated: "Of each of my days I have promised to make a life apart, distinct from the one that preceded it. March! March!"

That evil angel, that torturer, that demon, I only perceived then, had the features of Lalagé...

Certainly, if I had had such a dream in the temple of Hecate, when I awoke, the high priest of the goddess would not have failed to draw an elevated moral from it; but what event in life, and even of the Second Life, does not trail in its wake a scrap of some morality?

III. Astronomical Journeys

Where am I? What eager whirlwind is carrying me into the depths of the Heavens? I am floating, rising up with a speed that only the rapidity of the electric current can approach. The Earth vanished from my sight some time ago: poor wretched little Earth, I watched it shrink, gradually diminishing until it seemed no more than a schoolboy's ball, rotating after having touched the ground—and my heart was touched, my eyes moistened. Poor, poor little Earth, where so many grand passions seethe—and vanities no less grand!—little grain of sand from which I saw the sun for the first time, on which I have loved and suffered, shall I ever be allowed to return to you?

My emotion was not long delayed in changing its object. Still rising up, I was swallowed up by profound darkness, and the dread took hold of me that I might crack my skull on some unperceived celestial body. A feeble radiation dissipated the obscurity around me somewhat; I glimpsed a sort of reddish globe that was heading towards me. Was it a comet ready to crush me in its passage? What could I do to avoid it? I had no wings to regulate and direct my course.

With a vivid sentiment of joy, I then perceived that my own will was adequate in itself to move me the direction I desired. At first I had difficulty believing myself to be endowed with such power, but what could be more logical and natural, in accordance with the universally established order? When I was an inhabitant of the Earth, could I not cause my limbs to move solely by means of a mental instruction? Now my thought—my will, in the final analysis—was similarly steering my body: a body freed from the bonds of gravitational attraction, and consequently almost weightless.

Assured of this precious faculty, after having tacked back and forth for a while, gently cradled by the waves of the ether, intoxicated by that pure essence of life, I was emboldened to resume my ascent, continuing my course through the higher regions of space.

I saw that same reddish globe again, my first discovery in my voyage through the Heavens. It seemed paler to me. Whatever it was, it was definitely not a comet; it had neither the dazzling head nor the long atmospheric tail that is the obligatory accompaniment of all comets; no more was it a star, properly speaking, no scintillation within it indicated an active flame. What was it, then? Suddenly, a sort of grotesque face turned towards me; I recognized it. My reddish globe, my tailless comet, my ray-less star, was the moon!

On that subject, I had read all that dreamers had thought and all that thinkers had dreamed, from Pythagoras to Seneca, and from Cyrano de Bergerac and Fontenelle to Humboldt and Arago.

Among the scientists, one alone had not been content to think and dream; he had wanted to see with his own eyes.

From Easter to St Michael's Day,
He built a telescope
So large, so large, that Herschel's
Was myopic by comparison.[58]

---

[58] The first line of this verse, "De Paques à la saint Michel" is a popular way of indicating the summer months in France.

Then, he saw…what did he see? Huge bats in human form, *Homo vespertilio*—and I was consumed by desire to know that which all these scientists had thought, dreamed or seen, in the direct line of incontestable truth.[59] Could I ever hope to have a better opportunity to clear up my doubts? The moon was there, right there in front of me, accessible to me!

Exerting all my will-power to one unique purpose, combining all its force into a single impulse, I precipitated myself in headlong flight, and a few minutes later I touched down on a high mountain that presented hardly any other view than that of immense glaciers. The natural location of glaciers is on high mountains; I was not surprised.

I left these lunar Alps, or Cordilleras, to descend to the plain. There, the soil was covered with snow of dazzling whiteness, doubtless fallen the previous day; I had presumably arrived on our satellite in the winter season.

Winter could not be manifest everywhere, though. I visited the moon's four cardinal points; I descended into its valleys, and also into the craters of its volcanoes. I traveled over its seas, its gulfs. Everything there was rigid, motionless; it was all frozen. The place was fully illuminated by the sun, but the sun's light did not brighten or heat up anything there; its rays arrived there

---

[59] *Homo verspertilio* is featured in the celebrated "Moon Hoax" featured in the New York *Sun* in August 1835 and rapidly translated in French newspapers, where it caused a similar sensation. Joseph Méry wrote three satirical pieces inspired by it and the Fourierist Victor Considerant wrote an expansion and continuation as *Publication complète des nouvelles découvertes de sir John Herschel dans le ciel austral et dans la lune* (1836).

chilled, without the power to melt a snowflake, without awakening an atom of life. On the plains, there was not a tree; on the receding flanks of the rocks, there was not a blade of green grass or patch of moss; in the air, which was so clear that I could see every planet gravitating around its orbit, there was not a cloud, nor a bird in flight; no cry or insect hum could be heard there!

I could only perceive a single breath—that which emerged from my own breast.

The moon is dead, dead, dead!

"Has it, at least, lived its planetary life? Was it once inhabited?"

To that double question, I can give a bold affirmative response.

The cadavers of cities lie upon its plains; although covered by their shrouds of snow, the remaining indications of rounded shapes and rectangular lines are sufficient testimony to the hand of a constructor. Now, was that constructor Fontenelle's human being or Monsieur Nicollet's bat?[60]

To decide the matter, it seemed at first that I would only have to dig down into the layers of snow, to go into one of the houses, which must surely have retained traces of heir inhabitants, even better than those of Pompeii. Any tool that came to hand, of iron or wood, would be sufficient to the task. But one does not travel through the impalpable ether with arms and luggage—except in extraordinary cases, as we shall soon see.

I had brought with me neither a spade nor a pick-axe, and I could not excavate a path through those towns and ice-sealed tombs with my fingernails. Besides

---

[60] The Moon Hoax articles are credited to a fictitious French astronomer, Jean-Nicolas Nicollet.

which, the land's more-than-Siberian cold rendered me incapable of action. I was already thinking of leaving, and in thinking that, became depressed. Had I, then, undertaken this long journey only to register the moon's death-certificate? Would nothing help to enlighten me as to the nature of its former inhabitants?

Providence came to my aid!

Numbed by cold, with frostbitten fingers and chattering teeth, I was on the point losing all hope and was about to resume my flight, when a large corridor formed by high white rocks, decorated externally by a layer of ice that gave them the appearance of immense blocks of porcelain, opened before me. On the hardened ground and along the walls, a series of objects were scattered, the nature of which it was impossible for me to make out. I drew nearer, only expecting to find a few outcrops of rock or a few tree-trunks not covered by the snow— which would have been a victory in itself—but a much greater surprise and an unexpected triumph awaited me! I had before my eyes a complete specimen of the ancient population of the moon. Those sad specimens of an entire vanished race must have taken refuge there at the very moment of the great cataclysm. There were there still, conserved intact by the cold, with their last anguished expressions and in their final stances, perhaps hundreds of centuries old.

I therefore found myself in a position to answer, with complete authority, the great question of the inhabitants of the moon—a question that had so keenly preoccupied the scientific world and myself!

The moon had once been populated, not by giant bats, as Monsieur Nicollet had believed, or pretended to believe, but by beings much closer to the form and na-

262

ture of humans, although they were quite different in certain essential respects.

The double man, Plato's *homo duplex*, brought back into favor in our time as an anatomical reality by the savant Dr Serres of the Institut, was displayed there in the full expansion of his duplicate individuality.[61] Male in the right half of the body, female in the left side, the lunar human possessed two arms and two legs, exactly like the humans of Earth, but had in addition two distinct and separate heads, elegantly rising from articulated clavicles, capable of certain movements that are forbidden to us. Each of these heads had an elongated neck for a stem, which drew apart progressively from their bases. Evidently, this neck, instead of supporting only seven vertebrae, as ours do, must have accommodated at least twenty-two, like those of birds.

The broad chests of these strange beings presented, not quite in the middle but slightly to the left, two breasts, to which the double mouth of a bicephalous infant could be simultaneously applied. To the right, there was no trace of the vestigial nipple with which nature

---

[61] Plato's *Homo duplex* conceives humans as duplicate beings in terms of body and soul, although Plato had Aristophanes offer the diners in the *Symposium* a satirical fable "explaining" human sexuality in terms of the ancient division of a hypothetical hermaphrodite form. The anatomical observations of Étienne Serres (1786-1868)—in accordance with the remainder of the passage—had more to do with bodily symmetry. A similar calculated ambiguity forms the ideative basis of one of the chapters in Gaston de Pawlowski's *Voyage au pays de la quatrième dimension* (1912; expanded 1923; tr. as *Journey to the Land of the Fourth Dimension*, Black Coat Press, ISBN 978-1-934543-37-5 which might owe something to Saintine.

has decorated us, more in accordance with harmonic law than the law of necessity.

A double spinal column, branching from a junction, permitted the conjoined individuals to look one another in the face in order to smile, to talk—for I cannot doubt that they were possessed of the gift of speech—and to put their hand on one another's shoulder in a sign of friendship. That affectionate pose must have been habitual to them in moments of great stress. Almost all the poor coupled creatures that I had before my eyes gave me evidence of that.

The inhabitants of the moon were certainly the most complete hermaphrodites among the superior races, and love, among them, must have been practiced according to the strictest rules of moral hygiene. Brother and sister at first, later husband and wife, linked by custom and by blood, exempt from suspicion and jealousy, since they were never apart, unable to take a single step without one another, since they were born together and would die together, can they not offer perfect models of conjugality? If there were ever a Golden Age of happy households, it must surely have been on the moon.

At that point, before having reached my conclusion, I felt my thoughts clouding over because of the intensity of the cold, and I suddenly lost consciousness. I only recovered when I heard two voices: two quarrelsome voices, which increased in volume as they argued, replying to one another in the angriest possible tones. To the extent that I could understand, at first, the argument concerned furniture. How strange dreams are! One of the voices was that of my upholsterer; my upholsterer was arguing with someone, and that someone, who was shouting the louder, was me!

And yet, my astronomical voyage continued.

This is what happened.

IV. Another Visit! Another Planet!

Chilled to the bone, half-frozen, almost as dead as the moon itself, I took advantage of the feeble residue of my will to head for the first available planet. Desirous above all of warmth, rest and comfort, I had told my upholsterer—don't ask me how!—to send me all the furniture in my bedroom.

My upholsterer is punctiliousness personified. When I arrived at my planet, I found him waiting at the landing-stage with his baggage. It was the dead of night; without listening to his observations, of which I heard not a single word, and without even bothering to find out whether there was a hotel in the vicinity, I instructed him to set it all up in a beautiful grotto of slate-colored basalt, whose entrance, in the form of a portico, opened on to a lake.

Nothing was lacking in my improvised apartment, not even central heating; I perceived a gentle warmth there, which did not take long to bring me out of my glacial torpor. I could have believed that I was in Paris, surrounded by my furniture in the Renaissance style—I had a penchant for the Renaissance at that time.

Monsieur Durand, my upholsterer, had brought my old Gobelins tapestry, decorated with great characters of mythology, my Palissy faiences ornamented in relief with lizards, snakes and frogs, and even my famous Giotto canvas, *The Massacre of the Innocents*. I could certainly have been satisfied with less, but, I repeat, Monsieur Durand is punctiliousness made man; I had asked him for all my furniture, and he had brought it to me complete—and if he had not delivered the doors and windows along with the furniture, it was doubtless because the landlord had opposed it.

I threw myself on my bed, where I went to sleep immediately.

In the middle of the night, dull cracking sounds became audible above my head. The walls of rock seemed to be splitting noisily—and, from time to time, small flakes of basalt were falling on to my bed. Twenty other noises were not long delayed in mingling with these sounds; I heard sighs and all sorts of murmurs—even the murmur of water, which seemed to be lapping spasmodically against the entrance to my grotto.

"A fire has broken out, caused by my central heating, and the firemen are in the process of putting it out." That was my first thought.

Frightened, I hurled myself out of bed in order to get out of that inferno as quickly as possible. The exit was closed! The tall portico of rock had subsided, now leaving only a narrow aperture at its base, through which the hissing waves were coming.

"If it's not a fire," I said to myself, "then a storm has broken out over the lake—a tempest, most certainly, complicated by an earthquake!"

My situation, already terrible, was about to get even worse.

On going back into my room, I stood petrified by the spectacle that offered itself to me, which a phosphoric leakage from the rock permitted me to contemplate in all its marvelous horror.

All my furniture had come to life. Just as the high basaltic mountain into which I had come in search of shelter was cracking and moaning, and just as the little lake, my neighbor, had come swirling to besiege me in my refuge, every item of my household goods was playing an active role in its turn.

My four-poster bed, made of old oak-wood, entirely disarticulated in its limbs and joints, was attempting to return to its primitive and natural state. Its twisted feet and pillars were unrolling their spirals, standing upright, digging into the ground in order to implant themselves there; they were also implanting lively cuttings, by means of roots abruptly emitted by their nether parts, while a thin layer of bark began to cover each new stem as soon as it set itself upright.

Inlays in mother-of-pearl or tortoiseshell were detaching themselves from other items of furniture and becoming curved, rounding themselves off, and acquiring the forms of shells and carapaces. The leather and morocco upholstery of chairs was distending and taking on the appearance of the animals that had furnished it. The horsehair with which the armchairs were stuffed was escaping, in order to attach itself to strange animals, comprising their manes or fleeces.

All around me, everything that was conscious of a previous organic life, animal or vegetable, seemed to be trying to return to it. Nor did the miracle stop there. My night-stand started to dance; one by one, with a menacing air, it lifted each of its feet, which terminated in powerful eagle's claws—and these claws were opening and closing again as I approached, as if to seize their prey.

Further amazement! The mythological characters depicted in my Gobelins tapestry—Mars, Pallas and other gods of the first rank—were suddenly taking on a frightful three-dimensionality; their eyes were lighting up, their muscles stirring, and their mouths murmuring confused threats. The lightning-bolt that old Jupiter was holding flashed momentarily, and three times the mountain trembled on its base. Then, all those fallen gods began to flex their backs and stretch their arms in order to rid themselves of the weave that retained them—but they could not complete the task.

Less encumbered than the gods, the Roman soldiers in Giotto's painting launched themselves out of the canvas with wild-eyed gazes in pursuit of poor little innocents; I saw the blood running, and heard the screams of the victims and the imprecations of their executioners...

By means of a bizarre phenomenon, already observed by Pascal, I was momentarily conscious of my sleeping state. "I'm dreaming; it's a dream: a frightful nightmare, which my dear doctor would not hesitate to class among his *symplegadics!*"[62] I told myself—but after due consideration, I replied in the negative; "No, I'm awake, I'm fully conscious; it's all true, all real!"

And I continued to be subject to my dreamer's torment.

A formidable cracking sound warned me of the imminent collapse of that fatal rock, under which I had voluntarily imprisoned myself. From the obscure corner in which I curled myself up, with sweat on my brow, a violent shaking threw me back to the middle of the grotto; the cave, doubtless in consequence of an upset effected within the mountain, became narrower, gradually closing in until I was only left with just enough space to avoid contact with all the monsters by which I was surrounded.

Soon, enormous blocks of basalt detached from the ceiling fell upon the gods of old Olympus, who were

---

[62] As defined in note 12.

more entangled than ever in the threads of their tapestry, and the infamous Roman soldiers, who had not relented in their massacre of innocents. The trees and animals of my furniture, crushed and broken, were no longer anything but shapeless debris. Only my distraught night-stand, as if overcome by madness, ran away from that rain of rocks, using its powerful eagle's claws to clamber up the wall, scaling it all the way to the top.

To cap it all, the frightful reptiles—Palissy's lizards, snakes and frogs—which had retained for some time in the torpor habitual to them, were now sliding, running and hopping through the bloody debris; impregnated with that blood, they were swarming around and crawling up my legs, mingling their sinister hissing and frightful croaking with my cries of distress.

It was horrible!

However, the greatest suffering I endured did not arise from the perils I was running, nor from the spectacle before my eyes, nor from the venomous touch of the serpents; it came from the intolerable heat that reigned within the grotto. I was suffocating, choking; I thought I was dying.

In that supreme moment, a resounding voice burst out, overwhelming all those noises, all those rumblings and all those sobs.

The voice was my upholsterer's. "Quickly! Quickly!" he cried, seizing me by the hand. "The way out has been opened up for us again by a landslide. We haven't a moment to lose—hurry up!"

Would you believe it? At the very moment when I owed my salvation to the honest Monsieur Durand, I elected to inflict upon him the most unjust outbursts of temper. All my fears and all my suffering had just degenerated into furious anger. I reproached him for his disloyalty; I accused him of knavery. The furniture he had brought me could not be mine; it was bewitched!

He swore to me by his greatest gods that he had never played a practical joke in his life. I replied that he was a miserable liar! It was with malevolent, criminal intention that he had fired up the central heating to the point of asphyxiating me. I finished up threatening him to take him to court.

O triple Hecate! O Bombo, Mormo, Gorgo![63]

Fortunately, my brave upholsterer continued to drag me along with him, without paying overmuch attention to my recriminations.

Once outside the grotto, I looked for the lake that bathed its edge and could no longer see it. The lake had evaporated into steam, and now formed a large dark red cloud, in which the glow of a fire seemed to be reflected.

I scanned the high mountain of which my grotto was the base; it had been turned upside-down and twenty craters now open simultaneously along its torn flanks. The horizon traced in front of us was nothing but a circle of volcanoes.

"Where are we?" I asked, gripped by terror.

---

[63] Hecate is called "triple" here because she was thought by some writers to have three different aspects, being Selene or Luna in the Heavens, Artemis or Diana on Earth and Perseph-one or Proserpine in the Underworld; she was thus represent-ed, on occasion, with three bodies or three heads, one of a horse, one of a dog and one of a lion, and afforded such epi-thets as Tergeminus, Triformis and Triceps. Bombo, Mormo and Gorgo are all names associated with Hecate, as the intro-duction to the present section notes, but they are not normally used as if they applied to the three aspects detailed here.

"On Monsieur Le Verrier's planet, incorrectly called Neptune,"[64] Durand replied, with the utmost calm. "You've come from the moon, haven't you?"

"What! You know that?" I cried, interrupting him. "My dear Monsieur Durand, do you also know how the moon died?"

"That's an old story," he answered. "After having created the terrestrial globe. God put the moon at the service of the Earth, in the capacity of its satellite. It was charged with restraining and moderating the seas by means of its gravity, and for a few centuries things went according to plan—but the day came when, weary of turning on it axis, the moon broke its chain and tried to wander away from its regular orbit. Then there was the Deluge; in addition, to punish it for its disobedience, God struck it dead; since that time, it accomplishes its duties as a star entirely automatically, no longer doing anything but obeying the general laws of gravitation. Now, my dear client, let me resume what I was saying. Yes, as you have been able to verify for yourself, the moon is dead, and quite dead; here, entirely to the contrary, you have before your eyes a world in formation, where the forces of organic life are presently constituted with a frightful intensity. Here, due to the excess of heat, solid bodies liquefy and liquids evaporate into gaseous

---

[64] The planet whose position Urbain Le Verrier had previously calculated, on the basis of gravitationally-induced irregularities in the orbit of Uranus, was detected by Johann Galle in 1846. Le Verrier immediately proposed naming it Neptune, but British astronomers, who claimed that the priority of the predictive calculation rightfully belonged to John Couch Adams, preferred Oceanus. Rightly or wrongly, Neptune won and Le Verrier retained the credit.

form, thus forming the atmosphere indispensable to every planet that wishes to live."

I stood in front of my upholsterer, rapt. Never had I suspected him of being well-informed on these sorts of things.

"The brute matter has now been sufficiently warmed up and ground down," he went on. "Some of these volcanoes are beginning to die down; their fire is becoming central. The moment has arrived when the germs of animate beings can develop here, and they will develop, at first to excess and with prodigious rapidity. Examine the terrain on which we're treading at this moment; every atom of matter here is restless, avid for friction. Throw down an acorn here and it will germinate instantly, immediately growing and pushing up towards the heavens; tomorrow there will be an oak-tree, which will have taken on immense proportions in no time at all—but that gigantic tree will soon perish, empty and flaccid, exhausted by its effort.

"Instead of an acorn, set down the egg of a lizard here, or that of a hummingbird; out of it will come an eagle or a crocodile. This is the phenomenal epoch of monsters, of which Monsieur Cuvier had spoken to you, and the Marquis de Laplace before him. Here the globe is so avid to produce that everything that has form is alive. Here, a wooden horse will become a horse of flesh and bone, a doll will become a woman—and we ourselves, if we prolong our sojourn here imprudently, might well be transformed into giants."

I took three steps backwards. Monsieur Durand took hold of my arm again, with a smile full of irony. "Now, my dear client," he continued, "do you understand why, without any witchcraft on my part, the mother-of-pearl and tortoiseshell of your bed, the leather and horsehair of your chairs, the feet of your night-stand and Bernard de Palissy's frogs and serpents, as well as the people in your tapestry and Giotto's painting, tried to recreate their life, their form, their activity? And also why, without any other central heating but the volcano that warmed the ground beneath your feet, you almost died of asphyxia? Whose fault is that? Is it mine, who was only carrying out your instructions, eh? Answer me."

I gave him no answer; I had none to give. Besides, I was quite out of breath, with my tongue stuck to the roof of my mouth. The open air had become as hot as that of the grotto. Having almost died of cold on the moon, I didn't want to meet my end by virtue of an excess of heat; in any case, the prospect of turning into a giant was not at all tempting to my vanity.

I looked down at myself...my feet had already begun to develop considerably; my knees seemed to me to be more highly placed than before...

I hastened to quit Monsieur Le Verrier's planet, my mind anxiously full of the idea that creation is not yet terminated, and that God, instead of being at rest, as tradition affirms, is actively continuing his work.

V. What Is A Dream?

In leafing through my journal, I only wanted to extract a few new facts, a few rapid anecdotes, scarcely sketched; my astronomical journeys have taken me too far, I fear. However, I perceive there, in a margin, some poor verses, forgotten or disdained. Doubtless they seemed to me, at first, only to be a needless repetition.

At present, they appear to be to be a necessary summary, indispensable to the question. This is surely where they belong; let them be admitted, then.

In the night so calm into which slumber plunges us
What demon lives within us, and what, in sum, is a dream?
A dream, a deceptive mirror
That slips clarity beneath my closed eyelid,
Which makes the ground stir beneath my resting foot,
And casts my thought to the wind!

By nature active, troubled and, immortal,
When we are sleeping, is our soul alert?
Free, and deserting its prison,
With the lightning that shines, the bird that passes,
Does it go to play and lose itself in space,
And seek another horizon?

Perhaps, in fields, in cities and cabins,
When it has terminated its wandering,
It returns, and our mind
Adopts, unknown to us, the light visions,
Fugitive tableaux and temporary halts
Of the voyage it has made.

Hence those pure stars that shine for us in darkness,
Those steeples and palaces, and faces without number,
A prompt and mobile panorama
That whirls around us like a demented crowd
Disordered and confused, in an immense circle,
Which our awakening interrupts.

Hence presentiment, secret advice, foresight;
Hence, sometimes, a strange face in a dream,
    That charms you, and the next day
One sees the eyes again, a memory awakes
One thinks one sees a friend of the day before
    And extends one's hand, joyfully.

Who can explain the mystery of a dream?
When, bringing Heaven closer to the earth
    Our soul, invisible link,
Sometimes visits the dead to seek the beloved voice
That strikes our sleeping ear in the evening,
    And softly murmurs our name?

Who knows? That subtle fire stirring in my breast,
Might it not, outside me, haunt another abode?
    His God created it for me alone?
Perhaps, when I sleep, the one that I mourn,
My soul, visiting his last dwelling
    Reanimates him in his shroud.

Perhaps, warming up his icy remains,
To his desert brain it restores the thought,
    Sets him on his trembling feet;
Then, by night, on the edge of somber forests
Or along old walls, one sees shades wandering
    Faces covered by white veils.

But no, in revenants the era scarcely believes;
And incredulity, even gaining the vulgar
    Invades us from all directions;
When cold reason replaces the ideal,
Against the rising flood of the ocean of ice

The dream is our only rampart.

Let us dream, my friends! Immense, occult power,
Worth as much as life, from the dream results
　　　Real wealth, I tell you;
The black dream breaks us, plunging us into Hell,
But the tender white dream, however brief it is
　　　Takes us straight to paradise.

When spirit masters matter within me
Eyes closed, I arrange an entire existence;
　　　If someone comes to wake me,
We talk, but after that importunate truce,
The intruder departed, I resume my dream
　　　And fall back on the pillow.

Fortunate privilege of my adolescence,
Thanks to you, no more watchdogs or obstacles,
　　　Amours, this is your heyday...
Pardon me, although I retain the memory
I believe it ill behooves me to tell the story
　　　Of all that I dreamed at twenty.

In the night so calm into which slumber plunges us
　　What demon lives within us, and what, in sum, is a
dream?
　　　　A dream, a deceptive mirror
　　That slips clarity beneath my closed eyelid,
　　Which makes the ground stir beneath my resting
foot,
　　　　And casts my thought to the wind!

VI. Wellbeing at a Bargain Price

It is time to finish with dreams, sometimes good companions, sometimes also guides and dangerous benefactors. As a final moral, one more anecdote; it will be the last.

I once knew a man of sickly appearance, with a troubled and somber countenance. Among his relatives and in his vanity, everyone pitied him. He was believed to be poor—and perhaps that was not mistaken—uncivilized and an enemy of pleasures. He was nothing of the sort; all things considered, on getting to know him better, one might have proclaimed him one of the most fortunate people in the world. Something of an artist, something of a poet, although he lived in a hovel of sorts, he received good company there, without worrying about the visits to return; he gladly frequented salons, sure of always being welcome there; he shone there by virtue of his wit and his natural grace—which, generally, people were far from suspecting. There was not a celebration or a ball in the best society to which he was not invited; he showed himself there irreproachably costumed, dressed by the most fashionable tailors, who never permitted themselves to send him their bill.

At gambling, he won large sums, but he would have been ashamed to allow his household to profit from them. His gallant successes might have attracted violent quarrels on the part of brothers or husbands, but he was known to be an expert with all weapons; in any case, he prided himself on an impenetrable discretion, and even his wife was unaware of his numerous external relations. In order to dissimulate from her his frequent escapades, he used resources and means that only he had, and which testified to truly precious faculties.

If a hunting party, followed by a copious lunch, had retained him all day long, he only dined better when he went home, where he carefully refrained from taking his share of the game

In other circumstances, one might have thought that he was endowed with the gift of ubiquity. By night, while his wife was asleep by his side, he often quit her without her sensing his depart. Where did he go? What does it matter? The important thing is that when the lady woke up, she unfailingly found him beside her. To what did that man, so little considered in his entourage, owe so much good fortune capable of exciting envy? To dreaming! But dreaming was opposed to his becoming a good poet, a good painter, and even a good husband.

It is necessary that the Second Life dies not absorb the first; the thought that is immobilized easily turns to madness. It is necessary, above all, to refrain from putting too much faith in dreams.

Two words in support:

A young Spanish lord, having learned that one of his friends had dreamed about his mistress, went to demand a reckoning with him; they fought, and both were grievously wounded.

Another dreamer, a Portuguese, this time, saw his wife unfaithful in a dream and stabbed her when he awoke.

Those are excesses against which it is necessary, prudently, to defend oneself.

O Bombo! Mormo! Gorgo!

With that, reader, adieu! And may the white angel sent you good dreams.

APPENDICES

The Ballad of Jane Stilich

Vengeance is sweet in the heart of Montenegrins; even beyond the blue sea, vengeance is sweet to all the peoples who surround Montenegro.

In a casino in Xalasi-Mali, a fierce quarrel arose between Dragho Stilich and Arnold Mienesky, both rich men, one possessing a vast plantation of plum trees and white mulberries, the other numerous flocks of sheep with twisted horns. At the height of the dispute, Arnold drew his kandjar, and Drago fell on to a table murmuring: "Vengeance!"

Vengeance is sweet in the heart of Montenegrins.

When he was picked up he was dead. His eyes, however, remained open. Jane Stilich, his widow, had the body taken back to her home, where it was laid down on a mat. A pope came to bless him and sprinkle him with hold water; then his pipe and his weapons were placed beside him.

The sand-glass marked the fourth hour.

Then Jane Stilich went to find the sardar of Xalasi-Mali.

Vengeance is sweet in the heart of Montenegrins.

She said to him: "My son is scarcely in a state to life an ear of maize, and I have no brothers; you have brothers and four sons capable of handling a carbine.

You were Dragho's friend; punish his murderer. It is your duty, and I beg you to do it." And she got down on her knees before him.

The old sardar looked at her, and then replied: "Vengeance is sweet in the heart of Montenegrins. But Dragho Stilich was no longer my friend since he refused to give me four sheepskins last Christmas to make cloaks for my sons. However, as you are beautiful, my sons and I will set out on campaign; afterwards, you will marry me."

Jane darted a furious gaze at him and spent the night weeping beside the body of her husband, whose eyes were still open.

Vengeance is sweet in the heart of Montenegrins.

The next day, Jane went to the homes of the dead man's other friends, but all of them were also Arnold Mienesky's friends.

In her despair she returned to the house of the sardar, and said to him: "I accept the bargain."

He rubbed his hands in contentment.

When she returned home, Jane told the dead man everything, while sobbing, and whispered in his ear.

Then she closed his eyes.

The sand-glass marked the fourth hour.

Vengeance is sweet in the heart of Montenegrins.

"Quickly, my sons, let us make a provision of powder, bullets and food; let us put on our hunting boots and tighten our belts; let our cassocks be solidly fastened to our breasts, and above all, let us put on our sheepskin cloaks, to protect our weapons and provisions from the rain. Arnold Mienesky has retired to the higher mountains, and we are going to kill him, since he has killed Dragho, our best friend."

Vengeance is sweet in the heart of Montenegrins.

Skillful and wily, the sardar was soon on the fugitive's trail, but on the first day that he glimpsed him, one of his sons fell, shot in the head.

On the second day, another fell.

The sardar hesitated in his pursuit. For his part, the murder proposed to submit to a ransom.

A pope presented himself to the widow in order to obtain her consent to the reconciliation.

She refused.

The sand-glass marked the fourth hour.

Vengeance is sweet in the heart of Montenegrins.

In spite of her refusal, the ordinary price of a head, a hundred sequins, is sent to the vladika. The vladika convenes a kmeti.[65]

Everything is prepared in the church where the mass of peace is to be celebrated. The bells ring.

Twelve young mothers, carrying their children in their arms, knock on the widow's door.

"Jane, Jane! Open the door; we are bringing you the gold and embroidered kerchiefs."

The door does not open.

Vengeance is sweet in the heart of Montenegrins.

"Jane, neighbor Jane Stilich, in the name of our children, grant us the pardon! Arnold repents. It was only a dispute, not a hatred. He will kneel at your feet, bearing to his neck the kandjar that killed Dragho. The kandjar alone is guilty, and it will be broken and cursed by the priest. Open the door, Jane!"

---

[65] Author's note: "The vladika is the Bishop, the sovereign of Montenegro. A kmeti is a tribunal of reconciliation."

Jane remained inflexible. She had sworn something in the dead man's ear, and woe betide anyone who breaks her oath!

Dragho's murderer has returned to the forest. Aided by his brothers, this time, and the two sons that remain to him, the old sardar is forced to set out on campaign again.

Weary of fleeing and hiding, harassed on one side by ferocious beasts and on the other by his enemy, Arnold ceases to defend himself. He falls, struck by three bullets, and his vanquisher returns triumphant to Xalassi-Mali.

Vengeance is sweet in the heart of Montenegrins.

Jane learns of the sardar's return. She takes out her wedding dress from the chest where it is conserved in lavender and sweetscented bedstraw; she puts it on. She charges her fingers and ears with jewels; her hair-grip resounds beneath a double row of Turkish piastres; in one hand she holds her spindle, and in the other her bunch of keys.

"He has avenged Dragho in order to have his wife, and also his flock of sheep with twisted horns. What does it matter? I belong to him."

Vengeance is sweet in the heart of Montenegrins.

Already the bagpipe is announcing the approach of the sardar, his brothers and his two sons. Jane goes up to the highest floor of the house, and when the future husband gets ready to knock on the door she cries: "Here I am!"

And she falls beside him, her skull fractured.

The sand-glass marks the fourth hour.

The old sardar did not possess Jane or her flock of sheep with twisted horns.

Vengeance is sweet in the heart of Montenegrins; even beyond the blue sea, vengeance is sweet to all the peoples who surround Montenegro.

The Valley of Souls

According to Indian tradition, beneath the earth, in the second sphere of the inferior heavens, which the sun's rays no longer reach, an immense valley exists, half-somber and half-luminous. There, the blue-tinted foliage of the trees is illuminated by phosphorescent gleams; the plants, rigid and angular, are nothing but variously colored crystallizations, bearing for flowers blossoms of gems, umbels of garnets, topazes or amethysts, such as one can see in kaleidoscopes, and their prismatic facets reflect and multiply the gleams of the blue trees.

In that species of lunar twilight, all is silence. Neither the song of a bird nor the buzz of a bee can be heard; the soil there seems incapable of nourishing the smallest living animal. Even the plaints of the wind are silent beneath the motionless foliage.

A great lake, which is not alimented by any spring or steam, fills the lowest parts of the valley, not with flowing and sonorous waters but with a profound layer of white vapors, which bathe without moistening them the feet of banks and the bases of promontories, or spread like a light muslin scarf around scintillating isles

Movement is not, however, completely excluded from that silent world. Like a shroud rising up, the lethargic mirror of the lake sometimes swells and is animated at its surface. Forms are seen gliding through the vaporous wave, indecisive at first, so much does the substance of which they are composed seem to be mingled with the very substance of the lake; but soon, the principal dispositions of the human body, revealing themselves in their harmony, are detached from the veil of mist that surrounds them.

Those arms, those shoulders, devoid of muscles or epidermis, with dubious contours; those foreheads not shaded by any trace of hair; those faces that blood cannot color, which are not creased by a wrinkle or a smile, conserving nevertheless a physiognomy of shorts; those eyes scarcely indicated by a double brown patch, from which the residue of a gaze escapes; those faded lips, dull and closed, which only ought to open in response to a supreme commandment, are sufficient to give evidence of the difference of sexes among all those pale simulacra.

Once outside the lake, those cloud-men and women go to wander along the shore or lie down on the banks. The ground on which they are extended is visible through their diaphanous bodies; the onyx and topaz petals of the flowers, which are not even inclined, beneath their feet, can be seen shining.

And sometimes, adopting a melancholy pose, with an elbow posed on the ground and the head supported by the hand, those shades seem to be dreaming.

Of what are they dreaming?

Perhaps of their past existence; perhaps of their future existence.

For that valley is the abode of souls destined to submit to a new ordeal of life.

After having been judged by the terrible and incorruptible Yama, both the Minos and the Pluto of the Hindu Underworld, after having accomplished their time of tortures or delights, in accordance with whether they practiced vice or virtue during their last passage on earth, purified by expiation or recompensed for the courage deployed in their previous struggle, equal henceforth in the eyes of Indra, reconciled with Brahma, the creative power, and Shiva, the destructive and generative power, this is where they await the advent in the world of the infant into whose body their transmigration is to be accomplished.

One day, Chitra-Gupta, the green-hued angel with the triple shoulders, on whose back six pairs of wings are stacked, came in the quality of Yama's first minister to make his provision of souls. Before the diamond door by means of which one penetrates the valley, he encountered the goddess Shitala, protectress of children born or yet to be born.

The green angel, who saw her as a rival power, frowned.

"Have you come to importune me with your lamentations," he said to her, "and ask for gifts for your wards that only the superior gods can accord them?"

"I have nothing more to request," replied Shitala. "I have obtained from Brahma that which I desired for the happiness of humanity entire, and I have come to signify his order to you."

"What do you intend to do? What is it about?"

"Listen to me Gupta, and be proud of assisting me in my great and holy enterprise. If humans, during their terrestrial traverse, almost always complain of their lot, it is because, more often than not, their souls inhabit bodies that were not made for them, submissive to a condition that does not correspond to their instincts. Henceforth, informed in advance of its future destiny, every soul will have the right to accept or refuse the envelope of flesh in which it must accomplish its ordeal.

Such is the prayer that I addressed to Brahma, and he has granted it."

The minister of the Indian Pluto uttered such a burst of laughter that his six pairs of wings beat simultaneously on his triple shoulders, and he was unable to resume speaking for some time.

Finally, his great hilarity calmed down.

"Are you dreaming, Mother? Was Brahma himself, intoxicated by the perfumes of the Calamata or the sweet liquor of Amritam, dreaming when he made you that promise? By the rivers of the Underworld, I'm tempted to believe that he was making fun of you!"

For her only response, Shitala took from beneath her scarlet cloak the decree emanating from Brahma, carefully wrapped in lotus and cuscha leaves, and handed it to him, while he diamond door had just opened before them of its own accord.

"A curse on humans! The world is reaching its end!" murmured Chitra-Gupta, uttering such a sigh that all the light phantoms of the lake found themselves driven back to the other shore, like sea mist under a storm wind. "Giving humans the choice of accepting or refusing their future destiny! The excess of charity has rendered you mad, Old Mother! Henceforth, we shall no longer have souls to furnish, except to the children of the rich and powerful. Within half a century, the kings will be born without people and the Brahmins will be preaching in the desert."

"Let us try," said the goddess.

"Let it be so, since you wish it and Brahma orders it."

After having taken more exact cognizance of the divine decree, the green angel, somewhat reassured, approached the lake, consulted his register and, in a resounding voice, summoned six souls in turn, by their last terrestrial names.

As each name was pronounced the lake quivered, a slight seething was manifest at one of the points of its silver sheet, and then a shade, rising above the layer of vapors, slowly came ashore.

When he saw all six of them gathered around him, he informed them, along with Brahma's decision, the restriction that was included therein.

"By the refusal to become immediately the guest of the body predestined for it, the soul will lose its turn of life, and will prolong its sojourn in this valley of annihilation for a number of years equal to the one that it would have spent among humans."

It was that clause that had appeared to reassure Chitra-Gupta as to the consequences of the decree.

The first soul summoned was that of an old dervish who had left in Mysore the memory of a life spent not only in holy austerities but in the cruelest mortifications of the flesh.

"You," he angel said to him, "are to be born in the midst of an honest family of merchants, in a condition equally distant from the honors that trouble human reason and the poverty that depraves it. Rejoice!"

"Rejoice doubly," said Shitala, "for after having been gently inebriated by the light of the sun and your mother's kisses, you will escape the corruptions of the world; still enveloped in our robe of innocence, you will die an infant! This time, you will obtain the prize of the combat without having struggled, without having suffered."

"To die a child!" said the old dervish. "What! To place my lips on the rim of the cup without even being able to empty it by half! To see the doors of life open before me only to stop on the threshold! As well not to be born! I have savored the joys of Heaven; I want to savor those of earth. I shall wait."

And, with an indignant gesture of refusal, he plunged back into the lake.

"The old fool has been perverted in Heaven," said Chitra-Gupta, shrugging his triple shoulders.

"Is excessive virtue, like vice, subject to remorse, then?" murmured Shitala, having become thoughtful. "It's possible..."

Another soul succeeded that of the dervish.

Hazard—or, rather, destiny—is often pleased to contrive strange contrasts. It was the soul of a former bayadere, whose grace and voluptuous dances had once been admired by all Benares; she had even figured splendidly in the ceremonies of the temple, which, in spite of the disorder of her conduct, had earned her the protection of the Brahmins during her life, and perhaps the indulgence of the gods after her death.

She advanced lightly, almost bounding, toward the divine couple, who were sitting on a malachite rock veined with gold.

"You are to be beautiful," Yama's messenger said to her, "and your beauty will enable you to become the wife of a rich nabob, who will set treasures at your feet in order to satisfy the least of your caprices. Rejoice!"

The soul of the bayadere seemed to quiver as if under an impulse of you; rapidly, she darted her gaze around, over the bushes of jade and turquoise and all the rich gems that formed the floral decoration of the valley, doubtless thinking that she would find similar ones on earth with which to make necklaces, bracelets and belts, and to suspend them from the long tresses of her hair.

Before giving her complete acquiescence, however, she asked: "Will the rich nabob, my husband, be young?"

"He will be three times your age," Shitala replied, "but no matter. Rejoice, for, after having heaped you with his gifts, he will quit the earth, leaving you absolute mistress of your fate, free to choose a new husband, and that one will be young and handsome."

"Will that one render me a mother?"

"Your two husbands, the young and the old, will leave you childless."

The bayadere suddenly adopted a desolate pose. "Childless!" she repeated. "Again that shame!"

And, returning abruptly to the lake, she disappeared, uttering the words: "Living without children is not living!"

The green angel looked at the good goddess with a mocking smile. "That's a refusal you certainly wouldn't have expected, Mother? An old husband to enrich her and bent to her whims; a young one to satisfy her tastes…it's incomprehensible. Does your sex, worthy goddess, remain subject to caprice even in this empire of annihilation?"

"If a tree condemned never to produce fruit could speak, Gupta, it would reply to you: 'Sterility is shame!' For a woman, it is worse still. The divine Brahma, by an ineffable gift, deigned on the first day of the world to share his creative power with her; as soon as she emerges from the cradle she shivers with an aspiration of maternity; even as an infant, a woman is already a mother. Poor bayadere! I understand her refusal."

"Very good, worthy Shitala, but in the meantime, we're running the risk of not finding a soul that wants to quit this valley. We've already endured the refusal of the old dervish and the young bayadere; fortunately, we're going to deal with a former prince who was once devoured by the impotent desire to rise to the foremost rank. Ambition, the thirst for honors, is the great motive of the species; this time, I'm sure of the acceptance."

And with a gesture, the summoned the soul whose turn it was to appear.

"Rejoice!" Gupta cried to him, as soon as he started moving. "Rejoice and thank the gods; you are to be a king!"

"King!" said the soul, and stopped, shivering. "At the most, that was good once—it's a sad and cruel métier today! To become the executioner of one's family in order to maintain oneself necessarily before one's people, and, when one has merited the chastisements of Heaven and the scorn of men, to become the vassal or the prisoner of invaders from Europe...what a fate! My uncle, the powerful sovereign of the Deccan, had my eyes burned for fear that his subjects might judge me worthy to succeed him, and he died a humble pensioner of the English king. I'd rather be born in the humble cabin of a pariah than on the golden steps of the throne of Delhi!"

"The danger is even greater than I thought, since even kings recuse themselves," murmured Yama's minister.

"We're still only half way," Shitala said to him. "Let's continue."

Of the two souls that followed, one was to animate the body of a banker, unscrupulous as to the means of enriching himself, but who, as well as fortune, would be afflicted by a rude malaise that would hold him almost continually extended on a sick-bed; the other was destined to inhabit the envelope of a poor but laborious cultivator, and toiling in the open air would maintain him in flourishing health.

"To be both poor and healthy," said the latter, "is to possess a good stomach only to lodge the demon of hunger."

"Wealth in the company of suffering," said the former, "is a mantle of gold thrown over a cadaver."

And both refused.

"Well, Shitala," said the green angel, with the pride of triumph, "do you still think that it is just and sage to inform humans of the fate to come and leave them free to be or not to be? On that condition, I repeat, the world will soon be depopulated. Thanks to the imprudent prayer addressed by you to Brahma—by you, the protectress of children—there are already five poor mothers who will weep over their stillborn infants."

Then, seeing the good goddess, troubled by shame, lowering her head without responding, he added: "Believe me, let's not go any further, for the last soul that it remains for us to consult will go to plunge into the lake again at the first word—and this time, not without good reason."

Opening his ledger, he got ready to scratch out the six names inscribed there, but the remaining soul, seeing that it was alone, had not waited to be summoned to approach the malachite bench.

By its plaintive march, and the inclination of its head, tilted toward its shoulder, it could be divined that its memories of its previous existence only awoke within it dolorous or melancholy impressions.

It was the shade of a poor daughter of Patna who had only had painful duties to fulfill on earth. Having remained a stranger to the enjoyments that could be procured by rank, power or fortune, she had been the unique support of her poor impotent mother; and when Adismo, the god of misfortune, had appeared to allow himself to be momentarily disarmed by her resignation, when a young fiancé had presented himself for her, bringing her promises of wellbeing, she had died on the very morning of her marriage, bitten in the foot by a snake.

"Weak creature fatally predestined," the angel murmured, "I shall not say 'Rejoice!' as to the others, for I have nothing to offer you but a new existence of difficulty and privations. The two souls that preceded you here have refused their transmigration for want of not being able to possess fortune and health at the same time; to you I cannot promise either. You are to endure both poverty and suffering. Will you accept life at that price? Decide."

Without making a movement toward the lake, the shade remained silent and attentive, as if in the hope that another revelation might come to soften the cruelty of that one."

"Alas, alas!" said the good goddess, profoundly moved by pity, "profit from the gift of Brahma, dear soul; not only will poverty pursue you through the frailties of your body, but after incessant labor without result, and sickly, it will be necessary for you to exhaust the strength that remains to you in caring for your husband, also ill."

The young soul stood up straighter.

"That spouse, next to whom I must spend my future existence in toil, misery and malady, will he love me?"

"Yes, but not without division. A rival will be preferred to you; from the ashes of your happiness, scarcely glimpsed, new anguish and new suffering will surge forth for you, even heavier for you to bear than the others. You will be jealous."

"I will love him, then?"

"You will love him."

"Until the end?"

"Yes, until the end...for, alone among his wives, you will follow him all the way to the flames of his pyre."

"Blessed be the name of Brahma; I can live!"

To that cry of amour, to that passionate aspiration toward devotion, toward sacrifice, the mute and cold valley found an echo to respond; the trees shook off their immobility; the phosphorescences and the diamantine flowers redoubled their gleam, and all the phantoms that populated the depths of the lake rose above the surface at the same time in order to salute their companion with a final gesture.

Already, however, the good goddess was carrying the poor loving soul away beneath her crimson cloak, while Chitra-Gupta, rapidly deploying his six pairs of wings, lunched himself toward the seventh superior heaven in order to have Brahma's decree annulled by Indra, the god of Heaven.

Indra revoked the decree; but in his golden book he inscribed the name of the young daughter of Patna...and then, beneath it, that of the bayadere.

SF & FANTASY

Adolphe Alhaiza. *Cybele*
Alphonse Allais. *The Adventures of Captain Cap*
Henri Allorge. *The Great Cataclysm*
Guy d'Armen. *Doc Ardan: The City of Gold and Lepers; The Troglodytes of Mount Everest/The Giants of Black Lake; The Abominable Snowman*
G.-J. Arnaud. *The Ice Company*
André Arnyvelde. *The Ark; The Mutilated Bacchus*
Charles Asselineau. *The Double Life*
Henri Austruy. *The Eupantophone; The Olotelepan; The Petitpaon Era*
Barillet-Lagargousse. *The Final War*
Barbot de Villeneuve.*The Naiads/Beauty & The Beast*
Cyprien Bérard. *The Vampire Lord Ruthwen*
S. Henry Berthoud. *Martyrs of Science; The Angel Asrael*
Aloysius Bertrand. *Gaspard de la Nuit*
Richard Bessière. *The Gardens of the Apocalypse; The Masters of Silence*
Chevalier de Béthune. *The World of Mercury*
Albert Bleunard. *Ever Smaller*
Félix Bodin. *The Novel of the Future*
Pierre Boitard. *Journey to the Sun*
Louis Boussenard. *Monsieur Synthesis*
Alphonse Brown. *City of Glass; The Conquest of the Air*
Émile Calvet. *In a Thousand Years*
André Caroff. *The Terror of Madame Atomos; Miss Atomos; The Return of Madame Atomos; The Mistake of Madame Atomos; The Monsters of Madame Atomos; The Revenge of Madame Atomos; The Resurrection of Madame Atomos; The Mark of Madame Atomos; The Spheres of Madame Atomos; The Wrath of Madame Atomos* (w/M. & Sylvie Stéphan); *The Sins of Madame Atomos* (w/M. & Sylvie Stéphan)
Jean Carrère. *The End of Atlantis*

Félicien Champsaur. *Homo-Deus; The Human Arrow; Nora, The Ape-Woman; Ouha, King of the Apes; Pharaoh's Wife*
Didier de Chousy. *Ignis*
Jules Clarétie. *Obsession*
Jacques Collin de Plancy. *Voyage to the Center of the Earth*
Michel Corday. *The Eternal Flame; The Lynx* (w/André Couvreur)
André Couvreur. *Caresco, Superman; The Exploits of Professor Tornada* (3 vols.); *The Necessary Evil*
Gaston Danville. *The Perfume of Lust*
Camille Debans. *The Misfortunes of John Bull*
Captain Danrit. *Undersea Odyssey*
C. I. Defontenay. *Star (Psi Cassiopeia)*
Charles Derennes. *The People of the Pole*
Georges Dodds (anthologist). *The Missing Link*
Charles Dodeman. *The Silent Bomb*
Harry Dickson. *The Heir of Dracula; Harry Dickson vs. The Spider*
Jules Dornay. *Lord Ruthven Begins*
Alfred Driou. *The Adventures of a Parisian Aeronaut*
Odette Dulac. *The War of the Sexes*
Alexandre Dumas. *The Return of Lord Ruthven; The Man who Married a Mermaid* (w/P. Lacroix)
Renée Dunan. *Baal; The Ultimate Pleasure*
J.-C. Dunyach. *The Night Orchid; The Thieves of Silence*
Henri Duvernois. *The Man Who Found Himself*
Achille Eyraud. *Voyage to Venus*
Henri Falk. *The Age of Lead*
Paul Féval. *Anne of the Isles; Knightshade; Revenants; Vampire City; The Vampire Countess; The Wandering Jew's Daughter*
Paul Féval, *fils. Felifax, the Tiger-Man*
Charles de Fieux. *Lamékis*
Fernand Fleuret. *Jim Click*
Charles-Marie Flor O'Squarr. *Phantoms*
Louis Forest. *Someone is Stealing Children in Paris*

Arnould Galopin. *Doctor Omega*; *Doctor Omega and the Shadowmen* (anthology)

Judith Gautier. *Isoline and the Serpent-Flower*

H. Gayar. *The Marvelous Adventures of Serge Myrandhal on Mars*

Louis Geoffroy. *The Apocryphal Napoleon*

G.L. Gick. *Harry Dickson and the Werewolf of Rutherford Grange*

Raoul Gineste. *The Second Life of Doctor Albin*

Delphine de Girardin. *Balzac's Cane*

Emmanuel Gorlier. *The Nyctalope and the Tower of Babel*

Léon Gozlan. *The Vampire of the Val-de-Grâce*

Jules Gros. *The Fossil Man*

Jimmy Guieu. *The Polarian-Denebian War* (2 vols.)

Edmond Haraucourt. *Daah, the First Human; Illusions of Immortality*

Nathalie Henneberg. *The Green Gods*

Eugène Hennebert. *The Enchanted City*

Jules Hoche. *The Maker of Men and His Formula*

V. Hugo, P. Foucher & P. Meurice. *The Hunchback of Notre-Dame*

Romain d'Huissier. *Hexagon: Dark Matter*

Jules Janin. *The Magnetized Corpse*

Gustave Kahn. *The Tale of Gold and Silence*

Gérard Klein. *The Mote in Time's Eye; Starmasters*

Fernand Kolney. *Love in 5000 Years*

Paul Lacroix. *Danse Macabre; The Man who Married a Mermaid* (w/Alexandre Dumas)

Louis-Guillaume de La Follie. *The Unpretentious Philosopher*

Jean de La Hire. *The Fiery Wheel; Enter the Nyctalope; The Nyctalope on Mars; The Nyctalope vs. Lucifer; The Nyctalope Steps In; Night of the Nyctalope; Return of the Nyctalope; The Nyctalope and the Tower of Babel*

Etienne-Léon de Lamothe-Langon. *The Virgin Vampire*

André Laurie. *Spiridon*

Gabriel de Lautrec. *The Vengeance of the Oval Portrait*

Alain le Drimeur. *The Future City*

Georges Le Faure & Henri de Graffigny. *The Extraordinary Adventures of a Russian Scientist Across the Solar System* (2 vols.)

Gustave Le Rouge. *The Dominion of the World* (w/G. Guitton) (4 vols.); *The Mysterious Doctor Cornelius* (3 vols.); *The Vampires of Mars*

Jules Lermina. *The Battle of Strasbourg; Mysteryville; Panic in Paris; The Secret of Zippelius; To-Ho and the Gold Destroyers*

Maurice Level. *The Gates of Hell*

M.-J. L'Héritier de Villandon. *The Robe of Sincerity*

André Lichtenberger. *The Centaurs; The Children of the Crab*

Maurice Limat. *Mephista*

Listonai. *The Philosophical Voyager*

Jean-Marc & Randy Lofficier. *Edgar Allan Poe on Mars; The Katrina Protocol; Pacifica 1, 2; Robonocchio; Return of the Nyctalope;* (anthologists) *Tales of the Shadowmen 1-14; The Vampire Almanac* (2 vols.)

Ch. Lomon & P.-B. Gheuzi. *The Last Days of Atlantis*

Charles Malato. *Lost!*

Maurice Magre. *The Marvelous Story of Claire d'Amour; The Call of the Beast; Priscilla of Alexandria; The Angel of Lust; The Mystery of the Tiger; The Poison of Goa; Lucifer; The Blood of Toulouse; The Albigensian Treasure; Jean de Fodoas; Melusine; The Brothers of the Virgin Gold*

Victor Margueritte. *The Bacheloress; The Companion; The Couple*

Camille Mauclair. *The Virgin Orient*

Xavier Mauméjean. *The League of Heroes*

Joseph Méry. *The Tower of Destiny*

Hippolyte Mettais. *Paris Before the Deluge; The Year 5865*

Louise Michel. *The Human Microbes; The New World*

Tony Moilin. *Paris in the Year 2000*

Michael Moorcock's *Legends of the Multiverse*

José Moselli. *Illa's End*

John-Antoine Nau. *Enemy Force*

Marie Nizet. *Captain Vampire*

Charles Nodier. *Trilby and The Crumb Fairy*
C. Nodier, A. Beraud & Toussaint-Merle. *Frankenstein*
Oksana & Gil Prou. *Outre-Blanc*
Henri de Parville. *An Inhabitant of the Planet Mars*
Gaston de Pawlowski. *Journey to the Land of the 4th Dimension*
Georges Pellerin. *The World in 2000 Years*
Ernest Pérochon. *The Frenetic People*
Pierre Pelot. *The Child Who Walked on the Sky*
Jean Petithuguenin. *An International Mission to the Moon*
J. Polidori, C. Nodier, E. Scribe. *Lord Ruthven the Vampire*
P.-A. Ponson du Terrail. *The Immortal Woman; The Vampire and the Devil's Son; The Police Agent*
Georges Price. *The Missing Men of the* Sirius
René Pujol. *The Chimerical Quest*
Edgar Quinet. *Ahasuerus; The Enchanter Merlin*
Jean Rameau. *Arrival; in the Stars*
Henri de Régnier. *A Surfeit of Mirrors*
Maurice Renard. *The Blue Peril; Doctor Lerne; The Doctored Man; A Man Among the Microbes; The Master of Light*
Restif de la Bretonne. *The Discovery of the Austral Continent by a Flying Man; Posthumous Correspondence* (3 vols.); *The Fay Ouroucoucou* (2 vols.)
Jean Richepin. *The Crazy Corner; The Wing*
Albert Robida. *The Adventures of Saturnin Farandoul; Chalet in the Sky; The Clock of the Centuries; The Electric Life; The Engineer Von Satanas; In 1965*
J.-H. Rosny Aîné. *Helgvor of the Blue River; The Givreuse Enigma; The Mysterious Force; The Navigators of Space; Vamireh; The World of the Variants; The Young Vampire*
Marcel Rouff. *Journey to the Inverted World*
Marie-Anne de Roumier-Robert. *The Voyage of Lord Seaton to the Seven Planets*
Léonie Rouzade. *The World Turned Upside Down*
Han Ryner. *The Human Ant; The Superhumans*
Henri de Saint-Georges. *The Green Eyes*
Louis-Claude de Saint-Martin. *The Crocodile*

Frank Schildiner. *The Quest of Frankenstein; The Triumph of Frankenstein; Napoleon's Vampire Hunters*

Nicolas Ségur. *The Human Paradise; Penelope's Secret*

Pierre de Selenes: *An Unknown World*

Norbert Sevestre. *Sâr Dubnotal: Vs. Jack the Ripper; The Astral Trail*

Angelo de Sorr. *The Vampires of London*

Brian Stableford. *The Empire of the Necromancers (1. The Shadow of Frankenstein; 2. Frankenstein and the Vampire Countess; 3. Frankenstein in London); The Wayward Muse; Eurydice's Lament; The Mirror of Dionysius; The Pool of Mnemosyne; The New Faust at the Tragicomique; Sherlock Holmes and The Vampires of Eternity; The Stones of Camelot* (anthologist) *News from the Moon; The Germans on Venus; The Supreme Progress; The World Above the World; Nemoville; Investigations of the Future; The Conqueror of Death; The Revolt of the Machines; The Man With the Blue Face; The Aerial Valley; The New Moon; The Nickel Man; On the Brink of the World's End; The Mirror of Present Events; The Humanisphere*

Jacques Spitz. *The Eye of Purgatory*

Kurt Steiner. *Ortog*

Michel & Sylvie Stéphan. *The Wrath of Madame Atomos* (w/André Caroff); *The Sins of Madame Atomos* (w/André Caroff)

Eugène Thébault. *Radio-Terror*

Edmond Thiaudière. *Singular amours*

C.-F. Tiphaigne de La Roche. *Amilec*

Simon Tyssot de Patot. *The Strange Voyages of Jacques Massé and Pierre de Mésange*

Louis Ulbach. *Prince Bonifacio*

Théo Varlet. *The Castaways of Eros; The Golden Rock.; The Martian Epic* (w/Octave Joncquel); *Timeslip Troopers* (w/André Blandin); *The Xenobiotic Invasion*

Pierre Véron. *The Merchants of Health*

Paul Vibert. *The Mysterious Fluid*

Villiers de l'Isle-Adam. *The Scaffold; The Vampire Soul*

Gaston de Wailly. *The Murderer of the World*
Philippe Ward. *Artahe; Manhattan Ghost* (w/Mickael
Laguerre); *The Song of Montségur* (w/Sylvie Miller)